6/7/2017

Trilby Kent was born in Toronto and grew up in London, Miami, and Boston. A graduate of Oxford University and the LSE, she has worked as a rare books specialist at a leading auction house; a freelance journalist contributing investigative, arts, and feature writing to the Canadian national press and publications in America and Europe; an academic editor; and a creative writing tutor with one of the UK's leading distance learning schools. She has also contributed essays and interviews to such literary journals as *The London Magazine* and *Slightly Foxed*.

SILENT NOON

September, 1953. Fourteen-year-old Barney Holland is promised a fresh start when he is offered a place at a boarding school on the remote North Sea island of Lindsey. Instead, he is shunned by his peers both for his status as a charity pupil and for being the replacement of a recently deceased student, the popular Cray. The arrival of Belinda Flood provides Barney with an unexpected ally, and both outsiders soon fall under the influence of charismatic senior pupil Ivor Morrell, who reigns over the forbidden corners of the school. Gripped by mounting horror at his discovery of secrets harboured by the isolated school community, Barney desires nothing more than to escape the island — and its haunted past — once and for all.

Books by Trilby Kent
Published by The House of Ulverscroft:

SMOKE PORTRAIT

TRILBY KENT

◆

SILENT NOON

Complete and Unabridged

CHARNWOOD
Leicester

First published in Great Britain in 2013 by
Alma Books
Surrey

First Charnwood Edition
published 2015
by arrangement with
Alma Books
Surrey

A catalogue record for this book is available
from the British Library.

ISBN 978–1–4448–2238–0

Published by
F. A. Thorpe (Publishing)
Anstey, Leicestershire

Set by Words & Graphics Ltd.
Anstey, Leicestershire
Printed and bound in Great Britain by
T. J. International Ltd., Padstow, Cornwall

Every moment grows, like a plant with tangled, hidden roots, out of the soil of the past, and is invisibly shaped by it. What these children had suffered, uncomprehendingly, reached back further than their memories, back into the time before they existed and before their lives began.

And even that was not the beginning.

Anna Gmeyner, *Manja*

On the island one was driven back into the past. There was so much space, so much silence, so few meetings that one too easily saw out of the present, and then the past seemed ten times closer than it was.

John Fowles, *The Magus*

Oh! brave white horses! you gather and
   gallop,
The storm sprite loosens the gusty reins;
Now the stoutest ship were the frailest
   shallop
In your hollow backs, on your high arched
   manes.
I would ride as never man has ridden
In your sleepy, swirling surges hidden,
To gulfs foreshadowed through straits
   forbidden
Where no light wearies and no love wanes.

A.L. Gordon, *The Swimmer*

I

By the time the car arrived to deposit him, fourteen boys and a housemaster were already gathered at the makeshift terminus in Grimsby, the old building having been destroyed in the winter floods. The others cast dark looks at the newcomer, the one responsible for the fact that they'd had to sit in the draughty waiting room for two hours, dripping in their school-issue sou'westers, watching ferry after ferry disappear into the fog towards Lindsey Island.

Ten minutes into the journey, one of them detached himself from a knot of boys to ask Barney what year he was in. Over the engine's tinny drone, Barney told him.

'You're a bit big for the Second,' said the boy.

'I'm fourteen,' said Barney. And then, because his interrogator was not going to say anything, he added, 'I've been out of school for a while.'

'Huh,' said the boy, and wandered off across the open deck to rejoin his friends.

There was a big empty space below deck with wooden benches and misted-up portholes and rubber matting underfoot. Some of the boys hunkered down here, perching on their school trunks in groups of two or three, playing card games and swapping stories from their holidays over bottles of lemonade. The older ones paced about on deck in brooding pairs, collars turned up against the wind.

At one point the housemaster, Mr Runcie, sat down next to Barney on the creaking bench.

'Sir — dreadful business about Cray,' ventured one of the card-players. 'My old man says it sounds like the Russians, not an accident at all, sir.'

'A very sad thing,' said Mr Runcie. 'Whatever the cause.'

The card-player resumed his hand.

'First time away from home?' said Mr Runcie, turning to Barney.

'Sir.'

'You'll get the hang of it in no time. You've done the Eleven Plus?'

'Sir.'

No, he hadn't passed. The woman whose job it was to comment on such things said it must have been down to distractions at home. Home was Camden Town. It was all right. His dad — for some reason, Barney corrected himself here — his *stepdad* wasn't working at the moment, but he had a folk group that sometimes played in local pubs. Folk as in ballads, not Morris dancers.

When they had exhausted the conversation, Mr Runcie told Barney that he'd have to excuse himself to check up on the lads on deck. 'Wouldn't want anyone disappearing overboard on my watch, hey now, Holland?'

Barney tried to ignore the looks from the cabal of boys clustered nearby.

'*Hey now, Holland?*' sniggered one, which set off an echoing murmur from the others.

Barney let their voices disappear beneath the

throb of the engine while he drew patterns in the condensation on one of the portholes. With the tip of his finger he traced a tall ship, squinting at the distant horizon so that it would look as if the vessel was floating on the real sea outside. Then, using the corner of one nail, he filled in a series of tiny figures. When the picture was complete, he watched the ship of fools bob up and down on the green waves until fresh condensation started to collect on the inside of the glass.

As the vessel and its crew disappeared into the fog, he used his fist to obliterate the ship and everyone on board.

★ ★ ★

Barney didn't know much about Lindsey Island beyond what one of his dad's friends had told him when they'd found out he'd been offered a last-minute place at the Carding House School.

'We ditched them in the war,' he'd grinned, between swigs of bitter. 'Two weeks later, in come the Jerries, and they don't leave until '45. Right bastards they were, too.'

It didn't reflect well on the mother country, ditching the islanders like that, Barney's dad had observed. By his tone it was clear that this was just another way for Spike to say what he'd always maintained about Sheila and what he'd taken to calling 'her grand adventure'. The note left on the kitchen table had said she'd send for Barney and his little brother, Jake, once she had found a place to live. There had been just one letter after that, with a long bit about the ship

5

that was taking her back to Cape Town and the swimming pool on board where people who hadn't previously crossed the Equator were ceremonially dunked. It all sounded terribly raucous, and the boys had asked when they'd be allowed to join her. But the letter hadn't said anything about that, so Spike had told them that they'd just have to wait and see.

They'd been waiting the night one of the neighbours rang the health visitor because Jake was screaming with earache and a temperature and Barney hadn't known what to do. The next day, Spike came home to find a woman in flat shoes and cloudy spectacles standing outside the flat with the news that Barney was meant to be in school and his brother needed a doctor. Either they would both be taken into care, or Jake could stay under supervision if Barney could be found a residential place. That same evening, she called back with what she called 'good news': a spot had come up at a state boarding school on Lindsey Island — some distance, yes, but it was still England and the fresh air would do him good. Anticipating their ignorance, she had brought an atlas with her so that Barney could see exactly where it was. In fact, Lindsey Island didn't even fit onto the main map of Britain. Instead, it featured along with several other crown dependencies in boxes around the edge of the page: magnified beyond justification, plucked from their natural coordinates and lined up together like a drifting army of geological misfits. Lindsey Island appeared dislocated and empty; its neighbour, St Just, hadn't even featured beyond a black speck, like a seal's head poking out of the water.

None of this had bothered Spike, who said his boy deserved to go to a proper school, not a foundling home, because Barney wasn't a foundling and was old enough to know the difference too. It was decided before anyone asked Barney what he thought. And it was all Mum's fault.

Barney knew that if it hadn't been for the war Mum would have gone home to South Africa sooner, to a house in a sunny suburb by the beach. Then he wouldn't have had to be sent to a cold, grey island that was and wasn't England, and he wouldn't be just another weight tied to the wings of a beautiful bird: a dull man-child incapable of imagining a better life or understanding the one she had fashioned out of dreams and half-remembered memory.

★   ★   ★

It was too dark to see more than the shadow of a cliff overlooking the harbour as they clattered along the gangplank to the sound of water slapping against the sea wall. Glancing over one shoulder as the ferry lights switched off with an electric jolt, Barney was struck by the murky shine of the water and the blackness of the sky, which was dull with cloud. On the coach, the boys slumped into fuzzy, nicotine-scented seats, the youngest ones letting their heads loll against the rattling windows. Once they had left the town, a new kind of darkness opened up before

7

them — the headlights slicing a trail down the flat, hedged road, illuminating a pile of grey fur on the verge, or clusters of straw droppings imprinted with hoofmarks.

Finally, they turned into a driveway. Some minutes later, the coach braked at a house. Before it was a gravelled square and a fountain filled with green water.

While the others silently unloaded the luggage, Barney wandered towards the fountain and stood, hands in pockets, to consider the statue at its centre: a man and horse emerging from the motionless slime. The animal's outstretched neck and rolling eyes made it look as though it might unseat the naked rider, who grasped his mount's mane while pointing with the other hand at the rising moon.

How did the song go? Barney chewed at a bit of skin that had begun to peel beneath his fingernail, squinting even though there was hardly any light.

There is a fountain filled with blood
There is a fountain filled with blood
There is a fountain filled with blood
Flows from Emmanuel's veins!

He trailed a finger through the water before noticing that a lamp had switched on in one of the dormer windows: someone must have been woken by bars of light gliding along the wall. He froze. Did a hand clutch the lifted fabric? The harder he looked, the more convinced he became that someone was there, watching the boys emerging from their bus. A moment later, the curtain floated back into place, and the light switched off.

The school matron had appeared from the main building. With Mr Runcie, she led the boys across the square and into Medlar House. It was past ten, so the latest arrivals were given Ovaltine and digestive biscuits instead of supper. As they were emptying their mugs, a lad Barney's age wandered downstairs in a flannel dressing gown. The boy was pale and square-headed and moved as though a string was pulling him up by the collarbone. Mr Runcie introduced him to Barney as Robin Littlejohn. Barney felt himself being coolly registered by a pair of blue eyes set deep and slightly too close together.

'Holland's in your set, so I'll ask you to show him the ropes and make sure he goes to meet the Head tomorrow, straight after breakfast,' said Mr Runcie.

The last of the luggage was brought in, and the housemaster secured the front door. Giving the heavy iron latch a final, fond pat, he winked at the new boy as if they were already complicit in a marvellous secret.

★　★　★

Upstairs in the dormitory, a boy introduced as Hiram Opie flung both arms around Barney's shoulders, squeezing tightly. 'My favourite animal is the pteranodon,' he announced, before releasing Barney and turning to Robin with a triumphant expression. Hiram was the only boy

9

with his nightshirt buttoned to the top; his socks had been stretched to cover bony knees. 'It's rice pudding tomorrow,' he said. 'Rice pudding, pice rudding, mice running, cunning cunning mice . . .'

'Opie's simple,' said Robin as the other boy wandered back to his corner. 'He only learnt to tie his shoes this summer. But he's too old for primary school and too clever to go in a home, so his parents put him on the List.' He eyed Barney, taking in the tattered jumper, baggy shorts and mismatched shoelaces. 'You too?'

'He doesn't sound simple. What's a pteranodon?'

'Some kind of dinosaur, I expect.'

No one had mentioned assigned beds, so Barney took the one next to Robin. He would have preferred a corner spot, where there was more privacy, but Robin seemed to expect him to stay where he was.

'You're allowed five things on your side table,' he was saying — and Barney noticed how the other boys had already put out alarm clocks, comic books, Airfix models, family photographs. When Robin saw that he wasn't going to place anything on his table, he nodded in the direction of two boys on the other side of the room. 'That's Cowper and Shields,' he said. One boy was almost as large as Barney, with a downy shadow beginning to show over his long upper lip: he was the one who had interrogated him on the ferry. He had the other one in a headlock and was trying to stuff a sock in his captive's mouth.

10

'Percy.' Robin summoned a baby-faced boy. 'This is Holland. Holland, Percy. 'Weeps' to you and me. Brought his rabbit with him to school last year, and didn't we have waterworks for a month of Sundays after some owls got it one night . . . Did your mum remember to pack nappies this time, Weeps?'

'Shut up, Littlejohn,' mumbled Percy, casting a dark look at Barney before sloping back to his corner.

'Bed-wetter,' said Robin. 'Cowper spent last half-term at his place. Turns out Weeps is a bit of a Wild West fanatic. Has that wallpaper in his room covered in cowboys and Indians — the kind that looks like cat sick if you squint at it, you know?'

'Jesus.'

'That's what I said,' agreed Robin.

'No, it's my fags. I can't find them.'

Robin peered over Barney's shoulder, eyeing the muddle of grey pants, socks and shirts spewing from his battered suitcase. 'Was it locked when they brought it up?' he asked.

'There isn't a lock.'

'Well, that's your problem, then. Swift's probably been in and nicked them. You'll be in for it if he's found smokes in your case.'

He perched on the end of the bed to watch the new boy organize the contents of his suitcase into two drawers. Barney was the only one to have arrived without a proper trunk or tuck box. The school uniform he laid out on the chair was secondhand; the piping on the blazer was loose at the cuffs and there were holes picked in the

11

flannel where the previous owner had sported athletics badges.

'So it's London you're from?'

Barney nodded.

'What's that like, then?'

'All right. Where do we put our towels?'

'End of the bed's usually best. If you leave yours in the showers it'll get nicked.' Robin leant back on his hands. 'Poor old Cray was from London too.' He pretended to lift a piece of grit from under one fingernail.

'What sort of accident was it?'

'Plane crash, I heard — coming back from holiday. That's why you got his place, I imagine. Best not to think about it.' Robin heaved himself abruptly from the bed and consulted the clock that hung over the doorway. 'Ten minutes until lights out. Hey, do you want to hear a joke?'

'Go on, then.'

'All right, so there's this meeting between the Yanks and the North Koreans. They get together for a banquet, and during the meal this American general says to this Korean general, 'What are you planning to do after the war ends?' And the Korean chappie, he says, 'I will ride my bicycle all around my country, with my head held high!' And the American says, 'Well, that'll be just swell. And what will you do in the afternoon?''

Barney drew breath to say something but was cut off by a loud guffaw from Hiram. The boy with the elfin face clutched his sides and rolled onto the bed, his shrieks obliterating every other

12

sound in the room. Barney and Robin watched him with mounting embarrassment, until at last Robin shoved him off the bed and snapped, 'You're messing up the sheet, *retardus*.'

A knock at the door: the cue for lights out.

'The bell goes at quarter to seven,' said Robin. 'It's still the old air-raid siren, by the way. Takes some chaps a while to get used to, so don't be surprised if you wake up with a bit of a jump.'

Later, pinned beneath sheets that smelt of peppermint and lye, Barney reflected that the bed-wetter — he couldn't remember his name now — had watched him pull back the covers with wide, terrified eyes. And then he felt his insides churn: this had been the dead boy's bed. Robin had wanted him to take it so he wouldn't have to sleep next to an empty space — the kind of space where a ghost might turn up in the middle of the night, bloated and discoloured, with rotting eyes and bits of seaweed dangling from his fingers. Barney shaped his mouth around the name: Henry Cray. It felt like a cry in the darkness.

In this way he came to realize how he would be viewed from now on, as a visiting spirit from the future, an intruder resented for creating unseemly collisions with the past. And at that moment he began to feel himself becoming almost invisible — less real than the boy he imagined drifting in a sea of flotsam, in an ocean on the other side of the world.

★ ★ ★

13

Everyone had agreed that it would be better if the girl didn't return to school that term. There hadn't been time to register her for a place at Whitemoor Ladies' College, and the only other option had been to ask the Head if it would be possible for Belinda to attend classes with the Second Form at CHS, where her father Mr Flood was a housemaster. Belinda should have been in the First, really, but she was a precocious child, and the curriculum at St Mary's was known for its rigour.

'It would be unconventional,' observed Mr Pleming, when the request was put to him after the first housemasters' meeting of the year, just before the boys started to arrive.

'This is an unconventional place,' Mr Flood replied.

'You have a point,' said Mr Pleming, stroking his moustache.

Had the suggestion appealed to his competitive spirit — an attitude sharpened by the fact that St Mary's had not been requisitioned during the war? Fears of reprisals against English-born staff and boys had forced his institution's temporary relocation to Lincolnshire, while the girls' school had managed to maintain three mistresses and a student body of twenty native islanders throughout the Occupation years. Even today the girls lorded their pluck over his pupils, recalling tales of chemistry lessons undertaken covertly at night and the secret practice of using pages torn from *Juncker's German-English Dictionary* as kindling.

'It might even do the boys good,' ventured Mr

14

Flood, who felt that he might have lost the Head's attention.

'Quite right. Something to distract them from the Cray business.'

'That wasn't what I had in mind, exactly.'

The Head checked himself. *It is with very great sadness that we announce the passing of a student*, a last-minute addendum to his summer letter to parents had begun. *Although many members of the school community will remember those years when we mourned such losses with bitter frequency, in peacetime it is an exceptional occurrence and perhaps all the more shocking for this . . .*

'A civilizing influence, then?' he asked. 'But are you sure Belinda wouldn't feel slightly out of her depth?'

'She's had a difficult few months, Headmaster. She's grown up a lot this year.'

That spring, an illicit smog had floated over the high walls that surrounded the St Mary's estate and left its residue on the tennis courts and hacking trails. It had been carried indoors by girls fresh off the hockey pitch and infected their clothes and hair and the mugs of steaming cocoa that they carried upstairs at bedtime. Parents had once believed that the strong female example set by the Head and her retinue of bluestocking spinsters would constitute a solid barrier against attacks on their daughters' ignorance. But the pernicious cloud had penetrated even their best defences.

There was no secret that, in the absence of boys, some girls were more likely to make idols

15

of their teachers. The staff encouraged it, to an extent, as a means of fostering loyalty to the institution. Most would agree it was far preferable for a girl to spend several weeks mooning over a mistress or one of the prefects than to become entangled in mature liaisons with members of the opposite sex, of which, at St Mary's, there were next to none. A surly groundskeeper and the director of accounts — myopic and prone to spitting his sibilants — were the only men.

This had all been very well before the capsized boat and the rumours that subsequently began to circulate about a particular member of staff, the English mistress, Miss Gallo. The lot of it fuelled by adolescent hysteria, thought Mr Flood, who had been shocked to learn that his daughter was one of the girls being questioned over the affair. Of course, the questioning led to nothing — only tears from the other students and stubborn, stoical silence from Belinda. The child who had closed herself in her room for the duration of the summer was a stranger to him, a ghost.

But the fact remained that she needed an education, a point repeatedly stressed to him by his wife until he had finally capitulated and taken it up with Mr Pleming.

'Obviously, she would live at home,' said Mr Flood, following the Head out of the common room into the corridor. The smell of beeswax floor polish and long-neglected flowers gave the wood-panelled passage a distinctive pre-term odour, unsullied by boys' sweaty bodies, rubber shavings and adolescent experiments with pomade. 'She'd attend chapel, of course, and lessons. Not games, naturally.'

They had stopped outside the Headmaster's office, and Mr Pleming's hand was already on the brass doorknob. He stared at Mr Flood, taking in the droll mouth and hair combed, fine as a baby's, over his perfectly round head. Still not sure whether an agreement had been reached, Mr Flood extended one hand.

'We're very grateful, Headmaster. I'll make sure Belinda comes to see you first thing on Monday to express her thanks in person.'

'That won't be necessary.' They shook, and he opened the door. 'Now you go and enjoy what's left of the peace and quiet before the little rotters start to arrive.'

Returning to Ormer that evening, Flood had paused on the green to watch a nightjar cruise, silhouetted against an orange sky. The breeze that ran through the treetops felt like a long, slow letting-out of breath.

He let himself in through the side door and headed straight for the kitchen to tell his wife the good news.

* * *

Belinda worried at a string of costume pearls between her fingers, twisting the necklace in coils around one slender arm. It was a restless, unthinking motion, and after a few minutes her mother set down the tub of cold cream with a jerk.

17

'Do stop that, darling,' she said.

Belinda scowled and threw herself back onto the bed, dark hair fanning against the pink chenille. When this achieved no response, she pushed herself onto her elbows and studied her mother's bare back. The cotton nightdress had the narrowest of shoulder straps and scooped down low, revealing a single brown birthmark on her mother's shoulder blade. It made Belinda think of Miss Gallo's kimono, which the English mistress had worn to the beach like a child playing dress-up: a thick-heeled polymath in a concubine's nightie. Miss Gallo was not at all like the woman sitting at the vanity before her.

In the mornings, before she'd put on her face, her mother's naked eyelashes were brittle and her lips slightly too thin. There were two tiny scars and crinkling of skin under one arm, where she had cut herself falling into a shallow pond as a child, and a permanent bruise high up on one thigh, acquired in an adolescent riding accident. These marks were embarrassing to Belinda, because they hinted at places on her own body which she felt to be ugly and beyond her control. The neat, inward-turning navel and the black, square-topped bristles that peeped high up her thighs, around the pleats of her bathing costume — Belinda had grown inside that same body — were unintelligible and revolting to her.

There was a knock on the bedroom door. Lucia appeared, dressed in a pink bathrobe, her hair twisted into rag curlers.

'Is it true, Linda-Lou?' The child's eyebrows inched up into her golden fringe. 'Are you really

18

staying? Will you come to school with me now?'

'Your sister goes to big school,' said their mother, rising. 'You know that, Lucia.'

The younger child was ushered from the room with promises of one last chapter before bed, and so Belinda turned towards the dresser to examine the clutter of face creams, tonics and powders left in the wake of her mother's night-time regimen. Brushes, pencils and blotting pads; a jar of tablets labelled 'Pentazine'. Belinda picked up one pot and raised it to her nose. This was her mother's smell, she told herself, considering the label. Only then did she realize that, if this were so, it must also be the smell of countless other women.

For no obvious reason, the thought distempered Belinda. *A disruptive presence*, her headmistress had written. Suddenly it was all she could do to prevent herself from hurling the tub of cream at the nasty, frightened little face in the mirror.

⋆   ⋆   ⋆

Despite its pretensions to originality, The Carding House School was one of a breed of liberal institutions that had been forced to admit financial defeat after the Crash. The only thing that made CHS exceptional was the fact of its survival. That, and its remote location: on this austere island it was possible to keep costs low, while the ferry journey and fickle tides meant fewer visits from inspectors. The grounds had been bought outright after the Great War, death duties rendering it impossible for the Audley family to maintain the two-hundred-acre estate. The reception rooms were converted into the school's administrative centre, while the atrium doubled as a hall for concerts and assemblies and the larger kitchen served as a dining room. Classrooms had been adapted from the library, saloon and gun room, which were now connected to the main building by the old servants' corridor.

At first there were just three boarding houses — Ormer, renovated from the huntsman's lodge; Medlar, the stables; and Wool, so named for the carding house built early in the previous century for the first Lady Audley's amusement — but later a fourth had been added. Tern House incorporated a set of German barracks erected during the war years. Unrelenting North Sea winds and rain had left rust trails running down the corrugated roof. Its advantage, as the senior boys' boarding house, was that it overlooked both the forest and the green. On the other side of the main building the grounds became poorly lit and neglected, a smaller field here having been used as a timber store during the war. The Audley family vault and the disused old kitchens had remained under lock and key for as long as anyone could remember.

All of this was explained to Barney by Robin after breakfast. As they climbed the staircase from the dining room to the headmaster's quarters, the discussion moved on to the student caste system.

'Percy and Cowper are middle-class duffers,

like me,' Robin said. 'Too thick to pass the common entrance, so our people tell their bourgeois friends they prefer to send us somewhere *progressive*.' He spoke briskly, bored by the fact of knowing everything. 'Shields and Opie are military. They get locked up here because their people are always shuttling between Blighty and Malaysia, or Singapore, or Hong Kong — not like in the old days, where you'd actually get to live somewhere hot if your old man was posted there. You're scholarship, aren't you?'

'And Cray?'

Robin snorted. 'He'd have you think he was military because his hundred-times-great-granddad copped it at Waterloo. Cray was always a blowhard, though.' They had stopped outside a panelled door. 'Ratty's in there. Do you want me to wait for you?'

'It's all right.'

'Godspeed, Holland.' Robin rapped sharply on the door — more loudly than Barney would have done — before shoving both hands in his pockets and sloping off across the atrium. A voice from inside the office said something that Barney couldn't make out. He waited for several seconds, wondering if he should knock again or wait to be called.

'Come in!'

Barney put his shoulder to the brass panel already patterned with fingerprints and leant his full weight against it.

This was not the first time that Mr Pleming had watched a new boy struggle like a dung

21

beetle scrambling against a cowpat. He waited just long enough to be sure the lad wouldn't forget the indignity of this moment before crossing the room to pull the door open with a swift, hearty motion.

'Years of practice,' he said to Barney, who did not return his grin.

The Headmaster's office was all polished wood and thick-pile rugs and a ceiling like a wedding cake. There was a green baize-covered table in the centre of the room, flanked by bookshelves. Mr Pleming reached for the cues propped up on an umbrella stand.

'Do you play?' he asked Barney.

'Sir,' said the boy. 'In London the balls are different colours.'

'In London you must have played snooker. This is a billiards table.'

Barney chewed his lip and nodded.

'Sit,' said the Headmaster, indicating a chair in front of the desk and seating himself opposite the new boy. 'Holland.'

'Sir.'

'You came in with the last of the Medlar lads last night, did you?'

'Sir.'

'The crossing wasn't too rough, I hope?'

'No, sir.'

'Very good. And someone's shown you about?'

'Sir.'

'Excellent. You might have noticed, Holland, that unlike other schools our houses are separated by age. We find boys learn best when fraternization between older and younger chaps is kept to a minimum.' Mr Pleming tweaked his ear, shifting in the chair. 'A good house, Medlar. Mr Runcie never has any problems with them. You're not to worry about being a bit older than the lads in your form.'

'Sir,' said Barney, who felt that Mr Pleming didn't like him much, to judge by the way he had begun to shuffle his papers to and fro.

Mr Pleming set the file down on his desk and beamed at Barney.

'Have you any questions for me?' he asked.

Barney shook his head.

'Excellent,' said the Headmaster. He stood up and offered his hand across the desk. 'It's been good meeting you, Holland. I hope you'll be very happy here.'

★   ★   ★

'And then, just as I was about to go, he asked me if I'd misplaced a pack of Woodbines,' Barney told Robin later that afternoon, as they trundled towards the river path on their way to an induction at the boat house.

'What did you say?'

'I told him I'd never smoked in my life.'

Robin grinned at him and squeezed Barney by the shoulder.

'Cut out the tarting, Littlejohn,' barked the sixth-former in charge, catching the new boy's eye. Robin pulled a face before setting off at a jog to overtake the boys leading them on the rocky path. Exhilarated by the warm pressure of Robin's hand on his shoulder, Barney followed.

According to Robin, the island was like a sponge soaking up the ocean: saltwater rose through the ground so that one day the weight of it would drag the woods and everything else — school, masters, boys — into the sea. What was left of the pumping station, a mighty Victorian project designed to drain the surrounding fields, had already been mostly flooded by the river and its tributaries. A string of wire had been pegged along the opposite bank to prevent cows from wandering into the stream.

'You cross that line and you're trespassing for the next two miles,' warned Robin. 'If you keep walking, you'll reach St Arras.'

The six of them had broken off from the group after the meeting at the boat house and drifted downstream for their clandestine smoke.

'I lost my watch around here last term,' Robin told Barney. 'A silver Buren. You never know: it might turn up one day.'

Shields and Cowper were lighting cigarettes with a boy from another dormitory, Hughes, whose cheeks were blotched with rosacea. They didn't offer one to Barney, whose pride kept him from asking for a draw. Getting dressed in the dormitory that morning, he had discovered too late that someone had tied one of his trouser legs in a knot. As he struggled to push his foot through, Shields and Cowper had bundled him into the corridor and locked the door behind him.

'Nice one, Camden Town,' he'd heard them

snort on the other side of the door, as he tried to untie the knot before one of the masters passed by. Even now he felt the panic of hearing the lavatory door open, and Percy's startled expression at the sight of him, red-faced and shirtless, with one trouser leg on and the other contorted in a stubborn lump.

Hiram had joined Robin on the low bridge to chuck pebbles into the murky water. Before long, they had worked their way up from pebbles to stones and from stones to broken pieces of brick and concrete. They accompanied their attacks with ridiculous sound effects, the rat-a-tat-a-tat of machine-gun fire, the whistle of rockets and the hollow hum of V2s. Each successful strike was greeted with cackles and a scuffle after fresh ammunition.

'Look, Holland,' called Hiram, after a while. 'Look.'

Robin had clambered onto the highest ledge of the remaining wall and was brandishing a rock at the water.

'This is your captain calling,' he said through his other hand, which cupped an invisible loudspeaker to his mouth. 'We have reported failure in both engines. Repeat: failure in both engines . . . '

'That's not funny,' said Hiram. 'He's going to kill Henry Cray.'

'Mayday! Mayday!'

'Cut it out, Littlejohn,' said Shields.

'*Che barba*,' groaned Cowper, who had been to Venice in the summer and now peppered his conversation with Italian to make the others feel small. Hughes belched loudly.

'It's too late,' said Robin. 'We're done for. All hands on deck . . . '

The splash was disappointing. The others laughed as they turned their backs on the scene and began to wander up towards the towpath.

'Wait up, you lot,' cried Hiram, as he scrambled down from the bridge.

Barney wasn't invited, and following them would have meant leaving Robin, who was now staring with a deflated look at the rippling water. The sound of leaves twisting on their branches accentuated the silence.

'They're hypocrites, the lot of them,' said Robin. He still hadn't moved from his position on the ledge. 'You only get taken seriously here once you're dead. Everyone wants a piece of him now — everyone wants to be his best friend-in-mourning. If you ask me, it's sick.'

He dropped from the ledge onto the little bridge and walked across the brick walkway to Barney's end of the pumping station.

'This place will always be a shit-hole,' Robin said. 'The Krauts used Ormer as a brothel, you know. They diced up the bodies of their slave workers and used them to thicken the concrete for the walls.' He crouched by the stream and cupped his hands in the water. 'They're all a bunch of rotters. Cowper's a know-it-all prat who keeps Shields as a hanger-on because it's the only way he'll get Shields to share from his tuck. Weeps is as wet as a full nappy. Opie's thick as a plank. Hughes is downright revolting.' He sighed. 'Sometimes I wish that the Russians

26

would just get it over with and bomb us out of history. There's a fallout shelter in the woods, but it's not half big enough for the entire school. Sometimes I make a list in my head of the people I'd save, and the people I'd lock out.'

'Who'd you save?'

'Opie, I suppose. He's so pathetic it would be cruel not to, and he's got a heart murmur. And Morrell, because he's the cleverest boy in the school. He'd be good to have later on, once we'd survived the bomb.'

Barney nodded.

'Morrell's in Tern, two years up,' said Robin. 'Jonty — his brother — was there on D-Day. He stormed a German pillbox all on his own and took out four Krauts, just like that. The whole company would have died if it hadn't been for him.'

'So he came back? Jonty.'

'Do you think he'd have a plaque in the chapel if he had?'

'Oh.' Barney bent to tie his shoelaces. 'I'll bet your watch is here somewhere. If it's heavy enough it would just sink to the bottom.'

A siren's wail startled the cows from their spot of sunshine.

'Come on — Runcie will get testy if he sees the others back before us,' Robin said. 'We're not supposed to be out in groups smaller than three.'

Emerging from the forest gloom, they followed the path as it bent away from the river. They did not notice the housemaster's eldest daughter, now standing ankle-deep in one of the rock

27

pools, poking at something in the water with a long, bent stick.

★ ★ ★

Swift dropped the spoon into the saucer and leant back in his chair, reaching for the stack of papers he'd brought with him. They were sitting in the atrium beneath the inglenook fireplace. Recognizing the contrived camaraderie of a master sharing a pot of tea with his student, a pair of boys heading towards the dining hall exchanged grimaces. Already the institutional smell of cream-of-tomato soup had begun to waft up the kitchen stairs.

'*Les Peintures murales de Çatal Höyük*,' read Swift, withdrawing a single page from the stack. 'By Ivor Morrell, Esq.' He dumped it on the low table by the teapot. A handful of words, pencilled in angular, schoolboy cursive, showed through the thicket of red lines. Ivor opened his mouth to say something when the crash of books on floor tiles made them both look up. A junior boy was standing in the middle of the atrium, staring dejectedly at a pile of Latin primers strewn about his feet.

'Buck up, Tooley,' said Ivor. 'What a dreadful butterfingers you are.'

Blushing, the boy began to collect the books.

'Morrell,' said Swift. 'That's enough.'

'You were saying, sir? About my paper.'

'Frankly, Morrell, I found it rather *déplaisant*.' Swift reached for his tea, sipped and returned the cup to its saucer. 'You need to watch your use of the pluperfect. Particularly in the section about the *déesse des volcans*. Who, I might add, sounds rather less like Graves's poetic muse and rather more like something out of a penny dreadful.'

'Sir.' Ivor stirred his tea.

'Well, then,' Swift continued, leaning back in his chair and smoothing his hair with the palm of one hand. 'I take it from your reflection paper that you enjoyed *des bonnes vacances . . .* '

An explosion of laughter sounded down the hallway, followed by a patter of footsteps. Two laundresses wheeled a linen trunk across the atrium, stifling giggles when they noticed they had attracted glances from the French master and his pupil.

Ivor continued stirring his tea, concentrating on building a riptide against the current with his spoon. The laundresses were plain-faced girls, their features already taking on the same pasty cast as their mothers and grandmothers. None of the island girls who came to work at the school had yet managed to snare a sixth-former, although that wasn't to say it would never happen. Right now these two had contrived a reason to stop the trunk and fiddle with one of the wheels, which had turned askew. The younger one couldn't have been older than Ivor himself, and she threw quick, ostensibly surreptitious glances in his direction from where she knelt behind the trunk. Her companion widened her eyes and snorted back a fresh eruption of laughter.

The boy must have been aware that he was

attractive to them. Shyness was not the problem, noted Swift. There was disdain in his posture; distaste in the grim line of his mouth.

'*Et ta mère?* She is well, I hope?'

At last the laundresses moved off, and Ivor leant back in his chair. '*Beaucoup mieux.*' He swallowed. 'Apart from the seizures and the melancholy, sir. And the drink.'

Swift leant forward and said in a low voice, 'Morrell. That kind of talk doesn't do anyone any good, now, does it?'

'No, sir, it doesn't.'

They drank studiously, ignoring the dinner bell as though to acknowledge it might betray some kind of weakness. At last, Swift said, '*Ça suffit*, Morrell.'

'Thank you, sir.' He set about collecting the tea things onto a tray to return to the kitchen — languidly, to show that he didn't mind missing out on the freshest rolls or bagging a seat nearest to the buttery. Such concerns were for junior boys, not for Medes.

'Oh, and Morrell: see Matron about a haircut, would you? Before chapel tomorrow.'

★ ★ ★

When he had gone, Swift bundled the stack of holiday papers under one arm and returned to his attic set in Medlar House. As a student, he had boarded at Ormer, and he had been relieved to be assigned to a different boarding house when he returned as a master. His rooms were above the dormitories, so he was not bothered by the noise of pillow fights and scuffles over toothpaste and undeclared tuck; he could choose not to hear raids between neighbouring dormitories unless there was sufficient commotion to risk disturbing Mr Runcie, whose rooms were on the ground floor. In his little attic empire with the dormer windows framing two squares of sky, he might have been anywhere, far from here.

He lay down on the bed and closed his eyes, but the muscles in his face would not relax and his eyes trembled against his eyelids. Downstairs, a door opened and slammed shut. Footsteps crunched on the drive; someone yelled on the upper pitch. Swift rolled onto his side, torn between admitting defeat and getting up for a blanket and waiting out the draught until he was asleep and wouldn't care. It was to no avail. His meeting with Morrell had made him restless.

He undressed and put on shorts and a vest and a jumper. His plimsolls waited by the door.

He told himself that he wouldn't bother planning a route; his runs with the boys always followed roughly the same course, and today he intended to indulge in the luxury of venturing off school grounds. By the time he reached the lower pitch, there were no boys or masters in sight. He followed the towpath past the pumping station and over the footbridge into the adjoining field, where cows trundled halfheartedly after him, knowing deep in their bovine hearts that he would not stop to feed them. He was officially on another man's property now, though who that might be and whether he was likely to mind remained as much a mystery to Swift today as five years, ten years, fifteen years ago. It did not matter terribly.

Pausing to clamber over the stile at the far end of the meadow, he felt the sudden chill of being observed. Something on his blind side — not a movement so much as a presence. *If I don't look, I won't have to see who it is*, he thought. *Then I can carry on.*

He looked, and at first he saw nothing. The spaces between the trees at the other end of the meadow were dark and still. Only the uppermost branches moved, the leaves at the top flimsy against the leaden sky. Down below, the cows had moved off, leaving a space where only moments ago he had been, his footsteps leaving impressions in the flattened grass. There, now, stood a grey figure, watching him.

Swift blinked, and still the figure remained. Then he turned, and Swift saw that he was holding something long and bladed. Some kind of farm implement.

Krawiec had not been the school groundsman in Swift's student days. One of the other masters had told him that the taciturn Pole had spent the months after the war wandering the island, taking housewives by surprise when he pressed his face against their front windows to ask for food. Swift could not imagine why Mr Pleming should have offered Krawiec a job — perhaps out of guilt.

Now he was working his way across the field, using the long blade to slice the flattened grass, exposing layers of rock and rubble. Five years ago, he had found Swift in almost this precise spot.

Swift completed his climb over the stile, intent on resuming his run. Perspiration had turned cold against his skin; his heartbeat scooped into his stomach. Still Krawiec worked towards him, swinging his blade to and fro, looking up from time to time to regard Swift with an unchanging expression.

Swift waited until the groundsman stood within speaking distance.

'Picking up some extra work,' he said. It was a statement from which the Pole was supposed to infer a question.

'High time too,' continued Swift. 'Whoever owns this bit left it far too long.'

'Car needs a service.'

'Expensive business.' Swift swallowed. 'Of course. I don't suppose the Head's been terribly forthcoming.' He felt his pockets: sixpence. An insult. 'I'll see what I can do,' he said. 'This afternoon. I'll drop by this afternoon, shall I?'

Krawiec did not reply. Swift watched him turn and lever the blade high over his head, swinging it through the long grass with a grunt. He waited until the groundsman had worked his way down half the length of the meadow before clambering back over the stile and reeling back towards the school.

★   ★   ★

Robin had warned him that he'd better be on his guard, and sure enough on Monday morning

33

Barney was woken by four boys grabbing his wrists and ankles and hauling him out of bed. It was Shields and Cowper on his legs, and twins from the adjoining dormitory on his arms. They must have woken early, as they were already dressed. Together they bundled him downstairs and outside to the bin sheds, where Hughes was waiting with the lid of a compost box. The stench of rot — powdered eggs, potato peelings and fish heads — made the boys gasp as they lifted him in.

'The medicine, Hughes.'

While Cowper held his head back, Shields squeezed Barney's cheeks, forcing his mouth open. Hughes was holding what appeared to be a handful of small grey shells, and out of these he prised slippery white globs that he forced into Barney's mouth.

'Swallow,' ordered Cowper, as Barney sputtered and gagged on the horrible living jellies. 'You'll do five minutes in here before we let you out.'

There was no point in fighting them. Better to play possum. Barney closed his eyes against the darkness and covered his face with his hands while trying to breathe through his mouth. The limpets had left a salty aftertaste, and he scraped his tongue with his fingernails to erase their slimy trail.

It was hot inside the bin, as if all that decaying waste was oozing life, and his back soon turned wet with something that dripped down the sides. Outside, the others were standing guard, pretending to play at a ball game while chanting

34

a playground rhyme loud enough for him to hear.

> The worms crawl out and the worms crawl
> in,
> The ones that crawl in are lean and thin,
> The ones that crawl out are fat and stout,
> Be merry, friends, be merry!

Mr Runcie's voice summoned them to line up for breakfast, and there was a scuffle of feet. When he had begun to think that he must have been forgotten, Barney felt the bin rock as someone wrestled with the lid. It was Robin.

'Hurry up,' he hissed. 'They've had their fun. You've got about a minute to get dressed before Runcie notices you're not there.'

Cowper was straightening his tie and smirking as Shields and Hughes play-fought their way into line. They were standing in front of the large bay window, where a movement behind the glass caught Barney's eye. It was the French master, Mr Swift, standing with his hands in his pockets, staring straight at him. He must have seen the others too — must have made the connection between the boy picking the fish bones from his blazer and the crew of lads rough-housing not twenty yards away. He had seen and done nothing.

Barney knew that there was still a nasty whiff trailing him as he fell in behind the others. Filing into breakfast, he tried to ignore the other boys' delight at his humiliation and deflected with a shrug the pitying looks from the masters.

Eating a sandwich at the formica table, Belinda watched the last of the Medlar boys tumble into school. The mullioned kitchen window was closed, and their voices were muffled as they crossed the drive, the larger ones shoving their way through the doors ahead of the smaller lads when the masters weren't looking. Boys, she thought. Where did all that energy come from? And why did they expend it so stupidly?

She prised her sandwich apart and drizzled a slow trickle of syrup until tiny rivulets slid from the crusts. When the trickle had slowed to a drip, she squeezed the bread between her fingers and then took another bite.

Belinda's mother appeared in the kitchen doorway, head bristling with Toni perm curlers, just in time for *Woman's Hour*. The air was so close in here — why hadn't she opened the window? Before Belinda could object, the sounds and smells of the school drive flooded the room. It made her think of those days when the tall grass outside was whipped flat by the wind, when Miss Gallo would stop in the middle of the lesson to rush across the room and throw open the windows, so that in the dormitories at night the girls would giggle that she must have started the Change.

She watched her mother twist the ring from her finger, which had swollen in the late-summer humidity, and place it in a saucer on the window sill. The soap squeaked a complaint in her hands. Lather, rinse and re-lather — and then attacking

36

herself with the nail brush as well, scrubbing so aggressively that it was a wonder she had any fingers left at all.

'Syrup sandwiches again,' she was saying. 'Was breakfast not enough?'

Belinda reddened.

Thankfully, her mother didn't expect an answer: she was too preoccupied with her own impenetrable tics to launch a thorough investigation into her daughter's. In particular, tidying. Or rather, rearranging things — the sugar bowl, some letters, Mr Flood's cufflinks — into neat clusters, or columns, or piles. It was an infuriating habit, tinged with tragedy. *Sisyphean*, Miss Gallo would have called it. But Belinda was not at the age to wonder at the cause of her mother's unhappiness: only to be irritated by it.

Now there was the usual barrage of comments about crumbs and posture. Questions about the day's lessons and what time she would be home for lunch; a nudge between the shoulder blades, encouragements to work hard and smile when introduced to the masters. The same encouragements had been made five years ago, when Belinda started at St Mary's: only then her mother had been confined to her bed, pale and red-eyed with stomach flu so severe the doctor had wanted to send her to hospital for investigations. But Belinda's mother didn't believe in making a fuss — she had driven ambulances in the war, hadn't she?

By now the last of the boys had disappeared inside. Belinda waited for the siren's cry before heaving herself in silence from her chair and tugging her satchel from the hook by the door.

★ ★ ★

The laundry was at the end of the basement corridor. Robin had told him that the passage had once joined up to a network of German bunker tunnels: a concrete underworld now all but forgotten, sealed off from the things that grew and lived and died on the island. The walls were painted pea-green from the floor to shoulder height and whitewashed up to the ceiling. At the far end was a plastered-over doorway where the whitewash was a lighter shade than the walls. From the laundry there seeped a clammy smell of steam rising through hot linen. Human noises were muffled by machine ones: the roll and thump of pumping cylinders, the agitated whirl of spinning drums. Robin said that it became a lawless zone in the evenings, after the cooks and laundresses went home, so that the youngest pupils preferred to walk outside through the dark after prep.

It turned out that he had been summoned because Matron wanted to know why he hadn't registered a games shirt.

'If you think I'm going to spend half a day scrubbing grass stains out of a perfectly good school shirt, you've another think coming,' she said.

Then she asked how many handkerchiefs he'd brought with him, and Barney told her just the one: it had been a leaving present from Miss

Lynch in the flat across the hall.

'Just the one,' repeated Matron in a tutting voice. Barney could tell it wasn't a proper telling-off, but he made sure to look chastened.

Duly dismissed, he continued down the basement corridor with a dull dread of what awaited him upstairs. The morning's lessons stretched before him as no man's land stretches before a soldier in the trenches. He slackened his pace, concentrating on the flagstones and going out of his way to avoid the cracks, and began to whistle a favourite of Spike's from Friday nights at The Bull and Gate.

Is this your bride, Lord Thomas, she said,
Methinks she looks wonderfully brown,
When you could have had the fairest lady
That ever trod English ground . . .

At the top of the stairs stood a girl in a crumpled green gym tunic and T-strap sandals, her school tie twisted in a tight, angry knot. When she turned to face him, he saw that she was very young: all little-girl elbows and bony knees and black hair tied in a ponytail. She had a short fringe and a nose that sloped a little too severely. Was she ugly? She looked taken by surprise, as if caught out at some mischief.

'Do you know which one is Oakshott?' she asked. She didn't move aside to make room for him to pass.

'Who?'

'Oakshott,' she repeated. 'It's a room.'

There were two doors on one side of the

39

corridor, three on the other. Boys he recognized from his form were traipsing into the room nearest. A bell rang, and Barney forced himself past.

'Sorry. I'll be late.'

In the classroom where he joined his set, someone bumped Barney in the shoulder, pushing him towards the fray of ricocheting pencil stubs and India rubbers: detritus that plummeted into the waiting jaws of upturned desktops. The best places had already been colonized. Robin had paired off with Hiram in the back row. Hughes was sitting next to Shields, who was busy taking stock of his fountain-pen cartridges, and Cowper had left his satchel on the desk next to his in a way that suggested he didn't want the new boy anywhere near him. Barney decided to insert himself next to Percy the bed-wetter, who at least had found a neutral spot in the middle of the room, when a voice behind him sent everyone scattering to the empty benches.

'Preston, the windows.'

Barney turned to find his nose three inches removed from a silver tie clip. He stumbled backwards and nearly sat on Shields's fountain pen.

'Buzz off, new scum.'

'New boy, what?' The master's massive, pockmarked head teetered upon the collops of his neck as he considered Barney through thick spectacle lenses.

According to Robin, Doc Dower had worked in intelligence in Asia during the War, decoding telegraph messages in a dimly lit bunker. He'd

40

been captured by the Japs and escaped into the jungle only to be caught again a few days later. After that, they'd given him a complete torture treatment: bamboo shoots, starvation, water suffocation. If they'd been anywhere near the ocean they'd have trailed him behind a boat as shark bait — but luckily for Doc, the prison camp was up in the mountains, far from the coast.

Running both thumbs around the inside of his belt, he said, 'Holland, is it?'

'Sir.'

'Let's put you where I can keep an eye on you, what?'

The giant indicated a seat in the front row. As Barney sat, there was a hush of anticipation and delight: the girl from the stairwell had appeared in the doorway. The tips of her ears had turned a brilliant red.

'There's a spot behind Holland,' said Dower. 'You'll have no difficulty keeping up with this lot. Still making a hash of linear equations, aren't we, gentlemen?'

No sooner had Barney copied down the first sum than a crumpled ball of paper landed on his desk. Shields was glaring at him, shooting out his lip and indicating with jerks of the head that the message had been intended for Cowper. Barney balled the paper in his fist and let it fall at his feet. When he was sure that Dower's attention was focused on the boy at the board, he gave the paper a kick. After a while, another scrunched-up ball landed on his desk.

Heard the one about the St Mary's girls and the canoe?

Barney squashed the paper in his fist and propped his head on his knuckles, pretending to be lost in thought while twisting to steal a glance at the desk behind him. The girl was sitting with one elbow propped on her open book, chewing the end of a pencil, which she held between two fingers like a cigarette holder. Scrubbed and scentless, she was an anomaly among bodies that smelt of sweat, grass clots and burnt porridge skin; her stillness rankled.

Barney's gaze drifted across the tops of heads clipped short and parted smartly to the side to where Hiram and Robin sat in the back row. The smaller boy was hunched over his book, tongue poking out of the side of his mouth. Robin was staring out of the window at the pampas grass that bowed and swung in the late-summer breeze, idly tapping a pencil against his teeth.

'Eyes front, Holland. Have you finished?'

'Sir.'

Doc Dower rose from his desk and wandered over to look at Barney's work.

'That's a vertical line, Holland. It has an undefined slope, what?'

'Sir.' Now he had a closer view of grey hairs bristling from the master's large, drooping ears; of his pockmarked nose and magnified, watery eyes — and Barney wondered what it was that made him so popular among the boys. Maybe it was his cultivated brusqueness, or the knowledge that this fearsome giant was partial to Gracie

42

Fields and Lam-Dong tea.

'It's straight, boy, straight up and down. Like a telegraph pole, what? Erect.'

Behind him, Shields muffled a snort of laughter which quickly developed into a protracted coughing spell.

'So what's that *m* doing in here? *Ax* plus *By* makes . . . '

'*Stultior quam asinus*,' muttered Shields.

'Anybody?'

'C, sir.'

'Quite right, Cowper.' Doc Dower straightened, tugging at his belt again. 'I'd suggest you complete the questions in Chapter Two for Friday, Holland. Cowper will help you in prep. What, Cowper?'

'Sir.'

The master returned to his desk, and Cowper shot Barney a poisonous look.

'Books away, gentlemen. I can tell the grey matter is in need of a good stretch after a summer of inertia. Hands on desks.' Doc Dower began to pace up and down the rows, leaving a trail of musk — a sour smell edged with tobacco. 'A thousand rabbits inhabit two hundred acres of land. In January, twenty-five rabbits die of myxomatosis. Thereafter, one in every five rabbits is infected each month. At the end of the year, how many rabbits might I expect to find on a fifty-acre area?'

A boy in the middle of the room raised his hand.

'What is it, Fairborough? Sit up when you ask a question, boy.'

'Do all the infected rabbits die, sir?'

'So they do, the unfortunate beggars.'

'And don't they ever reproduce, sir? Isn't that what rabbits are known for, sir?'

Glances were thrown at the girl in the corner. Doc Dower removed his spectacles and used the end of his tie to remove a smudge from one of the lenses. 'Littlejohn! What about you?'

A bell rang, and there was a sudden scuffle of twenty bodies jostling to unpack desks. Over the din the housemaster barked, 'Will you be joining us at morning notices, Miss Flood?'

The room fell quiet again. Cowper, who had already reached the door, began to whistle 'She Wears Red Feathers', while Shields mimed a hula behind Doc's back.

'Mr Pleming told me to see his secretary first,' answered the girl, in a voice so small Barney had to hold his breath to make out the words.

'Quite right. If you come with me we might avoid getting tangled up with this lot, what?'

There was not time to tell whether her smile expressed relief or disappointment. She rose and, pressing her books to her chest, followed Doc Dower into the corridor.

'Fancy that,' said Robin, as they joined the tide of bodies flooding towards the atrium. 'A VIP. Just you watch the special treatment she'll get.'

Barney thought he sounded just like Spike, who never made any bones about the fact that Mum had always behaved as though she deserved better than she got. It had been wicked to say that the bombing had been exciting:

44

watching the sky light up and swarm with planes, waiting for death to rain from the air. Mum used to boast about the night she left Barney in a dustbin, when there hadn't been time to run for the shelter. She'd been disappointed, years later, when she asked him if he could remember any of it, and he was forced to admit that he couldn't. And because the war was the one thing that they should have been able to share, his mother had resented this, just as she had resented the boredom and indignity of being poor in peacetime.

Watching the girl's moss-green tunic disappear into a sea of grey wool, Barney wondered what it was that she had left behind, and whether she, too, resented her place here, among them.

Dear Spike,
Its Sunday night which means we all have to write letters home in prep. This is the first letter I've written so dont laugh or Ill deck you.

Schools not too bad. The food is cracking but you have to say it stinks or else people wonder what you get fed at home. Some of the lads get tuck which is jars of jam that they have to share with the rest of us. Cowpers mum makes brilliant lemon curd. Too bad her sons a complete idiot.

As you can imagine I'm a real hero and am extremly popular haha. Robin looks out for me all right. Opie doesn't get beat up because hes simple. The others are Hughs Cowper Percy (Weeps) and Shields who always thinks

45

that people are stealing from him.

Sagartians are Sixth formers. Below them are Medes and then us Lydians. Sagartians and Medes can wear any jacket or shoes they like. First formers don't get called anything. Jerry is the ghost in the basement corridor.

The masters are all right. Robin says Runcie isnt half as smart as Swift even though he taught Swift before the war. Swift got a First and worked in the Resistance in France if you believe that. Swift is a top sneak. He took my fags and binned some comics of Robins because we're not allowed Yankee stuff.

Tell Jake I miss him and dont touch my shrapnel while I'm gone. Have you seen Seven Days to Noon? Robin saw it in the holidays and said it was brilliant.

Times up. Ill write again next week. You can write back if you like but dont feel you have to.

Love,
Barn

'Who's Spike?'

Barney shoved the letter into its envelope, wondering how long Robin had been reading over his shoulder.

'My dad.'

'You call him Spike?'

'That's his name.' Robin grunted, but Barney could tell he was impressed. 'He's my stepdad, actually.'

'Oh. No, don't do that . . . ' Robin reached out and Barney froze, the tip of his tongue grazing

46

the dry envelope glue. 'Runcie seals them. You put it on the pile up at the front.'

Barney considered the letter in his hand.

'You go on — I just need another minute,' he told Robin.

But Robin showed no sign of leaving. Instead, he propped himself against the corner of the desk as Barney blacked out some bits. 'So your mum remarried?'

There wasn't much point in admitting that there had never been a ceremony. 'After the war.'

'What happened to your old man?'

'He died in Burma.'

'Hard luck.'

'It's all right.' Barney eyed the letter in Robin's hand. He was turning it along the edges against his knee, the corners pressing white spots in the skin. Outside, a thin rain had begun to hiss on the gravel drive.

'My dad was at Dunkirk,' said Robin. 'Well, almost. He got out just before. Supposedly, they stuck him in a desk job for the war, but really it was Intelligence — he's just not allowed to say so. He knew someone who won a Victoria Cross.'

'That's not bad.'

'So why'd you address it just to him? Do you write to them separately?'

'My mum's in South Africa at the moment.'

'What, on safari?'

'No, you drip. In Cape Town.' Robin continued turning the letter on his knee. 'She's gone away for the air. She'll be back for the holidays.'

'Long way to go for the air. My mum says

47

Thorpeness has the best air anywhere. It's expensive, though. My uncle's friend has a house there. It's a lot closer than Africa.'

'She has family there.' Barney pushed his chair out from the desk, sensing that Robin wanted to be impressed. 'The air in London kills people, you know.' Back home, the soot from coal fires mingled with bus exhaust and tobacco fumes to stain the buildings grey. Pigeons with stumps for feet where their toes had been burnt off on electric wires primped at wings made black and greasy by the filth.

'I've heard everyone eats snoek there,' said Robin. 'Fresh, though. Have you been to Africa, then?'

'I'm going soon. Next year, perhaps.'

'But you haven't been before?'

'No.'

They wandered up to the front and deposited their letters on the pile that had begun to accumulate on Runcie's desk. The housemaster smiled at Barney.

'Going for any teams, are we, Holland?'

'I don't think so, sir. Not unless there's football, sir.'

'Shame, that. I suppose it will have to be cross-country, then. Mr Swift takes the runners. I'll let him know to expect you on Tuesday, shall I?'

'Swift's a slave driver,' said Robin as soon as they were outside. 'He leads runs right down to the sea and back up across the chalk ridge. Four miles, sometimes five at a go. You only have to

48

look at that chest to know he has a horse's lungs. Are you fit?'

'I can handle it all right.'

'It's harder for smokers,' continued Robin. 'Here's a tip: the first circuit starts outside Tern. They cut through a footpath in the woods towards the main road. If you're anything like me, you'll be shagged out pretty fast. Swift will hang back to make sure none of the stragglers try to duck off. The trick is to keep yourself slightly ahead of the slowest ones, but not so far ahead that everyone's watching you. That way, no one will notice if you slip off to the bunker. You can't miss it — big concrete thing with a metal roof.' Robin slung his arm through Barney's. 'Morrell used to do it all the time. You hang around for half an hour or so, then you rejoin the group on the way back.'

★   ★   ★

He had already been warned about the horrors that awaited him on the chalk ridge — biting insects and tall grass that left razor marks on the boys' bare legs — but it was the pain in his chest which made Barney pay attention to opportunities for escape. On the approach to the woods, exactly as Robin had predicted, Swift fell back to bark at a cluster of first-formers beginning to wheeze and complain of cramp. Three Medes had already taken off into the distance. Staggering his position towards the back of the main group, Barney saw that Swift and the younger ones were still a good fifty yards behind.

By then, he had already spotted the glint of corrugated steel through the trees.

The bunker was larger than an Anderson shelter and roofed with galvanized panelling that sloped to shoulder height. Barney dropped to his knees and waited, pressing his hands against the cool concrete wall as he listened to the patter of feet squelching through wet leaves. There was a silence as the middle group disappeared over the hill — then fresh footfall as the younger boys shuffled past.

'Jocelyn! Vickers! West!' Swift bellowed. 'You have until the count of three to get to the top of that hill, or else you'll be doing circuits tonight . . . '

Within moments, they had gone too. The bunker's outer door had been left on the latch and swung to with very little effort. Inside, just a few feet on, was another, heavier door.

'You can't get in that way.'

Behind him stood one of the Medes who'd left the rest of the group behind earlier in the run. He had black hair combed to a dovetail and a crooked mouth. He was picking at his teeth with a twig. Barney tried not to stare. Robin had told him that younger boys were not supposed to smile at seniors.

'You have to use the other door,' the older boy said. 'This one's sealed shut.'

'Right. Sorry.'

'You don't need to apologize.' He stepped onto a log and held his balance, gripping with plimsolled feet. 'So why'd you bunk off the run?'

'I was getting tired.'

'Course you were.'

Barney bristled. 'What about you?'

The other boy slid off the log and wandered around the side of the bunker. 'I don't give a damn,' he said. 'Swift's a twat. Anyone who comes back to teach at the school where he was a student is a twat, if you ask me. Want to see inside?'

The air within the shelter was cool and dank. Because the entrances were built at right angles to the main chamber, even with one door fully open the farthest reaches remained in darkness. Floorboards creaked as the two made their way inside. After a moment, Barney heard the switch of a match being struck. He turned to see the older boy holding a cigarette between his lips.

'I'm Morrell,' he said.

'I know,' Barney said. 'Robin told me you used to come here.'

'Who?'

Barney began to feel uneasy. 'Robin Little-john,' he said. 'In the Second.'

Ivor snorted. 'Oh, him,' he said, seating himself on a bench that ran the length of the room and kicking his heels onto an overturned metal bin. 'A friend of yours?'

'Maybe.'

Ivor grunted, blowing smoke through his nostrils. 'And you are — '

'Holland. Barney Holland.'

'If you ask me, Holland, you don't want to be getting too involved with Littlejohn. Just between us, he's rather . . . fragile.'

'Seems alright to me.'

Ivor took a long, deep drag of his cigarette. 'He's untrustworthy. Attracts vulnerable types. That idiot kid, Opie . . . and now you: a charity case from the urban poor.'

'Sod off,' said Barney, who still hadn't decided whether or not he'd been invited to sit and so remained standing.

'Cheek.' Ivor leant his head against the wall. 'Tell me, Holland: how would you rather die — charging into battle on horseback or jumping out of a plane?'

'Neither.'

'Naturally. But if you had to choose.'

'On horseback, I suppose.'

'I think I'd prefer to die flying. Failing that, I should like to die of gluttony. I'd do it in here, and eat myself to death right on Ratty's doorstep.'

Barney remembered what Robin had said about his list of people to save and the ones he'd lock out in the event of a nuclear strike. 'You'd never fit enough food in.'

'I'd start outside, like animals do before they hibernate,' said Ivor. Then, with a smile as if he was swallowing something unpalatable for politeness' sake: 'Animals stuff themselves with food, and humans stuff themselves with stories. You'll have noticed that, here. Apparently old Cray was a brilliant spin bowler. That's a myth. Or people will say he was everybody's friend — a really popular, happy little chap. That's a myth too.' He squashed the cigarette stub into the floor and ground it with his heel. 'It's just the school's way of protecting its ghosts. No one can make a hero of Cray, because he didn't die fighting for anything. But you can't tell boys that, because we're supposed to believe that death happens for a reason. For glory, for eternity.'

'What's it like having your name on a plaque in the chapel?'

Morrell withdrew another cigarette from his pocket. 'Do you smoke? You shouldn't, you know.' He handed it to Barney, struck a match. 'Seeing as you ask, it's an existential conundrum. I imagine it's a bit like being a backwards ghost. Dead-to-be. Tomorrow and tomorrow and tomorrow . . .'

'Like the Jerry in the basement corridor?'

Ivor laughed, holding the match out. 'Who told you that?' Barney didn't reply. 'Littlejohn again. Well, a bit like that, I suppose. You know why half the school's not here, don't you?'

'Robin said there was dry rot in the walls.'

Another snort of laughter. 'The Germans blew up the entire west wing before they left. It was Ratty's idea that the students should help to rebuild it. He had everyone hauling these bricks up from a pit on the other side of St Arras, like Pharaoh's slaves building the pyramids. Now, that's what I call fascistic.'

Barney didn't know what to say, and so he said nothing.

'Is that Dolly's daughter in your form?' asked Ivor.

Barney nodded. 'Her name's Belinda. She's in my set for Maths.'

'Does Dolly teach you?'

53

'No, we have Doc Dower.' Barney decided to take his chances and sat down, even though Ivor hadn't told him to. 'Is it true he was tortured by the Japs in the war?'

'Not unless there were Japs fighting in Italy,' replied Ivor. 'Honestly, do you believe everything those idiots in the Second tell you? They'll say he bludgeons mice with a cricket bat for sport too.'

'How do you know?'

'Because Dower had me over to his set when I was in my first year.' He cast a scornful look at Barney. 'He's not a pederast. He taught me how to make spaghetti carbonara like they did in Rome. No cream, lots of pepper. It's better with real eggs, of course. And bacon, not mutton.'

Barney struggled to imagine Doc Dower and Ivor Morrell cooking dinner in the master's kitchen.

Ivor clenched his cigarette between his teeth and pulled a comb from his back pocket. 'That Belinda goes walkabout at night,' he said, smoothing his hair on either side. 'I've seen her wandering past Tern after lights-out.'

Barney stubbed his cigarette against the wall. 'Where to?'

'I haven't a clue. Perhaps to join a witches' coven in the forest.'

'You could follow her one night.'

The older boy looked up at Barney with a look that was almost fierce. 'Could I? And why would I want to do that?'

The shadows began to shift, and Barney glanced at the open door. The patch of forest floor outside the entrance had darkened. 'That lot will be getting back soon,' he said.

'You go on. Wait at the hill, but make sure Swift doesn't see you. Best to slip in behind him.' Ivor flicked his cigarette at the upturned drum. 'Nice meeting you, Holland.'

★　★　★

Waiting by the mound of freshly turned earth, Mollie Flood reflected that the tree was a vulnerable-looking thing, dwarfed by the plaque emblazoned with Henry Cray's name and the dates *1940–1953*. One or two people had proposed a panel in the chapel, but the consensus had been that there simply wasn't enough space — and besides, tree-planting supported irrigation, vital to managing the island's water levels.

Next to the cakes table, a group of junior boys flapped restlessly in their still-too-large uniforms. At their first school tea the youngest ones always affected a toughness that disagreed with their tidy partings and round faces. Before the year was out they would be unrecognizable, transformed into loafish adolescents. This was the week in which several would fall victim to the Sagartians' midnight dormitory raids: the smallest lashed to the wall bars in the athletics hall and left until morning. Her husband had been the one to discover them once: two boys hanging from the gym bars, pale and furious and exhausted. Both had refused to reveal their tormentors' names. They would grow up to form cosy

55

gangs and practise the same laughing cruelty in their own time.

Behind the juniors stood three larger lads drinking Kia-Ora. One was in a second-hand uniform, while the other two wore civvies: point-collared white shirts, wool blazers, shorts and knee socks. Mollie did not recognize the first, who was stolid and glooming, but the others — a red-haired boy with an obvious developmental problem and another with the face of a Fra Angelico seraph — she remembered from the previous year. The taller two were trading insults, while the delayed one grinned stupidly, revealing pointed teeth stained a bright orange.

Michael Swift had paused nearby to speak to them in a fellow-to-fellow sort of way. There were lines at the corners of his eyes now, drawn by the wind on long runs across the chalk ridge. Just five years ago, Mollie had mistaken the blue-eyed French master for one of the older boys.

'Got there in the end.' Her husband, spruce in a summer suit that had perhaps become just a little snug around the middle, appeared at her elbow with the tea and a plate of meat-paste sandwiches.

'Is that a new boy?' She settled herself on the blanket. The tea was lukewarm and weak.

'Ah, yes. Holland. Scholarship chap from London.'

'I see he's hit it off with Henry Cray's old friend.'

Her husband didn't reply, focusing instead on

56

blowing imaginary steam from his cup. He had never understood her questions about the boys' private lives — his term for their friendships and personal interests — as if they were fully formed human beings worthy of considered discussion. He did not see the point in spending time analysing them as individuals, when it was the disordered mass that he was tasked with handling in the classroom and the dormitories.

'I thought I'd do a roast chicken tonight — the girls will like that.'

'Sounds lovely.'

Mollie waved a fly away. 'Belinda's been eating like an ox lately. I caught her chewing blotting paper the other day.'

'Must be another growth spurt.'

'I think she's bored.'

Flood turned to look at his wife. 'What on earth has she got to be bored for?'

'I suspect she misses her friends. There's not much here for a girl of her age. She doesn't make any effort to pretend to enjoy coming to the shops with me on the weekend. All she wants to do is have baths. I caught her running her third of the day last night. And she's been hideous with Lucia the last few evenings . . . '

'That's perfectly normal.'

Mollie peered into her teacup. A gnat was floating in what remained of her tea, drifting on the cloudy brown tide as it slapped against the sides.

'Is he awfully deprived?' she said. To look at him one might have thought they'd lost the war. She ignored her husband's sideways glance as

57

she tipped the dregs of her tea onto the grass. 'He's not at all troubled? Coming from London, I mean.'

'Not that I've been told.' The youngest boys in the school tended to be less complicated than the ones old enough to have experienced bewilderment or grief for fathers returned from abroad or dead in the war. They didn't feel entitled to the same battle-weary attitude, these lads who had to be evacuated with their mothers, or in some cases hadn't been evacuated at all. 'You'd have heard about it if there was anything untoward in Belinda's set.'

'Would I?' This was not the sort of place where word spread quickly: *loose lips sink ships* was a hard mantra to forget. The masters' wives were friendly, of course — they hosted tea parties and knitting circles — but these were cagey affairs dominated by shows of unflagging loyalty to their husbands. Mollie didn't understand their forced jolliness or the smiles that said *Aren't we lucky never to have left school?* — but she tried to emulate their matter-of-fact pride at being too busy with their own families to bother trying to be substitute mothers for the boys. Mollie had never got along particularly well with the Head's wife, although she pitied her for being married to a man whose overbearing solicitude concealed what Mollie considered to be a transparent contempt for women.

The three boys, meanwhile, were picking their way across the green, scattered with clusters of students enjoying their tea in the sunshine. Mollie noticed the young seraph nudge the new boy in the ribs, nodding in the direction of Ormer House. Her elder daughter was emerging from the side door: barefoot, in Peter Pan blouse and blue capris. Belinda ignored her mother's eye as she cut across the green, making a beeline for the cakes. That morning, she had said she wouldn't be attending the tea because she was stared at enough during school.

'You see, her greed won out,' Mollie remarked.

The three boys had finished eating, and now the seraph and the scholarship lad had begun to tussle on the grass. Belinda filled her plate with scones and a slab of crusted yellow cream before traipsing along the perimeter of the green to enjoy her spoils in privacy. Several of the students looked up at her with little interest: as a master's daughter she was off-limits to them. Yet something about that lonely figure skirting the chattering crowds filled Mollie with pity, and also resentment at what she perceived to be unnecessary furtiveness. Without thinking, she called out after her.

'Darling!'

The cry made those standing nearby stop to look at the girl, who froze with a startled scowl. For a moment she seemed to stare straight through them all — before turning and continuing towards a copse of trees in the shadow of the abandoned east wing.

★ ★ ★

Swift was the next person to see her, an hour later, squatting on the steps leading up to the old

59

kitchens with her head in her arms. He knew the girl by sight, but had not spoken to her since the drinks party at Flood's five years earlier, when the French master had arrived as a new member of staff. She had been a recalcitrant only child at the time, and Swift had not warmed to her.

'What's this?' he said — and by 'this' he clearly meant her, here.

Belinda looked up. The fine, almost translucent skin around her eyes was blotchy. She stared at him with a closed look, pressing her palms onto the concrete step.

'Well, now? What on earth is the matter?'

The girl's face turned even redder as he crouched on the ground in front of her. She shook her head, mouth crumpling to rein in fresh tears.

'If it's to do with any of the boys, you must tell someone,' he said.

Again she shook her head — impatiently this time, angry.

'Shall I take you home? Perhaps it's something you'd prefer to tell your mother?'

'She can't do anything about it,' said Belinda. She nodded at the far side of the kitchen, where weeds grew among the rubble. 'It's too late for anyone to do anything about it.'

'About what?' asked Swift. Despite himself, he set off to investigate beyond the kitchen wall. Belinda stood up — but then she hesitated, hanging back while the master disappeared around the corner of the building.

What remained of the walled garden was now overrun with tall nettles and building debris:

60

broken bricks, bits of tile and thick pieces of green glass mixed in with clumps of chalky soil. The ground was spotted with holes dug by small, burrowing creatures. He told himself that she had probably come across a snake, or a rat. Perhaps she had been stung by the nettles.

A trowel had been left on a ledge of wall, next to which was a pile of freshly turned earth. Over the ledge, something wrapped in a newspaper, preserved from the elements by a piece of patterned oilcloth. Brownish skin like leather, an open mouth, two arms folded like tiny wings.

By the time he returned to the kitchen steps, the girl had disappeared.

★ ★ ★

'What I don't understand is how it could have taken this long to turn up,' said Pleming, handing the French master a tumbler and settling in the larger of the two armchairs. 'Half the island buried their silver before the Germans arrived, and half the island dug the place up again once they left. You'd think somebody would have come across it long ago.'

'One would, yes.'

'Poor old Flood — as if they'd not had enough troubles already.' Pleming arched his back to get a better view of the window. 'What are that lot doing?'

From where he sat, Swift could make out the tops of several heads still milling about the police car in the drive. 'Medlar boys.'

'Get them to clear off, would you? On your

61

way down.' This would be the second time this year that he'd have to be interviewed by the police superintendent. Pleming was tired of Hastings's face: the sallow cheeks and petulant mouth. 'I imagine he won't be much longer with the girl.'

Recognizing Swift's expression as he emerged from the main building, Robin tugged at Barney's sleeve.

'Buck up,' hissed Cowper, who had also seen the French master approaching. Immediately the others began to drift away from the police car — all except Opie.

'Is it true, sir?' he said. 'That there was a Jerrybag baby buried behind the old kitchens?'

'For Christ's sake, Opie,' muttered Shields.

Swift planted himself in front of the group. In the excitement, Hughes's rosacea had flared to a dazzling scarlet. Percy looked as if he was about to cry. Littlejohn was regarding him sourly, as usual. The new boy was more interested in peering into the police vehicle.

'Get away from there, Holland. Superintendent Hastings will be out soon, and he shouldn't have to fight his way through your little mob to get to his car.'

'Well, sir?'

'Opie, whoever's told you that is spouting a load of old rubbish.'

'Was it really a mummy, sir? Like the Tollund Man? Is it true that babies mummify if they've not eaten anything before they die, sir?'

'I shouldn't think it's any of your business, Cowper. All of you should have been back in

62

Medlar half an hour ago. Where's Mr Runcie?'

'He's gone into town, sir.'

'It was Dolly's daughter who found it, wasn't it, sir?' said Robin.

'I shouldn't think it makes the slightest difference who found it, Littlejohn,' snapped Swift. 'The next person who asks about it will be put straight on the Head's List. Get back to the house, all of you.'

Watching them slouch off, he was tempted to call after Cowper to pull his hands out of his pockets — but he resisted. And it was because he decided not to raise his voice that he heard Littlejohn mutter to the new boy, in a whisper that was meant to be heard, 'Everyone knows a woman on board a ship is bad luck.'

★ ★ ★

The joint had been stewed and gave off a rotten smell that drifted from the head of the table where Mr Runcie, in the housemaster's weekly ceremonial, carved. The blade struggled against the grain, working deep grooves into the meat before finally piercing down to bone. The meat was an anaemic colour and the size of a small dog or large cat, but without clear signs of rib or socket it might have been anything. Perhaps this was intentional: perhaps someone in the kitchen had realized that, under the circumstances, there would be little appetite for something identifiably dead before its time.

Next to Barney, Opie's mouth hinged open in unconcealed delight, his tongue flat and red and

63

shining. He was watching the plate now approaching, passed hand to hand down the table. 'Lovely,' he murmured.

According to Cowper, it had been a collaborator's child. 'Either that, or it came from one of the French tarts the Jerries brought over.'

'Why shouldn't it be one of ours?' asked Hughes.

'That's what I said,' Robin reminded the others. 'I said that before — didn't I, Holland?'

Barney couldn't remember, but he nodded anyway.

'It could have been one of the girls who work in the laundries,' said Shields. 'Affairs and that, you know.'

'What do you know?' said Cowper. '*Non molto*, I'd say.'

'More than you do.'

'Oh, shut up.'

Shields leant across Robin to present Cowper with a full view of the contents of his mouth: a glistening, sticky mess of half-chewed brisket and mash.

'Stop that,' snapped Robin, who'd been in a mood all morning.

'We weren't talking to you, so put that in your cake-hole,' said Shields.

Cowper reached across to grab the piccalilli. 'With relish. The beef's foul.'

'You should be grateful we have any meat at all,' said Opie. 'When you think of all those poor orphans in Poland and Romania and *Hungary*.'

Shields snorted and bounced one leg beneath the table. There were pen marks scribbled on his knee, just below the cuff of his shorts, from where he'd been playing a game of noughts and crosses against himself during Latin.

'What I don't understand is why anyone thinks it's fair that we're worse off now than we were before, thanks to all those poor orphans in Poland and Romania,' said Cowper. He cut a glance at the dark-haired figure at the end of the table. 'Though some can go home whenever they like to be fed by Mummy. Cheese soufflé and baked bananas with blancmange every day of the week.'

'Even Flood can't get cheese off ration,' said Shields.

'With pins like that, his missus can get whatever she wants.'

Barney had only ever heard his dad's friends talk about the black market. 'I've heard she goes wandering in the woods after dark,' he said. Five pairs of eyes flickered up at him before consulting with each other in silence.

'Who told you that?' ventured Shields.

'One of the boys on the Tuesday run.'

Robin straightened. 'Morrell, you mean,' he said. His face had a pinched look. 'He does like to play with us, you know. Pretends to take a paternalistic interest, but really he's just messing about.'

Barney didn't know what 'paternalistic' meant. 'I don't think he made it up,' he said. And then, feeling his confidence boost, he added: 'Anyone can see she's a queer kid. Perhaps she was looking for it.'

'Honestly, Holland, I wouldn't take anything

Morrell says too seriously.' Robin's voice had acquired a high note of protest.

'I had him for a six-o'clock once,' said Shields. 'When I found out he was on duty I considered asking Runcie for the lash instead. Morrell had us doing press-ups in the river.'

'One boy broke his arm trying to climb off the gym bars after Morrell tied him there,' said Percy. 'If that wasn't bad enough, when he came back to lessons he had to let Morrell sign his cast.'

'He should be in borstal after what happened last year,' said Cowper. 'Psychopathic, that's what. But because Ratty knows he's the first boy in the school's history to have a shot at Oxford, even the pig Hastings can't touch him.'

'One day, he'll be the chap with a finger on the button that will destroy us all,' said Hughes between inhalations of semolina. 'Speak of the devil.' At the table opposite, the Mede had risen to return his plate to the kitchen. It was the first time Barney had seen him in his school blazer, and only now did he notice the black band stitched around one arm.

'It's for his old man,' said Hughes, seeing him stare.

'Copped it in the war?'

'Hardly. The old devil deserted on Crete.' Hughes sucked his teeth. 'The Stukas start bashing up the airfields, right? And he's so busy picking off the Kraut paratroopers tangled up in olive trees that he misses the evacuation to Egypt. Spends the next three years with a Greek family and comes home after the liberation.

66

Finds out that his first-born son got killed in Normandy, so he takes to drink, just like his missus, and finally croaks of a heart attack.'

'Not very edifying,' said Robin, using a word unfamiliar to Barney for the second time that day.

'Mrs Morrell is drugged up all the time now,' continued Hughes with indifference. He pressed the back of his spoon into the yellow lump on his plate. 'Religious nutter.'

Shields nodded at Cowper's fork. 'Your turn today, Cowper.'

'Bollocks. I took one the day before last. And I'm running out of space.'

It had been Shields's idea that they should take turns smuggling an item of cutlery out of the dining hall after each meal, a prank they were determined should acquire the status of school legend before the end of term.

'Old Baggage checks our drawers, you know.' Cowper slid the fork into his sleeve. '*Va bene*. I can't keep wrapping them in socks for ever.'

'Come on, Holland,' said Robin, who was now able to pretend that he was tired of the conversation. 'There's a load of fellows going into town this afternoon. If we're quick we can nip in to catch the second half of whatever's on at the Palace.'

'*The Cruel Sea*,' said Cowper. 'Saw it last week.'

'Good thing I didn't ask you, then.'

Robin had stored enough pennies in a sock under his mattress that he was able to make up the difference with Barney. 'We can get in

67

upstairs for one and three,' he said. 'If there are still a few Medes in town by the time it ends we can catch the beginning of the second show before coming back. It'll make a change from all that mummy talk, anyway.'

They cut across the playing fields and followed the river to the towpath. As he clambered over the wall, Barney realized that this was the first time he'd been off school grounds. He was surprised not to feel anything like liberation. The main road was framed by earth-bank hedgerows, and although it was possible to hear the churning of the North Sea, there was nothing to see but an arc of slate-grey sky.

The cinema was in St Arras, half an hour's walk away.

'It didn't get bombed like Port Grenen,' Robin said. 'London never told Fritz the island had been demilitarized, so the Huns dropped some whoppers before the invasion. Boom!' He mimed an explosion with his hands — palms up, fingers splayed — in front of Barney's face. 'Body parts everywhere. Turned the sea red.'

'Anyone from school?'

'Of course not. Except for Swift, they all ran back to England to be scout masters at the first sign of a Stuka.'

Where the hedgerow began to thin some farm buildings came into view, huddled in the crook of a windswept hillock. There was a wooden barn and a stone farmhouse with a thatch roof. The buildings were hardy but graceless, hunkered into the land like barnacles.

They were standing on a ridge that scarred the

northern half of the island. Far below lay sand dunes and a rocky precipice. The patchwork of crofts ended abruptly in pearly sky where the cliff dropped to the sea. Between the ridge and the farm buildings, grey-green scrubland shelved down towards the water, pockmarked with tiny canyons.

'Those are the chalk pits where the Wehrmacht put their prisoners of war to work.' Robin pointed at a grey bump rising out of the sea. 'And that's St Just, where the Yids and the Wogs were sent.'

'Who lives there now?'

'Inbreds, I suppose.'

When they reached the high street, Robin pointed out the sweet shop and the post office and the café that sold the best iced buns on the island. The café windows were large and undressed, and by each one was a table and two chairs. A man was wiping one of the tables, while at the other a solitary woman sat with both hands laid, palm down, before her.

'There, see?' Robin said, pulling Barney to a halt. 'That's Flood's missus.'

Cowper, in his crudeness, had overstated her looks, thought Barney. She was nicely dressed but too thin, and pale. Her nose was red and her eyes puffy.

'Come on — we might make it in time for the start if we're quick.'

In the musty darkness of the cinema, Barney stole a glance at his friend in the next seat, outlined in profile against the glow of the screen, and thought that perhaps they weren't so different after all — that perhaps they had more in common than their shared vulnerability.

'Here we go,' whispered Robin, as the lights dimmed and the projector crackled.

This is a story of the Battle of the Atlantic, the story of an ocean, two ships, and a handful of men. The men are the heroes; the heroines are the ships. The only villain is the sea, the cruel sea, that man has made more cruel . . .

So there had been POWs here too. Barney tried to concentrate on the film, but soon — because he couldn't help it — he found himself thinking of the military cemetery in Rangoon and all the war graves filled with composites of more than one soldier. After VE Day, no one had wanted to talk about the prisoners still languishing in jungle camps in the East: the thought was too depressing, and by that point people were desperate for something to celebrate. Mum had told him she had danced in Trafalgar Square with a tall Italian-American — and that night, listening through the thin walls to the sounds of laughter and tomfoolery, Barney had felt as if he was the only one who did not know how or why to be glad.

On the walk home Barney left the talking to Robin, encouraging him with grunts of agreement whenever the tide of conversation began to wash in his direction. Now he was saying that the mummy could be a Polish baby, perhaps even a Russian one. The school groundsman, Krawiec, was a Pole, Robin said. Last year he'd been

70

invited to speak to the First Form about how he'd been interned on St Just. He and twenty others had been abandoned there to starve. Because there were no guards — the island was trusted to do the Germans' dirty work for them — five of them had tried and failed to escape on a raft. That was two weeks before the end of the war. When peace was declared, he'd gone to America, but no one had told him he'd have to share a room with his employer's Negro footman — so Krawiec had spat in the face of the American Dream and come back here, to work at a school where there weren't any blacks.

A riot of seagulls wheeled about the cliffs, and Barney thought how strange it was that their cries only drew more attention to the surrounding silence. They were bigger than any seagulls he had seen before, with longer wings and necks and heads that were slightly yellow.

'My old man says you can always tell a Pole by his cheekbones,' Robin was saying.

Drowned out by the gulls, his voice evaporated into the moist air. Barney imagined the words being carried up into the sky in tiny droplets and wondered if the prisoners interned on St Just had noticed the unusual sharpness of sounds out here, in the middle of a grey sea.

★ ★ ★

As the Headmaster often reminded his pupils, space was a precious commodity at the Carding House School, just as it was on the island and, increasingly, across the face of the Earth itself.

71

There was no better illustration of this than the library, which doubled as a detention hall and room for play rehearsals and communion lessons. Five rolling bookshelves were all that distinguished it from the other classrooms. It was here that Barney discovered the red-jacketed history of St Just.

The pamphlet appeared to be the work of a local historian, privately published and donated to the school by the author himself. No one had bothered to paste a borrowing list to the inside cover. It contained a poorly referenced yet painstakingly detailed account of the island's history from the late Bronze Age to the turn of the twentieth century, recording the lost whistling language of its prehistoric inhabitants, Norse invasion, occupation by the Danes, annexation to the Spanish Netherlands and eventual handover to the British — as well as various pirate attacks, bootlegging exploits and mysterious disappearances. Drawings of the lost indigenous people — flaxen-haired, with sunken eyes and tugboat jawlines — accompanied diagrams of long-term coastal erosion and maps describing two penal settlements that had been established and then abandoned on its shores.

The pamphlet had been published in 1936, and so did not offer any information on the labour camps to which Robin had referred during their walk.

'I didn't have you down as a swot, Holland,' said a voice. Barney poked his head around the shelf to find Ivor Morrell moving a leather-bound tome onto a nearby desk. He left it open before joining Barney behind the stacks. 'It's rare to see a Lydian with his nose in anything but the latest Dan Dare. What have you got there?' Not waiting for a response he took the pamphlet, sliding a finger between the pages that Barney had marked with his thumb. He lighted on the picture of a witches' coven. 'Smutty. The one on the left looks like old Baggage.'

He flipped through the pages, but his attention seemed elsewhere. 'How is she?' he asked.

'Who?'

'Flood Junior.' He looked at Barney. 'It's not every day a girl discovers a dead baby on school grounds, is it?'

'Do you think the police will tell us, when they find out whose it is?'

'I doubt it. I should tell your friends in the Second that they might as well forget about the whole thing.' He returned the pamphlet to the stacks without checking the shelf number, then went back to the book waiting on the desk.

'*The Secret History*,' he said. 'Despite having a bear tamer for a father and a mother who was hardly better than a prostitute, Theodora managed to become Empress of Byzantium by the time she was twenty. Women's charms and all that.' A look of distaste. 'Procopius saw through it all, of course. Without power she'd have just been a whore. Here, read this.'

The text was dense, the paper almost translucent.

'Often, even in the theatre, in the sight of all the people, she removed her costume and stood nude in their midst; then she would sink down to the stage floor and recline on her back. Slaves would scatter grains of barley from above into the calyx of this passion flower, whence geese, trained for the purpose, would pick the grains one by one with their bills and eat.'

★ ★ ★

Barney looked up to find the older boy waiting for a reaction. 'What's a calyx?'

Ivor snapped the book shut. 'I shouldn't be keeping you like this. Junior prep ends soon, if I'm not mistaken.'

'At eight.'

Ivor was tracing lines scratched into the desk with his fingernail.

'I'm going to follow her tonight,' he said. 'I thought you might be interested.'

'Why should I be interested?'

'I didn't say you should. I said you might. To judge by the way everyone's been going on about the mummy, I'd have thought you'd be up for a little sleuthing.' He sounded irritated. 'Apparently, I misjudged.'

Barney swallowed. 'Let me come with you.'

'I don't know,' Ivor said. 'You've made me think that I'll probably come to regret it.'

'I won't tell anyone.'

'Not even Littlejohn?'

Barney nodded. Ivor scooped his book under one arm and wandered over to the window. 'It might be useful to have an extra pair of hands,' he said. 'And no one ever suspects the unpopular lad — do they, Camden Town? That's what they

74

call you, isn't it?' Barney didn't reply. 'Meet me at Tern,' he continued. 'Do you know where the bins are kept, under the stone hutch? Don't bother with a torch — she always brings one. Come at eleven.'

★ ★ ★

Lights-out was at half-nine. After that, there would usually be somebody who had forgotten to brush his teeth, and tonight it was Percy fumbling through the darkness towards the basins. One boy was always left to listen at the corridor in case of a raid from one of the other dormitories. This week that boy was Opie, who had moved his pillow to the foot of his bed to catch any movement in the sliver of light under the door.

Fortunately there would be no questions from Robin, who was in the San with a sore throat. After the last of the whispering between the beds had died down, Barney sensed the others slowly retreating from consciousness until the only sound was of water churning through an outdoor pipe and, beyond it, the steady trickle of rain pressed by the wind into rivulets against the windows. At half-ten the last rustlings came from Opie, who was chewing at his fingernails and spitting the parings at the basin opposite his bed. By the time the clock struck a quarter to eleven, Barney could make out the still shape of his head lolling against the iron bed frame, his breath whistling through his nose.

Wincing at the creak of bedsprings, Barney

pulled a jumper over his pyjama top and slipped his feet into his plimsolls. He crossed the drugget in three strides and managed to release the catch on the door without making any sound at all.

'All right, Holland?'

Opie stared up at him through the ribbon of light from the corridor.

'All right. Just going to the bog.'

This appeared to satisfy the sentry, who gave a gentle grunt as he rolled onto his side. 'To the bog,' he mumbled. 'Foggy boggy. Dog in a bog . . . '

Within seconds Barney descended the staircase and had his hand on the iron latch on the front door. Only then did he remember the housemaster turning the key in the lock on his first night.

The clock chimed eleven as he tested the windows in the common room. Two were painted shut; the third was locked and took several moments to release. Dreading the telling-off he'd get from Morrell if he were late even more than the thought of being caught breaking out of the boarding house, Barney shoved himself head first through the window and landed with a thump on the cold ground. The rain had stopped, at least. Brushing the dirt from his elbows, he turned to confront the darkness.

Normally, to get to Tern the boys would cut across the drive and pass over the green. Worried that he might be heard crunching on the gravel or spotted by some solitary master working late in the library, Barney decided instead to go the other way, around the deserted east wing.

He had just reached the bin hutch behind Tern when the rumble of an engine stopped him in his tracks. A car had braked outside the old kitchens, headlights dimmed so that the shadows only reached halfway up the stone walls, thrusting the top half of the building into darkness. There was a distant beeping and the crackle of a radio signal. Perhaps it was the police. Maybe they'd received a tip-off that there were other bodies buried here: not just babies but full-grown people too.

He slid himself inside the hutch, a trickle of sweat beading up around the elastic of his pyjama bottoms. The only sound was the clattering of beetles he'd disturbed by shifting the bins: flat, shiny bodies that rustled through the pile of dead leaves clogging the corners of the hutch. The stench was a blend of residual baked beans and lindane mousse. Something sharp struck the back of his head.

'Get a move on,' hissed Ivor, flicking his finger against Barney's ear.

'Did you see it?' whispered Barney. Ivor was wearing mufti, and immediately he felt ridiculous in his pyjamas and plimsolls. 'The car . . . ' He scrambled out from behind the bins to follow Ivor, who was already making a beeline for the forest.

'Never mind them. They're not here for us.'

By the time Barney caught up with him they had reached a part of the forest that was unfamiliar to him even in daylight. He followed Ivor blindly with arms outstretched. A steep mist hung in the spaces between the trees, and the air was wet and cool on his fingers.

'What took you so long?' demanded Ivor, when the school lights were no longer visible through the thicket. He remained focused on some point in the distance. Barney wondered if Ivor could see something which he didn't.

'I had to wait until everyone was asleep. And Runcie had locked the front door — '

'Luckily for you our little friend was also running late.'

A branch snagged Barney's jumper, and he winced at the thorns that caught his fingers as he pulled himself free. 'You saw her?'

'She made a dash for it when she heard the car.'

They marched on in silence for several moments, and Barney began to wonder what Ivor had meant about needing an extra pair of hands.

'I thought you said she'd bring a torch,' he said, trying not to sound petulant.

'She did. She won't need it now, though.'

'I can't see a bloody thing.'

Ivor grabbed him by the arm and pulled him to the ground. 'Look.'

Just a few feet from where they crouched, the forest floor fell away to reveal an inlet needling into the shore. Black water stretched before them and, high overhead, a crescent moon obscured by gauzy clouds shone in a sky the colour of dark-blue ink. The beach was bare of any foliage; the trees hung behind them at the top of the precipice.

A figure was working its way down one side of the inlet towards the rock pools. It looked as if she was wearing a robe, but it soon became clear that this was actually an unfastened gym tunic. Her sandals clattered on the rocks, and twice she had to steady herself as she slipped on the slick. When she paused, there was a grey noise: the crackle of the tide dragging at the pebble beach.

'There's just the one route down to the water, and that's the one she's taking.' Ivor shimmied forward on his stomach. 'Let's see what our little Melusine does next.'

The girl had removed her sandals and was pulling the tunic over her head. Underneath she wore a bathing costume of knitted wool. In water it would grow heavy and coarse. As she stepped into one of the rock pools her arms and legs seemed almost too long for her body, bony and vulnerable as a bird's, and in the sea glow they gleamed whiter than the moon. Her shoulder blades spiked and flattened as she rinsed herself with cupped hands. When she had finished, she stood waist-deep in the water with palms flattened on the surface, as if feeling the sea for something lost.

'If she was going to top herself she'd have done it by now,' said Ivor.

Sure enough, the girl had begun her retreat from the water. She shivered as she wrapped her gym tunic around her shoulders and slipped her feet back into her sandals. A coil of black hair stuck to her cheek as she bent to fasten the buckles.

'Hurry up — before she sees us,' whispered

79

Ivor, jabbing Barney in the ribs. Pressing themselves onto all fours, the boys scuttled towards the forest. They waited for the sound of the girl's sandals on the rocks; when it came, they slipped back towards the footpath.

Weaving past the slender trunks of trees connecting sky and earth, Barney felt a rush of elation, as if he and Ivor and the girl were the only people on the entire island. The ground was soft beneath his feet, and as he ran he remembered the picture in the book on St Just depicting the underwater streams: invisible, unmappable Lethes forging tunnels through the limestone. It was only when he caught up with Ivor behind the bin hutch, as the other boy grabbed him by the shoulders and pressed him against the wall, that he remembered to be afraid.

'Breathe one word to anyone about this and I'll tell them you wanted to jump her,' said Ivor.

Barney was so surprised he bit his tongue. A metallic taste filled his mouth as he nodded his agreement with watering eyes.

Ivor pushed him to his knees, ducking at the sound of footsteps drawing near. They waited in silence until the sound of a door closing on a latch prompted him to release his grip on Barney's jumper.

'You have one minute to get back to your dormitory without anyone noticing. If I see your name on the Head's List in the morning you'll be sorry.'

As Barney made to leave, he was overcome by the sensation that he had been implicated in something not only secret, but shameful. The car that had stopped outside the old kitchens was no longer there, but the rutted tracks survived as confirmation that he had not dreamt it. *They're not here for us*, Ivor had said — as if he had known everything all along. Barney told himself they had done nothing wrong; indeed, if anything had happened to the girl, if she had been swept out to sea or hurt herself on the rocks, it would have been thanks to him and Ivor that she might have been saved.

★   ★   ★

Spike had often told him that things happened in their right order. Spike believed in cycles and spirals and figures of eight: the rhythms of the tides and time recorded in tree rings. According to him, there was very little about life that was linear. He hadn't cried at his own mother's funeral, he once told Barney, because human emotions don't work like that: you feel things at all the wrong times and that's all right. You remember things out of order, too, but that just means you're finding a way to make sense of it all. So, when in August the letter had arrived confirming that the school would be delighted to welcome Barney into the Second Form — and would his guardian please see to it that the vaccination checklist was completed as soon as possible — his stepfather had tapped the paper with one finger and said, 'You see, Barn? To *everything there is a season.*'

Rain bulleted against the window high above

81

Barney's head. The glass was frosted and cobwebbed, so it let in just enough light to read by if he stood on the toilet. Barney had learnt by now not to turn on the electric light — it was only an invitation to Shields and Cowper to start drumming on the cubicle doors or climbing onto the bogs in the adjoining cubicle and dropping spitballs in his hair — and in the evenings the light from Runcie's study, directly below the washrooms, was just strong enough to penetrate the window glass.

A Land For All Seasons! blared the yellow text on the front of the leaflet, which contained four pages, each headed with words in the same elongated, hand-lettered font: *Sun, Sand, Savannah, Society.* On the first page was a picture of a man and woman drinking orange juice on a patio; on the second, a family building a sandcastle at the beach. A rhino charged towards the viewer from the third page, flanked by an elephant and a lion; and on the reverse, two women chatted as they walked down a city street, shopping bags jostling between them.

Spike talked a load of bollocks. Seasons were all well and good at the other end of the world, but they didn't count for much in the middle of the North Sea. Time had slowed to a crawl on Lindsey Island, where even the sunlight seemed to slouch. Nothing happened in the right order here, or back home. Everyone was always saying that things were about to get better — they were bound to, weren't they, with the war won and a new government? — and still they managed to get worse. No wonder his stepfather was so obsessed with songs by dead people, revived by blokes like him who dwelt in times gone by because they didn't have a future to look forward to. That was why four generations of the Copper Family kept droning on the way they did: to fill the silence, the horrible spectre that was the future, with the noises from the past.

Mum's plan had always been to become an air hostess, flying with SAA between Johannesburg and Bulawayo before returning to the family home in the shadow of Table Mountain. She had described this plan to Barney a hundred times while they waited in long bread queues and at bus stops in the mean London drizzle, and afterwards while she luxuriated in the bath for hours at a time — baths so hot it shocked him to watch her skin turn red: the only way she could satisfy her longing for heat. Now it seemed as distant a dream as the one he'd nurtured as a little boy, when he had watched the porters at Euston station and longed to wear a uniform with red piping and provide the answers to all the questions that travellers would ask, such as 'When is the next train to Liverpool?' and 'At what time does the tea room open?' Now the uniforms had changed so there was no red piping, and a sign in the tea room showed its opening hours for everybody to see.

Although he knew his mother's dream by heart, Barney still struggled to imagine the whitewashed house she described to him, with its curling gables and dark-wood panelling, the grand chandelier in the hallway and the gardens in the back that sloped all the way down to Hout Bay, the swimming pool with its inflatable ring in the shape of a swan and the staff quarters in the corrugated box behind the work sheds.

The pamphlet's corners had turned white where the paper had been bent, dog-eared in bed late at night, perhaps, or folded in his mother's vinyl pocketbook as she queued for ration cards. Barney had found it in the wastepaper basket the morning that he had woken to find her side of the mattress empty.

'Got it!'

Barney stumbled against the cubicle door as the pamphlet leapt through his fingers. The scuffle of feet alerted him to Cowper's presence in the next cubicle. Shields was crammed in with him, along with a boy from the other dormitory, Sanger — at this early stage in his school career distinguished for little more than being the only Jewish pupil at Carding House — who was balanced on Shields's shoulders. Cowper stood on top of the toilet, the pamphlet in his hands.

'Planning a holiday?' He tore off one page and dropped it in the toilet bowl.

'That's *mine*.'

'And there we were, thinking you were a proper socialist scab. Do you hear that? Holland's got *property*.' Cowper tore another page from the pamphlet and let it drift into the grey water.

Barney charged, but Shields blocked him and Sanger pulled at his hair. Cowper tore the third page and crumpled it into a ball before dropping it into the bowl and pulling hard on the chain. The roar of water drowned out Barney's shouts.

'Come on, you lot.' Cowper slipped the remaining leaf between the buttons of Barney's shirt and gave his chest an impertinent pat. He let the cubicle door slam as he followed the other two out.

Barney ripped the page from his shirt and considered the sandcastle family with sudden, vicious contempt. While the others were still within earshot, he added it to the toilet bowl and gave the chain another hard yank.

★ ★ ★

He had not intended to set out alone — the boys were not allowed on solitary walks past the boathouse — and it was only as he reached the lower pitch that Barney felt uncomfortably conspicuous. It was a grey afternoon, and as he picked his way along the sticky towpath, he imagined that his school coat might help him fade into the forest gloom.

No such luck. The figure digging at the far corner of the pitch had spotted him: straightened from his work to watch what he did next. If Barney turned around, it would be obvious that he knew he should not have been out alone; so he continued to walk, hands in pockets, down the edge of the pitch.

He had assumed that the figure was Krawiec, but as he approached it became obvious that this man was significantly larger than the Pole. He carried himself straighter too, and wore spectacles.

'Holland, what?' Doc Dower plunged the

spade into the yielding turf.

'Sir.'

'Out on your own? No one's told you the rule about that?'

'No, sir.'

'There's a rule. No unaccompanied walks past the boathouse. Now what will you do?'

'I'll go inside, sir.'

'Quite right.' He turned back to his digging, grunting as he heaved his shovel against a hump of turf stretching like a worm along the border. The fringe of his wool cap was damp on his forehead; his spectacles misted with his breath.

'What are you doing, sir?'

'What does it look like, Holland? I'm giving a tea party, that's what.'

'No you aren't, sir.'

'Impudence!' Doc Dower tested the hump with his boot. 'Independent thinking, what? They won't like the sound of that.'

Barney surveyed the field, which appeared to be sinking under the weight of an expansive mud pit. 'Are you draining it, sir?'

'My intention is that it shall drain itself in future.'

'Clay holds the wet in, doesn't it, sir?' Doc Dower paused. 'My father used to pump mud out of the Thames, sir. Mum said the clay was the only enemy he ever had.'

'Is that so?'

'That and the Japs, sir.' Barney watched Doc Dower return to his digging. 'Morrell says you weren't in Asia, sir. Only Italy.'

'Do you play rugby, Holland?'

'No, sir.'

'Messy business, rugby. Cricket: now that's a gentleman's sport.'

'My dad supported Sussex, sir.'

'He did, what? I had an aunt who lived in Liphook.'

Barney hopped across the barrier, his feet sinking into the wet ground. For once, he didn't care.

'Don't you have proper boots, Holland?'

'No, sir.'

'Keep to the flat there, then.'

'Can I help, sir?'

'I thought you were going back indoors?'

Barney bit his lip, glanced back at the school ruefully.

'So you weren't in Asia after all, sir.'

'Morrell is quite wrong on that point, Holland. Italy, '43-'44. South-East Asia Command '44-'46.'

Barney's heart leapt. 'Burma, sir?'

'Indochina.'

'No bamboo shoots then, sir?' Barney thought perhaps Doc Dower suppressed a smile — but when he turned to wipe his glasses on his cuff there was only the usual distracted frown. 'My dad built roads in Burma, sir. He died there. Up in hill country, sir.'

'I'm sorry to hear that, Holland.'

Barney waited for a war story — or, at the very least, questions about his father: which company? Did they have people in common? — but none was forthcoming.

He watched Doc Dower pause morosely over

the sinking pile, buffing it with his boot before heaving a tired sigh.

'Terrible trouble with mice, as I remember,' he said. 'Finger food for pythons, what?'

'Only pythons don't have fingers, sir.'

'Quite right.' Doc Dower joined Barney on his side of the ridge. 'What we need here, Holland, is a two-per-cent slope. I'd thought one per cent should do the trick, but the water still won't drain.'

'Sir.'

'How do we calculate slope, Holland?'

'With height, sir. And distance.'

'Too vague. Wouldn't pass in the jungle.' Doc Dower clicked his tongue. 'You try and build a road on fuzzy logic like that, and watch what happens.'

'Sir.'

'We calculate slope by dividing the *change* in height by the *change* in distance, Holland. The larger the result, the steeper the line. A horizontal line is — what?'

'Nought, sir.'

'Quite right.' He squatted to judge the depth of the trench. 'I'd call that a foot. What would you call the length of the pitch?'

'A hundred yards, sir.'

'I think you're being generous, Holland, but we'll agree on a hundred, what? In feet?'

'Three hundred, sir.'

'You're not as dim as you look, are you Holland?'

'No, sir.'

'Good. Decide what depth this needs to be to

88

make a two-per-cent slope, and you can have a *piastre*. Do you know what that is?'

'No, sir.'

'Currency, Holland. Lucre. A coin from Indochina. Wouldn't buy you a crumpet in town, but I'll wager Cowper hasn't got one.' He did not look at Barney — there was no wink, no conspiratorial smile — and when Barney blinked, wondering what the master had meant by that, he coughed. 'Well, Holland?'

'Thank you, sir.'

'Don't thank me yet. Thank me when you've come up with an answer.'

'No, sir.'

'Well. I thought you said you were going indoors?'

'I was, sir. I am.'

'Hop to it, then, Holland.'

★   ★   ★

While the class waited for the gale to blow over, Hiram Opie set up a game of Captive Queens at the end of one of the long workshop tables. At the other end, a pot of glue bubbled on a hot plate in readiness for the next lesson. For more than half an hour they had been hoping for permission to return to the house, and a fractious spirit had begun to build in the interval between organized activities. The air inside was warm and the rain seemed to sweat through the walls, flushing out colonies of centipedes that scuttled along the skirting boards.

'You build the castle around them,' Opie was

explaining, placing the queens in the middle of the table and proceeding to surround them with cards selected, solitaire-style, from the deck. 'You have to save the kings and jacks for the top, to watch the queens. To protect them.'

'It's to keep them from escaping,' interjected Shields. 'That's why they're *captive*.'

'No, it's not.'

'Captive Queens my arse,' snorted Cowper. 'Idiot's Delight, more like.'

'Lay off him,' snapped Robin, from behind his book.

'Don't be such a prig, Littlejohn.'

A rush of wind and sea rain pressed against the windows, making the glass buckle and creak, sharpening the classroom smell of chalk and glue.

Barney wandered round to the other side of the table to sit next to Robin. 'What's that?' he asked in a low voice. Robin tilted the book so that his friend could see.

'Nasty, eh?' he said.

On the left-hand page was a photograph of a bulbous statue of a woman with enormous breasts, gourdish thighs and no feet. To the right was a paragraph describing the Venus of Willendorf.

Robin pulled a face. '*Pig-woman* of Willendorf, more like. I found it on the shelf by Nunn's desk. You think he fancies fat birds?'

Barney scanned Robin's face for any sign of the ferocity he'd read in Ivor's eyes the night at the shore, and was relieved to see only fascinated revulsion. In the same moment, Robin glanced

90

at the girl sitting at the end of the workshop table.

'It wouldn't kill her to make an effort,' he said.

Belinda's legs were crossed at the ankles beneath her chair; her fingers toyed with a pencil over a blank sheet of paper. Every now and then she would shift her weight, sliding one hand beneath her legs to smooth the pleats of her tunic. She looked up when someone banged a desk or burst into raucous laughter, but otherwise remained indifferent.

'She's probably still upset about the mummy,' said Barney.

'I doubt it.' Robin continued leafing through the book. 'She thinks she's better than us because she discovered something important and got to be interviewed by the police. Not to mention the fact that she knows she won't be here for long.'

'She's stuck in here like the rest of us.'

'That's different. If she went outdoors right now the wind would sweep her clear to Denmark.'

From her seat by the creaking windows, Belinda heard nothing of this conversation. Although to everyone else she looked to be doing nothing but staring into space, she was in fact deep in concentration. Only that morning, she had begged her parents to let her give up the cello so that she could play the piano instead, like Joan Fontaine's character in *September Affair*. Every evening she would practise the autograph, copied from a *Modern Woman* photo essay, and devise new signatures combining their names. *Belinda Cotten,* or *Mrs Joseph Cotten?* She had seen *The Third Man* three times already, scrutinizing his breath through the cigarette smoke as he waited for Harry Lime under the ferris wheel.

For the last fifteen minutes she had been mentally rehearsing the knock on the saloon-room door: one of the older boys would come in to say that there was a visitor waiting for Belinda Flood in the atrium. Joe would be standing by the enormous palm in the gilded pot outside Mr Pleming's study. He would have stubbed out his cigarette on the steps before entering, and as he waited for her he would be noting the liver-coloured tiles with faint pity, thinking how pleased he was to be rescuing her from this dingy, forgotten place . . .

'Hungry?'

Belinda looked up to find Cowper standing over her with his hands behind his back. The others remained where they were, only now they were silent, watching her. The glue spat bubbles in the pot.

'Not really, no.'

'Go on.' He rattled something in one fist, like a person tempting a dog. When she didn't reply, he edged closer and opened his hand. It was filled with grey shells.

'Those are limpets,' she said. Then, recognizing the silence from the other side of the room, she added, 'You probably think you're being clever.'

A few of the boys snorted at this.

'Have one.'

'I don't want one.'

She hated the feeling of all those eyes on her. Last year, after Cathy Duggan had fainted in the toilets and Miss Home had to restrain Suzette Marx from rushing down the coast road to swim out after her sister Audrey, Belinda had climbed up into the enormous cedar tree and stayed there after the dinner bell had rung twice, thinking of bodies never quite making it to shore, teased back and forth on the waves. Eventually, a cluster of girls had gathered at the front of the school, and then Miss Haugherty had arrived, her square face even more creased and crumpled than usual. The tree shook when the groundsman leant his ladder up against the trunk, and she had heard the girls' whispers and the exasperated edge in the Head's voice.

Cowper picked out one limpet and smashed it on the countertop. He dug out a grey, slimy lump from broken bits of shell before slurping it from his fingers.

'Go on,' he said, rattling the shells in his hand. 'Tell you what: if you do — ' and he leant in closer to whisper something in her ear.

It was a moment before the others registered the sound of her hand hitting his face — and even then it was easier to believe that a ruler had been snapped, a book slammed shut. Only when Cowper lifted his hand from his cheek, revealing the bright red outline of four slender fingers, did a jeer rise from the ranks.

'You bitch,' said Cowper. Belinda lowered herself into her seat and picked up the pencil.

'You little bitch,' repeated Cowper, loudly

enough this time for the others to hear. 'Don't think we don't know why you're here. What gets a girl sent to a school for boys? Funny business, that's what. You ugly, no-good little *bitch* — '

She lunged, then, but not at him: towards the pot of glue, which she grabbed by the handles and raised high over Cowper's head.

It was only too possible to imagine what might have happened next — but then the door swung open, and as Belinda brought the pot crashing down onto the hotplate, Cowper leapt away from the desk. The shells scattered across the floor as he retreated across the room.

Belinda looked up to see a dark-haired Mede in Wellington boots and glistening sou'wester. His cheeks were wind-ruddy and damp. He did not notice the limpet shell spinning on its point at the foot of the long table.

This is it, Belinda thought. '*Which one of you is Flood?' he'll ask, and I'll put up my hand and then he'll say, 'Visitor for you in the atrium, Flood. Chap called Cotten in a long coat and fedora. Says he's come to sort out a bit of scum by the name of Cowper . . . '*

But instead the Mede was withdrawing a clipboard and pencil from his satchel. 'Runcie has sent me to take the roll,' he said. 'Once everyone's accounted for you're to scram back to your house. Abbott?'

'Yes, Morrell.'

'Ainsley?'

'Morrell.'

The Mede continued through the list without so much as glancing up.

'Flood?'

'Here, sir.'

There was a silence before a couple of the boys suppressed snorts of laughter.

'I say, *sir* . . . ' began one of the smart alecs in the front row.

'Shut up, McEllroy, or you'll take a brown slip.' Morrell returned to his clipboard. 'Holland?'

'Here, Morrell.'

'I've an errand that needs running this afternoon. Runcie said you could come up to my set once we're done here.'

Visits to a senior's set were expressly forbidden. Sensing an opportunity to deflect his shame onto someone more vulnerable, Cowper whistled lowly, prompting sniggers from one or two of the other boys as Barney looked down at his hands and answered, 'Yes, Morrell.'

'Jessop?'

When all the names had been called, the Mede returned the clipboard to his satchel and consulted his watch. 'You lot have five minutes to report to your house.' He waited for the scuffle towards the door before summoning Barney with a jerk of the head.

Although the rain had let up, there was still a high wind as the boys hurried across the drive, shielding their faces with their cloaks. The barracks block that was Tern House gleamed white against the pewter sky.

'You can leave your shoes on the hot-water pipe and borrow Potts's slippers for now,' said Ivor as they ducked inside. 'Baggage will flip if she sees the state of your socks.'

It was his first time inside a private set, and Barney was disappointed by its Spartan appearance. Some Medes were said to keep Baby Belling stoves, even though electric appliances were forbidden in the dormitories. There were no such accoutrements here — no posters of Hollywood starlets, no popular magazines — just an empty fire grate, a stack of books piled in one corner and a desk in the other, bare apart from a postcard and two photos in paper frames. A record player sat, closed, on the floor. The book on the bed bore the words *Roth Memory Course*. Noticing the tilt of Barney's head as he considered the subtitle — *A Simple and Scientific Method of Improving the Memory and Increasing Mental Power* — Ivor picked up the book and returned it to the pile in the corner.

'The trick is to make a mental catalogue of things by placing them in the rooms of a house,' he said. 'Soon I shall be able to recall the order of an entire deck of cards. A little wager I'm having with Potts, you see.'

He hauled off his boots and sou'wester and shook the rain from his hair. Then he unsheathed a record — *The Rite of Spring*, said the cover — and set up the player. Moments later, the silence was broken by a clash of aggressive rhythms, a wild pulse syncopated with furious accents. It was music designed to agitate: it made Barney afraid.

'Drives Headington barmy,' said Ivor, indicating the room next door.

He set to work pulling out a trunk from a tiny

cupboard in the corner under the eaves. Barney meanwhile looked at the postcard stuck in the mirror between the frame and the glass. It depicted two floodlit and very naked men: one restraining the other by the wrist, forcing his knee into the arc of his back and clutching at his side with raked fingers as he bit the other on the neck. Overhead hovered what looked like a winged monkey, and behind the struggling duo stood a pair of dark figures, one of whom was covering his mouth in alarm. Hesitating, Barney slipped the postcard from the frame and turned it over. Nothing had been written on the reverse. The title was printed in small type in one corner: *Dante and Virgil in Hell*, followed by the name 'Bouguereau'.

He returned the postcard to the mirror frame.

The larger of the two photographs next to it was of a much younger Ivor, his parents and an elderly woman Barney took to be his grandmother. The setting was a rather grand drawing room; the boy Morrell was crouched on a deep, brocaded carpet. The women perched on armchairs and his father, dressed in military uniform, hovered behind them. The mother had a strained appearance and the grandmother wasn't even looking at the camera: her mouth was slightly agape and her eyes seemed to be searching out something to the right of the frame. The boy's hair was shortly clipped, revealing protruding ears. He could not have been older than four or five.

The other photo was a portrait of a young

man of seventeen or eighteen, smartly turned out in cap and high-collared military jacket, gazing beyond the camera with stern eyes.

'Is this your brother?' he asked.

Ivor didn't look up from the trunk. 'I don't suppose you've had the pleasure of hearing Pleming's Armistice Day speech yet? In a year's time you'll have the roll call of the school's Glorious Dead by memory.' He rolled his eyes up to the ceiling and took a deep breath. '*Coatsworth, Comfrey, Curless, de Bock, Dockett, Frankland, Hess, Just, Kors, Kingsley, Lennert, Loft, Morrell, Overbay, Previn, Potts, Savin, Standring, Thorup, Thrane, Voigt, Voysey, Widdows, Williams, Wilbermere.* And the greatest of them all was Morrell.' He snorted, though it could have been involuntary. 'Jonty'd have hated knowing that he'd end up as part of some set-piece propaganda drill. He only went into the military because Runcie sat him down for a chat one evening and told him it would make Pater proud.' He closed the lid of the trunk so that Barney could see the words printed in white across the lid. *Effects of Cpl. Jonathan W. Morrell*, it read. He reopened the trunk and withdrew a box tied with elastic bands. 'Ah. There you are.'

He unfastened the box and picked out something wrapped in crushed paper. He handed it to Barney, who discovered that it was a pot of jam. 'Blackcurrant, I think,' said Ivor. 'Granny's finest. You'll give it to her for me.'

'Who?'

'Flood.'

Barney considered the pot. 'I . . . suppose so.'

'As an apology for embarrassing her in front of the class today.'

But you didn't embarrass her, Barney wanted to say *She called you sir. She embarrassed herself.*

Ivor closed the trunk and returned it to the closet under the eaves. He stood up and joined Barney by the desk, pointing at the larger of the two photographs. 'Big ears,' he said.

'It's a nice photograph,' said Barney.

'When he saw that picture, my father insisted that I have them seen to,' continued Ivor. 'The next week I was sent to have my ears pinned at an army surgery near our house. I recovered in a ward next to the burns unit. Can you imagine?' He didn't wait for a reply. 'Grown men returning from battle with the most ghastly wounds, and a five-year-old having his ears pinned so his old man needn't be ashamed.'

'Did it hurt?' asked Barney.

'I don't really remember.'

They stood staring at the photograph for a few moments, saying nothing.

'I suppose I should go,' said Barney.

'Take care with that.' Ivor indicated the pot of jam. 'If I hear about any Medlar scum getting their fingers in you'll find yourself in Ratty's office for six of the best before you can blink.'

When he stopped Belinda on the drive later that afternoon, Barney told her he had something from Ivor Morrell in the Fifth before handing over the pot, still wrapped in paper. It was the first time he had spoken to her, and he hated himself for sweating so. *What did it look like?* he wanted to ask. *What does a dead thing look like?* She received the bundle with white fingers, a cleft digging between her eyebrows as she registered its weight.

'Is this a trick?' she asked, looking up at him. Barney shook his head, realizing only now that it might seem this way. 'What is it, then?' she asked.

'Blackcurrant, I think,' said Barney, starting to wish the girl would just accept the gift and walk away. 'Jam.'

There was a flicker of excitement as she examined the jar.

'Well,' she said. And then again, 'Well.' She tucked the pot under one arm. 'Thank you. Tell him I say thank you.'

'I will.' He turned to go, then stopped. 'Cowper was asking for it,' he said.

For a moment, she seemed about to smile.

'Holland, yes?' Barney nodded. 'Would you like some?'

Barney remembered Ivor's warning. 'No, it's all right,' he replied. 'Really. It's for you.'

The girl narrowed her eyes. 'Then how will I know he's not put something in it?' she said.

'He didn't. His gran made it.'

'Is that what he told you?' Barney shrugged. 'Come on,' said Belinda, making for Ormer House.

'I don't think I should come in,' said Barney.

The girl's expression hardened, and Barney swallowed.

'How about the shelter?' he said.

★ ★ ★

It was the most protracted apology he'd ever known. Twice that week, Ivor summoned him to collect another bundle — a bag of pear drops, a tin of Wagon Wheels — and between the end of lessons and first prep the new boy and the housemaster's daughter met in the shelter behind Ormer House to divide the spoils.

At first they ate in guilty silence, but by their third rendezvous the girl had realized that Barney was not as dull-witted as he looked and began to probe him for information about their benefactor. She hadn't noticed Morrell before, she said, because she'd always been away at school in term time.

'He looks terribly old to be in the Fifth,' she said. 'Out of school clothes he'd easily pass for twenty.'

'I'll be done for if he finds out you've been sharing his gifts with me.'

'I can share what's mine with Pleming's dog, if I like.' She pulled on a liquorice whip, stretching the black lace between sharp teeth.

'Makes a difference from the pig swill they serve us in hall,' said Barney. Lately, he had begun testing out Robin's sneering tone. 'The tapioca yesterday — '

Belinda made a face. 'Frogs' eyes in pus, you mean.'

He was dying to ask her about the body she had discovered by the old kitchens, but every time he came close she started talking again.

'Are they alive, do you suppose?' She was

101

pointing at a cluster of black spots rising like a rash up the concrete wall.

It seemed strange to Barney that a girl everyone said was terribly clever shouldn't know what mould looked like. 'I don't think so,' he said.

'Oh, but they must be, if it's a fungus.' She touched the plaster with her fingers.

'*Down in the dungeon six feet deep,*
Where old Hitler lies asleep,
German boys tickle his feet,
Down in the dungeon — '

'Very funny,' said Barney.

Belinda considered the empty paper bags. 'Why don't we invite Morrell next time?' Barney looked doubtful. 'For a proper feast. We could come on Wednesday.'

There was to be a fireworks display that night: school would break for half-term the following day.

'I promise I won't tell him you've been sharing all along. God's honour.' She unwound her scarf, licked her index finger and drew a sign of the cross on her throat.

'I'll have a word.' It would be something to tell Spike over half-term when he asked to hear about all the fun things the boys got up to. Then, he had a thought. 'But first you have to tell us why you're here.'

'Because there wasn't anywhere else for me to go. Because Daddy — '

'No secrets.' Barney crossed his arms, hoping

that Morrell wouldn't kill him for playing this game. 'Not from us.'

She stared at him as if trying to guess what he wanted to hear. In this light, the blue veins that travelled to her temples resembled branches caught in a flash of lightning, delicate and perfect and pulsing with life.

'Whatever the others are saying is probably true,' she said. 'I pushed a girl down some stairs.'

The admission filled him with a weird relief. 'That doesn't get people expelled.'

'What did you expect?' She began to gather the empty bags. 'If Cowper had hit me back, he'd get the sack too.'

'That's different.'

'Is it?' She shoved the bags into her satchel.

And then she told him about Minty.

That spring, someone left the gate to the coast road unlatched, and the headmistress's little schnauzer had escaped. The headmistress had assumed that Minty was sleeping out of sight until a craven-faced young man and his sobbing girlfriend were spotted traipsing up the drive carrying a limp bundle of grey fur. The dog had darted onto the road out of nowhere, they said, probably chasing after some fulmars that had gathered on the sea wall. The young man had slammed on the brakes and the car had skidded almost to the cliff edge, but by the sound of the thump under the passenger seat they had known that it was already too late.

As soon as Minty had been laid to rest under the ash tree in the headmistress's garden, some girls began to whisper about who could possibly have left the gate unlatched. Within hours of the funeral they were sewing the letter 'M' onto the backs of their ties and leaving elegies to the little dog's memory at the foot of the ash tree, while those not so inclined to sentimentality focused on hunting down the culprit.

'So it was you who left the gate open? That's not so terrible.'

'We weren't allowed on the coast road.'

'Then why were you there?'

'I was running away.'

Barney snorted. 'Not many places you could go. Unless you were planning to swim to St Just.'

She shrugged, slinging the satchel over one shoulder.

'I'm not that good a swimmer,' she said.

After she'd gone, Barney noticed that her scarf had slipped behind the bench. He picked it up, noting the anxiously braided tassels, the greying school stripes, and cupped the wool to his nose, breathing in the lingering scent of her mother's perfume.

★ ★ ★

She did not acknowledge him in prep, and for an instant he felt rebuffed: caught in a smile that was not returned, publicly wounded by rejection. Cowper spotted it, of course — Cowper was finely tuned to others' humiliation — but instead of raising a jeer he beckoned Barney over with a comradely grin.

'Seat's free,' he said, indicating the space next

104

to him. Barney took it and began to unpack his books.

'Playing hard to get, is she?' said Cowper, with what sounded like genuine sympathy. Barney looked at him.

'Grow up.'

'She's a snotty little madam, if you ask me.'

Barney made a show of looking over each shoulder. 'Who asked you?'

'Very funny. I saw you smile at her, and she turned away. That's rudeness, that is. Her parents ought to have taught her better.'

'I didn't smile at her.'

'Oh, give over, Holland.' Cowper surveyed the room, noting the empty desk directly behind the girl. There was no master present; the classroom door was open and Swift was in the library, listening for any disturbance in the low hum of boys halfheartedly doing their evening preparations. 'Let's have a little fun, shall we? And teach her not to be quite so vain in the meantime.'

Before Barney could speak Cowper was out of his seat and striding calmly towards the front of the room. Passing by the master's desk, he took a pair of scissors from the pencil pot. Then he slipped into the vacant seat behind the girl, who still did not turn around. She sat perfectly straight, black ponytail hardly moving even as she tilted her head to look between her Latin primer and exercise book.

Several of the others had noticed that something was afoot, and a wave of telegraphed messages rippled between the benches. One by one, they looked up to see Cowper brandishing

105

the scissors in the air behind the girl, pulling a ridiculous face begging encouragement. *Shall I?* it said. *Shall I do it?*

Barney could still pretend not to be watching: he could still say nothing and so risk neither accusations of attempted gallantry nor retaliation from Cowper. The scissors widened, and Cowper mimed snipping the girl's ponytail. Despite himself, though, Barney looked on, noting the tendons of her slender neck, the china-white skin behind her ears.

Someone — it might have been Opie — stifled a laugh, and in that instant the girl turned just sharply enough for her ponytail to leap between the gaping blades. There was a metallic slicing sound, a hush of breath . . .

. . . and then she saw Cowper fall back in his seat, letting the scissors fall to the desk as he flung up his hands in the air in mock surrender. 'I didn't do it,' he said.

Only now did she look down to see the straight black fringe of hair on the floor, like the mane lopped off a toy horse. One, two inches at the most — her mother would not even notice it — but still it was an alarming sight. She felt the blunt brush of hair at the base of her neck and her mouth opened.

'Liar!' said Barney, jumping from his seat. 'Liar!'

'Liar!' joined in Opie, who was now able to cackle freely. 'Liar!'

'Liar! Liar!'

'We were just joking about,' Cowper told Belinda, who had yet to say anything. 'If you

106

hadn't turned around like that — '

'What's going on in here?'

There was a communal thump of bodies hitting their seats as the boys feigned concentration. Only Belinda and Cowper remained where they were. Mr Runcie stood in the doorway, hands on hips. 'Cowper. Where is your prep?'

'Over there, sir.'

'Then what are you doing out of your desk? Miss Flood?'

Beneath sullen brows, eighteen pairs of eyes watched her.

'It was nothing, Mr Runcie.'

'Turn around, then — you have work to do too.' The housemaster scanned the rows, and his distracted gaze alighted on Barney. 'Holland: my study, please.'

★   ★   ★

His first thought was that someone had spied him going into the fallout shelter with Belinda Flood. But if it was to be a caning, Runcie would have waited until after lights-out to call him. By then the boarding house would be still, the boys in bed upstairs listening to the swish of the birch and the yelps below, pretending to be asleep when their chastened comrade returned.

The housemaster greeted him with a smile and invited him to sit. That was when Barney knew that it could only be bad news.

'We've had a telegram from your father,' said Runcie, withdrawing a piece of yellow paper from his inside pocket. 'Spike, is it?'

'My stepdad. Is Jake all right?'

'Everyone's fine,' said Runcie, smoothing the yellow paper on the leather padding of his desk. 'But I'm afraid it means you won't be able to go home for half-term. Apparently your stepfather has business in Manchester . . . '

A gig, thought Barney. *One of his mates at The Moon and Sixpence must have cut a deal with some landlord . . .*

'And he'll be taking your brother with him. They leave tomorrow, and considering the distance and the fact that we don't have an address where they'll be staying — '

Sleeping on Mick Allen's sofa, thought Barney, *or beneath the bar . . .*

' — we've agreed that you should remain here for the week. I'm sorry, Holland — it's rotten luck.' The housemaster steepled his fingers. 'To make up for it, I thought you might like to stay with one of our neighbours: that way, you won't be all on your own in an empty dormitory at night, and you'll have some company in the day.' He peered over the rim of his reading glasses. 'There could even be some pocket money in it.'

Barney blinked at him.

'A lady who lives on the road to St Arras needs help with a spot of housekeeping. Mr Krawiec, our groundsman, was doing some work for her a while ago: it was he who passed on the request. There's two pounds a week in it for the right man.'

Until now Barney had been worrying at a piece of skin at the corner of his thumbnail. At the mention of payment in pounds, not shillings,

108

he stopped. 'You're interested, I hope?'

'Sir.'

Runcie flashed a grin revealing teeth that were small and square, like a child's. 'Good. I shall run a message to Miss Duchâtel to let her know to expect you on Friday evening.' He stood up, and so Barney did too. 'I'm sorry about your disappointing news, but perhaps it's for the best. Krawiec will drive you down once the others have cleared off.'

'Sir.'

'Good lad. Think of it as a little holiday, won't you?'

Of course he wouldn't. It sounded like work, dull work, and loneliness tinged with shame. Screw Spike. No doubt he thought Barney would be happier here, just as he'd convince himself that Jake enjoyed caroming from gig to gig in a haze of hunger and boredom. The last time they'd stayed at Mick's, one of the band members' girlfriends had taken pity on them and brought a chess set. The boys had passed the next three days launching battles between the black and white pieces, scattering sentries along the window sills and planting hidden commandos beneath the furniture, while Spike and his mates played their music to empty taverns on the other side of town.

At least there was still the feast to look forward to. When Ivor heard that the plan was entirely Belinda's, he seemed to warm to the idea, even promising to pick up a few supplies in town that afternoon. The prospect of the fireworks display had put everyone in buoyant spirits, and with half-term just around the corner some risks seemed worth taking.

It was customary for students from the girls' school to join the masters and boys on their playing field to enjoy the best views of the fireworks. The junior boys commandeered the stone wall that ran from the chapel to the pumping station, swinging their legs at latecomers and increasing the volume of whistling and cheering whenever one of the girls came into view. The St Mary's students set up camp in the middle of the field, laying out blankets and waterproofs on the cold ground and anchoring these with baskets filled with thermoses and packets of biscuits.

From the edge of the field where the ground dipped towards the river, a group of girls silently appraised Belinda, who had drifted over to say hello to one of the mistresses. Some already had the thick-heeled, lumpish figures of middle-aged matrons, their young faces showing the early signs of puffiness from too many sweets and starch — a diet of peacetime privilege. The ones sitting in positions that allowed them a comfortable view did not take their eyes off Belinda when they opened their mouths to speak in low voices; the ones with their backs to her did not turn around, but waited for their friends to narrate for them, at once shunning and scrutinizing their former classmate.

Watching them at a distance, Flood noticed with a pang how small his daughter looked, how entirely lacking in self-possession. She had never rushed, as others did, to show off her friends to her parents at sports days and music recitals — those strange occasions, cruel in their cultivation of aspiration, when he found himself wondering what, exactly, those girls were being prepared for. Flood sensed that she may not have learnt the usual techniques for suppressing her loneliness and fear — the camaraderie of games, or the mysterious arts of schoolgirl cruelty (banishment to Coventry, Chinese burns beneath the dining table) — and this filled him with a sudden pity. But then a girl with a shiny forehead and hair twisted into slick plaits rose and joined Belinda with the mistress, the deputy head, she of the equine features and pungent lavender eau de toilette, whose most distinguishing characteristic was a propensity for speaking in subordinate clauses. The girl with the plaits squeezed her hands under her armpits while Belinda fiddled with her bracelet — a cheap thing she must have picked up in town, made of blue glass beads — shifting her weight from one leg to the other, feeling the cold. After a few minutes she embraced the girl with the plaits and accepted a gentle pat on the cheek from the mistress before peeling away from the group. Flood called out to some boys squabbling over a lawn chair before turning to find his daughter already waiting to speak to him.

'I've an awful headache,' she said, not looking up. 'I think I might go to bed.'

'The fireworks will be starting any minute.'

'I'll see them from my window,' said Belinda.

She did look rather pale, thought Flood, touching her forehead with the back of his hand. The smooth skin felt cool as marble. 'Poor Linda-Lou,' he said.

She smiled wanly. 'I'll be fine, Daddy. I just need some water and a little quiet.'

He watched her trudge up the slope towards the drive, arms hugged across her chest, skirting a crowd of juniors. There was Hughes, who had boils lanced every half-term, and the inseparable Shields and Cowper. Behind them was sloe-eyed Littlejohn and the new lad, Holland. Both were leaning back on the cold grass, not speaking, their fingers almost touching. Flood took a step forward. Was it Holland's hand that was searching out Littlejohn's? Hard to say, in this light. *So that's how it is,* he thought. Just as well that Runcie wasn't on to them, or he'd make a bloody show of it in front of the entire Second Form. Still, it wasn't the sort of thing he could ignore — and so he wandered along the edge of the pitch until he was within shouting distance of the two.

'Holland!' he barked. 'What's happened to your jacket, boy?'

The lad turned with a start, tucking both hands beneath his knees. 'It's inside, sir,' he replied.

'Well, go and get it, then,' ordered Flood. 'What were you thinking, coming out in shirtsleeves at this time of year?'

'Sir,' said the boy, scrambling to his feet. He said something to Littlejohn, who laughed, before scuttling up the slope towards the drive.

As he disappeared into the crowd, the first of the fireworks cut a tear through the starless sky.

★   ★   ★

On the drive, Belinda passed Matron and two maids carrying trays of rum cocoa to the masters on the lower pitch. It would take them at least ten minutes to reach the field, and another ten to return, and in between no doubt they would pause to admire the fireworks and partake of a drink to warm up. The kitchens would still be open, and empty.

She did not begin to suspect that she was being followed until she was halfway down the basement staircase. Hers were the only footsteps on the stone floor, but a shuffling noise, the sound of breath nervously restricted, made her pause. Then she remembered what her father had said about the kitchen mice — a couple of them had multiplied to entire tribes of rodents, too many even for Doc Dower to eradicate with his cricket bat — and forced herself to carry on. She was not afraid of mice.

It was only as she leant upon the heavy kitchen door that something spun her hard against the wall so that for a moment she was winded, incapable of making a sound. The corridor was unlit, the figure before her shrouded in submarine shadows, and before Belinda could protest she was shoved into an adjoining room. By the powdery smell she knew it must be the laundry — she felt with blind fingers the slats of the airing cupboard — but whereas the kitchen

113

had been alight with electric lamps, this room was quite dark. Her knees were knocked from behind and buckled — she fell forward, landing on a pile of sheets.

'You can hit me properly this time,' said Cowper. 'Or is it not as much fun without an audience?'

Using her own movement against her as she twisted against his grasp, he flipped her so that her face was pressed into the sheets. As if by instinct she knew that if she went limp, rather than rigid, she would feel like a corpse to him, numb. The smell of her own breath hit her through the linen. She gripped his wrists, but did not try to push him away. Frustrated by this refusal to struggle, he used his lower half to pin her down. Then he pressed his mouth against her neck and whispered, 'But you're not half a mutt.'

He released her. She waited for another blow, but all she could hear was the sound of his footsteps on the stone slabs and the door closing.

She lay in the darkness for several minutes, waiting for her heart to stop thumping, and then crept to the door. He would have been a fool to lock her in — but still, it was a relief to feel the handle yield under her hand, to step into the corridor and see the lights on in the kitchen.

★ ★ ★

Morrell brought lemonade, a chocolate cake and something in a flask; Barney a canister of Van Houten's Cocoa nicked from Shields's stash and half a box of stick-jaw Robin hadn't wanted.

They had been sharing a cigarette as they waited, hungrily filling their cheeks and breathing clouds at each other through the frosty air. The girl was late.

When at last she emerged from the antechamber into the candle-lit bunker, she seemed to have arrived empty-handed. She registered the boys from the doorway before ducking out and returning with a basket.

'It's a bit of a jumble,' she said, without a hint of apology. 'I had to pinch a few things from the kitchen.'

Barney reached for the basket: pilchards in oil, liver paste, jellied ham, tinned pineapple. He hesitated, feeling Ivor's gaze.

'Honestly,' Ivor said. He flipped a penknife from his coat pocket. 'Go on — you can serve me some of that armoured cow.'

'Serve yourself,' said Belinda. 'Is that stick-jaw?'

Seeing Ivor's surprise at this bald impudence, Barney braced himself for a reaction.

'We'll toss for it,' said Ivor. 'Heads I have it, tails you don't.'

'I'm not stupid.'

'Halves, then.'

'It's Holland's, isn't it? Let him decide.'

'You two go halves,' Barney said.

Belinda took the box from Ivor and broke off a piece while the other two watched. She tested the gold toffee with her teeth, the pink tip of her tongue curling around it, eyes screwed shut. Then she popped the whole piece in her mouth and sucked down hard. In that moment, the atmosphere in the shelter transformed. Even Ivor's authority seemed suddenly equivocal.

'We were waiting for you for ages,' he said, watching her reach for the cake.

The girl kissed chocolate crumbs from one finger.

'Half expected you wouldn't turn up,' Ivor continued.

Belinda looked at him. 'I ran into the ghost coming out of the kitchen,' she said.

Both boys laughed, although Barney found he had to think about it first. Ivor took the penknife from him and stabbed at the tinned pineapple.

'Did you, now?' he said, turning the tin in one hand. 'Seems to me you have a knack for things with a whiff of death about them.'

The girl's face closed into a hard look. 'What's that supposed to mean?' she said.

Ivor set the tin down. 'Digging up school skeletons,' he said. Barney held his breath, but Belinda only looked frightened for an instant.

'Oh, that,' she said, hardly moving, even though their knees were now touching and Ivor had pinned a corner of her dress to the bench with the heel of his hand. 'You can get into the old kitchens through the cellar door. Mrs Kenney told my mother that her dad had buried some fish knives there, so I thought I'd see if I could find them.'

'Must have been some surprise.'

'Mother says plenty of tiny babies died during the war because there wasn't enough milk and their mothers were all half starved. It was horrible. It looked like an alien.'

'More horrible than seeing a ghost?'

'Of course.' She shifted, tugging her dress out from under him, and took another bite of cake. 'The ghost is harmless. It's only the boys who are frightened of him.'

'What did he say?' asked Barney, unscrewing the cap on a thermos for the cocoa.

'He doesn't say anything. He flutters.' She watched them sternly 'He's trapped in the walls where the doorway's been filled in.'

For a moment they were silent, listening to the distant crump of fireworks and the rustle of dry leaves against the outside door. One of the candles had starter to gutter, spitting wax as it melted in on itself, and Ivor squeezed the flame out with his moistened fingertips. There were now just two candles left on the table they had set up in the centre of the shelter. The corner by the sealed door remained dark.

'Robin told me rotten stuff goes on down there,' said Barney at last. 'In the laundries.'

'One time,' started Belinda, 'the other girls tried a seance. It was a bit like this, with the candles, only it was in our dormitory, so it wasn't terribly frightening. My friend Joyce told us we could raise the Devil by saying the Lord's Prayer backwards. *Amen, ever and ever for, evil from us deliver —* '

'That's stupid,' said Barney.

Belinda nodded. 'I know,' she said. 'They tried to levitate one girl, but she was so fat they only managed to shift her leg a bit. It was obvious she was bluffing, anyway.'

'Girls,' said Ivor.

'They liked scaring each other,' said Belinda. 'Passing around a peeled grape after lights-out and saying it was a dead man's eye. There was one mistress, Miss Albert, who was supposed to have seen a ghost once, and if she thought you were trustworthy she'd tell you about it, but only once you were in the Sixth. But Miss Albert was always making things up. She wrote a filthy book, too, once.' She tossed her head. 'The ghost story was just for attention, of course. None of it was real.'

'But you believe in ghosts?' asked Ivor.

'I've heard the fluttering in the basement corridor. Once I felt something poke me in the back, like a thorn.'

'The Cruel Mother felt a thorn in her back,' said Barney. 'In the song. She murders the baby with a knife. When she gets home she sees his ghost and he sends her to hell.'

Ivor turned to Belinda. 'Does that sound like the ghost you heard?'

'The ghost in the basement corridor is a man,' she said. 'Haven't you been down there yourself?'

'Robin has,' began Barney. 'Robin says — '

'Shut up, Holland,' snapped Ivor. He passed the tinned pineapple to Belinda, who dug out a piece with her fingers. 'And you weren't frightened?' he said.

'Should I have been?' she asked — and for an instant Barney heard a flicker of coyness in her

118

voice, something older than her years.

Ivor unscrewed the cap from the flask and used it as a cup for a splash of the brownish liquid inside.

'Is that brandy?' she asked.

'How did you guess?'

'My mum keeps a bottle of cognac in our kitchen cupboard, behind the spice rack.'

Barney watched Ivor sip the excess from the brim of the cap and offer it to the girl, who shook her head. 'It smells horrible.'

'It's a very fine brandy, this. Holland?'

Barney took the cap, feeling he'd be in trouble if he didn't. The liquid made his tongue burn, but he handed the emptied cap back to the other boy with an appreciative grunt.

'Lady Flood's fond of a tipple, then?' asked Ivor. 'Bored, is she? Lonely? That's what women are always saying.'

'Mainly when Daddy's not about. She hates this place.'

'The school?'

'The whole island. She cries when she thinks no one is around. I caught her just the other day, coming out of the loo. She wishes we'd stayed in England after the war. She used to drive ambulances, you know.'

The pineapple was finished now, and there was only a corner of cake left. Barney looked at the empty toffee box with pride, feeling that he'd pulled his weight. No one seemed interested in the pilchards, so Ivor passed another capful of the brandy around. This time Belinda took a sip, pulling a face and declaring it vile as soon as she could speak.

'Tell us about your school,' said Ivor. 'Do you miss it much?'

'Hardly.'

'You must have had friends.'

Seating companions, dormitory buddies, tennis partners, agents to collect birthday donations in a pillowcase after lights-out. In an environment where friendship was too often reduced to expressions of loyalty, her only ally had been a muckle-mouthed girl who wasn't allowed to attend dance lessons because of a heart condition — one of those children who always seemed to be suffering from some kind of affliction: a sprained ankle or ingrown toenail or earache brought on by damp. Joyce had irritated Belinda, because she acted young for her age — she still read *Girl* magazines and could be reduced to tears by someone stirring the jam into her rice pudding so that the milk turned pink.

'Not really.'

'Pashes, then? What about the older ones?'

'Don't be stupid. Most of the girls were horrible,' Belinda said.

'Well, then, what about you?'

'Am I in trouble here too?'

'Certainly not,' Ivor said. He made a show of collecting the empty tins, fitting one inside the other, and Barney wondered if he was thinking of a way to ask her about her midnight trip to the rock pools. Before he could, she spoke again.

'Your brother liberated one of the concentration camps, didn't he?' she said. 'I heard he shot

120

a captured German just for looking at him.'

'He didn't make it to the camps,' said Ivor.

'In that case, someone should tell the First Form.' Unrepentant, Belinda fixed him with a knowing look. 'My dad says you can't decide what to do with your brains, so you do nothing.'

'Does he?' Ivor looked pleased. 'Well, you might cut Holland some slack. He's come to take Henry Cray's place.'

'I think it's best to die young,' said Belinda. 'Not that young, though.'

'Anyone who wants to die young is bound to live for a very long time,' said Morrell. 'You'll live to a grand old age. I predict at least three children and a brood of grandchildren, if you're terribly unlucky.'

'I can think of at least one person I wouldn't mind disappearing,' said Belinda to Barney. 'That brute in our year.'

'Cowper? He was just messing about the other day. I don't think he meant to cut your hair. It wasn't that much, anyway.'

'That's easy for you to say. At least you've made friends here. The funny one — '

'Opie,' said Barney.

' — and what's-his-name. Little — '

'Littlejohn.'

Belinda nodded. 'You were watching him in maths this morning,' she said.

Barney felt his neck grow hot. She began to speak, and then seemed to think better of it. 'Is that a poem?' she asked, pointing to the words on the wall behind Barney's head.

The lines followed the concrete bulge,

appearing to have emerged through the plaster by mysterious alchemy. Belinda moved closer, holding one of the candles to the wall.

Tears of the widower, when he sees
A late-lost form that sleep reveals,
And moves his doubtful arms, and feels
Her place is empty, fall like these.

'Tennyson,' said Ivor.

'Is it about his wife?'

'Not exactly.' The candle hurt Morrell's eyes. He took it from her and placed it on the ground.

'Who died?'

'I put it there after someone went away. A friend back home. His family worked for us, but we had to let them go when Pater came back from Crete. It was a stupid idea.'

'I'm sure it wasn't,' said Belinda, in a tone more bossy than pitying. Then, 'I like this place. It feels like somewhere you'd plan things. Like a Resistance.'

'No one bothered with a Resistance here,' said Ivor. 'They let the Boche in without a fight and turned a blind eye to a labour camp right under their noses. No matter what the plaques in chapel say, they're only there to make us wonder if we'd have been braver.'

There was a brief, chastened silence.

'Swift fought in the Resistance in France,' said Barney at last.

'Who gives a shit?' said Ivor.

'I'm just saying.'

'I know Swift,' Belinda said. 'Mother likes

him. I can tell.' She was undoing the ribbon from the toffee box, flattening the twisted sections against her lap.

'He's a tosser,' said Ivor.

'A brave tosser,' said Belinda, and Barney thought how foreign the word sounded coming from her. She tied the ribbon in a bow around her ponytail. 'He's very handsome. His eyes are so blue — '

'I shall tell him you think so.'

Even in the dim light, Barney could see the girl turn red. 'Don't you dare.'

'He's Holland's deputy housemaster, you know. And my personal tutor.'

Belinda was already thinking how much she'd like it all to come tumbling down: the school, the shelter, the cliffs themselves crumbling into the sea. She looked away, at the door.

'Pax?' Ivor's hand hovered in the empty space, waiting for hers. 'Of course I shan't tell.'

'Die on oath?'

He crossed his heart. 'Die young, if I'm lucky. Like Chatterton and Keats.' They shook, and Ivor felt the small bones of her hand, which was hot and smooth. 'Come on, Holland,' he said. And so Barney placed his hand on top of theirs, and they stood there like that for a moment in silence, until at last Belinda stifled a self-conscious laugh and the other two withdrew their hands, not looking at each other.

They decided to leave the basket and boxes and tins in the shelter, to clear out the next day. As Ivor drew the door closed, the other two stood in the forest gloom feeling the cold air and the darkness. The rumble of bus engines sounded like distant drums, and Barney thought of the abandoned pumping station at the other end of the forest, and how the river was at once here, under their feet, and elsewhere, flowing into the sea.

'Next time we should go down to the rock pools,' said Ivor. 'I'll find a way to bring proper meat, not this tinned crap.' It was the 'next time' that made Belinda look at Barney, who was at that moment grateful that the darkness concealed the guilt in his face.

Before either of them could reply a peal cut through the silence, and a second later a lone rocket exploded above the treetops, bathing the forest in silver and lighting their hands and faces white. Barney thought he saw something move through the trees — something near, something terrible — and then he realized that it could only have been his own shadow, thrown long against the ground by the light of Ivor's torch. In the distance there were cheers from the boys and yelps of delight from the departing girls, but Barney remained as still as Ivor and Belinda, making no sound as they lifted their eyes to the crackling sky fire, watching the last embers fizzle into the darkness like so many falling stars.

★ ★ ★

Half an hour after Shields accused Percy of stealing his cocoa from the common-room cupboard, four boys were committed to the San complaining of stomach cramps. The youngest, a first-former called Bellamy, had been reduced to tears by the pain. His howls could be heard from across the green as Swift carried him from the boarding house to the main building.

'It was the limpets,' Robin told Barney over lunch. 'Those idiot juniors don't know that you have to build up slowly. I saw three gobbling them last night behind Ormer as if they were chocolates.'

'I heard even Morrell's succumbed. Odd business, that,' said Cowper.

Barney looked over at the Medes' table. Sure enough, there was a space on the bench where Ivor should have been.

'Shields took your last spud,' said Robin, as Barney turned around.

'Shut your mouth, Littlejohn,' groaned Cowper.

'Shut your own — it's closer.'

In the half-hour that they were supposed to spend packing their bags, Barney asked Mr Runcie if he might be allowed to visit one of the boys in the San. The housemaster nodded and said of course, provided he asked permission from Matron.

On the first floor, the San door had been left ajar, a sign screwed to its centre insisting 'Strictly No Talking'.

'Don't just stand there, you dunce — come in and shut the door.'

Ivor was in the closest bed, propped up against two pillows and looking not at all unwell. There were ten bays in the room, which was large and bright, and all but one was occupied. Another boy, the editor of the school magazine who was rumoured to be writing a book, was propped up in the bed opposite Ivor. Barney recognized a chronically homesick first-former by the name of Pike reading a smuggled copy of the *Beano* at the far end. The others lay curled beneath starched sheets, feverish or asleep. Motes danced in a beam of sherbet sunlight which sliced the room in two, and shadows from the mottled-glass windows lapped against the wall behind Ivor's head.

'We were playing Name that Underground Station,' said Ivor. 'Potts here got stuck on the one between Hammersmith and Stamford Brook — and for the life of me I can't be sure whether it's Ravenscourt Park or Turnham Green.'

Barney considered the unwaxed forelock feathering into Ivor's eyes, the top two buttons on his pyjama top undone, and saw him for the first time as a boy like himself. Suddenly he wanted more than anything to be able to clamber into the vacant bed, to cocoon himself in this drowsy world of sunlight shapes playing on the walls and gentle games whispered between the sick bays.

'Aren't you ill, then?' he asked.

'As far as old Baggage is concerned I am,' replied Ivor, running his knuckles across his chest. 'Thank the Lord for syrup of ipecac. Made a nice mess in my set, but it convinced her I wasn't bluffing. At least I shan't have to go home tomorrow.'

Barney's mind shot to the photograph of Ivor's tight-lipped mother and absent-looking grandmother. 'It wasn't the limpets, then?' he asked.

'Don't be an idiot. Limpet-gobbling is a stupid game for stupid little boys to play. For God's sake, take your hands out of your pockets when you're talking to a senior, Holland.'

'So why can't you go home?' pressed Barney. Then he noticed Ivor's jaw tighten, and he realized that this was not the way to be seen talking to a Mede. He glanced at Potts, who was watching them both with interest.

'Ours is not to reason *why*, ours is but to do and die!' Ivor said. 'Life's a lingering fever, and all that. Isn't that so, Potts?'

'Couldn't have put it better myself, Morrell.'

'Do you have any of that stuff left?' asked Barney.

'What stuff? The ipecac? Sorry, old boy — I polished off the last drop.' Ivor was still grinning, but his jeering tone had softened. 'What's your excuse?'

'I can't go home. Runcie is sending me to stay with some old woman on a farm. I didn't know you could stay in the San over half-term.'

'Sagartians and Medes are allowed to keep on in their sets if they like. Baggage will telephone Mater and Pater to explain that I'm simply not up to the ferry ride. Chin up, old man. Once I'm up and about I might wander down to watch you pitching hay — how's that?'

Potts snorted, but Barney could tell that Ivor had meant it. 'That'd be alright,' he said. He wanted to say something about the night before — partly to show Potts, and partly to convince

127

himself that he hadn't dreamt the walk through the forest, behind the girl and ahead of Ivor, who had lighted their way with his torch — but he knew he shouldn't, and in the end he didn't, because at that moment Matron's footsteps sounded on the landing.

'You'd better make yourself scarce,' said Ivor.

Barney let himself out, closing the door behind him.

A cracking noise drew him towards the window, where he saw that the flag which had been lowered at half-mast since the start of term was now snapping in the wind. It was the first time he'd had a chance to get a proper look at the emblem: a warship teetering atop a coat of arms that was set against two fat stripes of orange and blue. The flag danced against the grey sky, and the ship bobbed on its orange sea, and it seemed to Barney that the window pane was humming:

> Then three times 'round went our gallant
> ship
> And three times 'round went she —
> Three times 'round went our gallant ship
> And she sank to the bottom of the sea.

II

The woman on the farm wasn't as old as Barney had expected. Having been told she had poor eyesight, he had imagined an ancient crone with bunions and an ear trumpet. But Miss Duchâtel was the same age as his mother, more or less.

The farmhouse where she lived was built low to the ground and had a round thatch roof. The clay floor was laid with horsehair. On that first night, Barney only noticed two items whose purpose was purely decorative: a pair of porcelain bookends cast in the shape of the Babes in the Wood, and a painting of a woman that wasn't his host, because she had long dark hair while Miss Duchâtel's was a brilliant red, shorn into a brush cut.

She was writing a history of the island, she told him, and she needed someone to help her organize four large boxes of papers into chronological order. Almost two decades' worth of accumulated scraps: some mercifully typed, many others written in a tight, sloping cursive, and a few in a hand that was small and square and thickly inked.

'But that can wait until tomorrow,' she told him. 'Tonight, you'll want to eat — and then you can tell me about yourself. Barney Holland,' she said. 'A good name.'

She spoke with an accent he didn't recognize. She had a largish nose and a prominent chin:

131

features which in a younger woman might be described as handsome, but which had become severe with age. He had never seen a woman with such short hair.

She poured the bean jar into two shallow bowls and brought them to the table. He asked if she had always lived on the island, which made her laugh. When she smiled, her small green eyes turned up at the corners like a Chinaman's.

'My parents were from Paris. I used to play the accordion in the 18th Arrondissement. For a while I modelled for Pascin. I was so poor then, he used to pay me in beef skirt. You've heard of him?' He hadn't. 'That was long before your time. After he died I came here.' She broke the stick loaf into four pieces and divided these between their plates. 'For the last ten years I've bred ducks and geese on this farm. You can meet them tomorrow, if you like.'

She wanted to know about his family, and he told her about London — about Spike and how he was going to front for the Tony Donegan Jazz Band one of these days. She said that she imagined London must be a very exciting place to live. And he had nodded yes, not bothering to mention the shrapnel-scarred shopfronts or the smell of oatmeal burgers that lingered in the alley behind their building — nor the corridor where the linoleum had begun to peel, the squat where it cost a shilling in the radiator slot to keep warm for two hours, and once you were out of matches that was that. He didn't mention the Jamaican family across the hall, the ones that had dog shit shoved through their letterbox every week for a month until they finally moved out.

She said the Carding House School had a very good reputation, did it not? He nodded and said nothing. She asked if he had made many friends, and he said one or two. He didn't tell her that Cowper and Hughes still wouldn't let him take his place at the dinner table without double-punching him in the ribs, or that Shields routinely lingered over his shower when they were the last ones in from games so there wouldn't be any hot water left for him. She asked where his friends lived, if there were any islanders among them, and he said they were all from England. One of them was in the San for half-term. She said that they must certainly have him come to visit, and Barney perked up at this a bit. He had second helpings of bean jar and then she said that she'd show him his room.

'But first,' she said. 'I have something that you might find interesting. Over there.'

It was the painting of the dark-haired woman. The face was not very good. More compelling was the fact that she appeared to have a horn growing out of the back of one hand.

'It's called a cutaneous horn,' explained Miss Duchâtel. 'Sunlight makes it grow.' She pointed to a plant in the foreground — its leaves translucent discs like paper, their seeds visible within — and said, 'In Denmark it is called a *Judaspenge:* 'coins of Judas'.'

He stared at the picture. 'What's it doing here?'

'When your school moved onto the mainland they left various bits and pieces with the islanders to look after. I got the painting.'

'Why haven't you given it back?'

'No one has asked for it. And I've grown fond of her. I've looked after her very well. If it had stayed in an empty school all this time, the mice or carpet beetles would have had her by now.'

'Oh.'

'Now you have seen her, and that's something the other boys can't say.'

'No. Well, thanks.'

'You must be tired. Come, you'll be wanting to see your room.'

When at last she left him, having explained where to find the outhouse — there was a chamber pot under the bed, he wasn't to be shy, but if he preferred she would leave the kitchen door unlocked — the first thing Barney did was draw the blackout curtains. He had never slept in a room of his own, and for the first time he saw just how dark the island night could be without the protective halo cast by lights from the masters' common room. The farm sat at the top of the ridge that ran down the middle of the island. Without any woods or fields or river nearby, just a chequerboard of crofts leading to the edge of the cliff, the sighing of the sea was loud enough to rumble at the walls.

It was a relief not to have to talk any more, not to have to listen, but he wasn't tired enough to go to sleep. He was also dreading the moment when he would have to turn down the lamp on the dresser by the door and cross the room in the darkness to get to his bed. Every few minutes, the house would creak as if he was in the belly of

134

a ship. He pulled back the blanket, which felt damp and released a whiff of something grey and musty, and began to undress, positioning himself near the door, because it had no lock. Then he practised his route to the bed — he could keep one hand on the wall, so it would be easy to find his way back to the lamp just in case — before sliding under the covers to stare at the cobwebbed ceiling.

He tried not to think about the lady with the horn growing out of her hand. Instead, he thought about the other boys on their way to homes in England: Percy in his room with the garish wallpaper; Cowper eating a five-course dinner surrounded by millefiori bowls and other *objets* his parents brought home with them from Murano; Shields taking stock of his Airfix parts and *Eagle* magazines. He struggled to imagine families and homes for Robin and Hiram and Ivor. Belinda would have a proper girl's room, he supposed, with stockings and ribbons draped over a pouffe, a bed cluttered with satin pastilles and posters of matinee idols pinned to the walls.

There was nothing much to look at here: the dresser drawers were empty, lined with faded violet paper, and the only pictures on the walls were two framed collages of pressed flowers. There was the lamp, and the curtains, and a small bedside table.

Idly, and without expectation, Holland reached for the handle of the table drawer, only for it to come loose in his fingers. He sat up and edged across the bed to reattach it. But the spindle had fallen inside the drawer as

135

soon as the handle had come off. There was nothing to be done but try to work the drawer free with his fingernails — and this he did, for several minutes, until at last it gave way with a pained whine.

This drawer, like the others, was lined with violet crêpe. Unlike the others, it was not empty: a few blue glass beads rolled down one side, hitting the edge with a clatter — although it was not these that gave Barney pause. Something long and black had been shoved to the farthest corner; if he hadn't reached his fingers in to grab the spindle, he might not have noticed it. But before he had decided to see what it was, it was there, in his palm: a lock of hair, coarse like a horse's tail, with just one grey strand running through it, tied with a piece of string.

After a moment, the hair began to feel unnatural in Holland's hand, grotesque, and he bundled it back in the drawer with a shudder. He switched off the lamp and tumbled beneath the covers before he could lose his nerve, and soon he slept.

★   ★   ★

When Barney arrived in the kitchen that first morning there was a plate of fried sausages with onion and apples and eggs and white bread with butter waiting for him on the stove top, and next to it a note that said, 'Feeding the girls, back soon. This is for you'. There was coffee in the pot too, and he helped himself with only the slightest twinge of guilt that Jake was probably having to make do with powdered milk and fried potatoes as usual. He polished off every morsel and then he washed his cup and dish in the sink, before pausing to consider what he should do next. It felt wrong to be alone in a stranger's house, even with permission.

The boxes Miss Duchâtel had shown him the previous night remained in the sitting room, open and waiting. She might not have liked it if he'd started nosing through them without her, so he sat in the straight-backed chair and studied the photograph that had been left on the top of one pile.

It was a group portrait of an infants' school: seventeen boys and girls arranged into three crooked rows in front of a severe-looking brick building with shuttered windows. The little boys sitting cross-legged on a rug in the front row hugged their arms to their chests in a pose of stubborn resistance. They wore wool tights under short trousers and identical grey smocks, and they squinted at the camera like shrunken old men. The girls wore dresses beneath grey pinafores: one or two had begun to outgrow these, and the square edges of too-long bloomers peeked out over patched stockings and rolled socks. Two had linked arms and were the only ones attempting smiles: the one dark, shy and gap-toothed, the other taller, fair and coquettish. Several wore beaded bracelets that might have been rosaries. All were strapped into stiff, heavy boots, as if in readiness for some gruelling mountain hike. They also all shared the same short bowl cuts, although one pin-faced girl had managed to work a twist of ribbon into her hair to set herself apart from the boys.

'Have you found me yet?' asked a voice over Barney's shoulder, and he started. It was Miss Duchâtel, red-cheeked from the cold, standing in a lumpy cable-knit jumper and a pair of men's trousers that bulged over the tops of rubber boots. 'There,' she said, pointing to the fair girl. 'And that's my sister.'

They agreed a method for Barney to sort the papers in the first box, and then Miss Duchâtel got up to put on another pot of coffee.

'I'm afraid I don't have a wireless,' she said. 'It's bound to seem a little quiet here. You must be so used to the noise of other children. And music, yes? You said your father was a musician.'

Every so often she would come out with something like that, something vaguely apologetic, perhaps in an attempt to draw him out of his silence, which he realized made her nervous. Finally he asked her if she had ever been to St Just.

'A long time ago,' she replied, setting the mugs on top of a book before kneeling in front of one of the unopened boxes. 'We went there on day trips. Not that there's much to see: it was barren before the Germans came, and just as barren when they left. The Todt took over the quarries for a while. Those poor people. The water was muddy and undrinkable, and the workers were treated like slaves.'

'Inbreds, Robin said.'

'Who?'

'The people on the other island. Oh, sorry

138

— my friend, Robin. From school.'

The woman opened her mouth, closed it again and turned to look at the clock on the mantelpiece.

'Would you like to see the girls?' she said.

The poultry were muddy and garrulous. 'You didn't expect so much noise, did you?' said Miss Duchâtel. 'They are better than watchdogs.' Barney nodded. He preferred the geese to the chickens, whose throaty grumblings had woken him in the early hours and whose scaly feet gave them the appearance of feathered reptiles.

'The fellow who lived here before was a photographer,' said Miss Duchâtel, as she lifted the feed bucket from behind the door. 'He poured all his chemicals out here in the yard, so now nothing can grow. The girls don't mind. But every so often I think of that stupid man and wonder if his pictures were any good.'

She showed Barney how to change the water troughs. 'They never usually get fed twice in the same morning,' she said, as the geese jostled against his legs, considering him with unblinking, orange-ringed eyes. The wind pressed her jumper to the sharp angles of her body, and for the first time he noticed how spare she was. She cuffed one of the taller geese gently about the head, separating it from the flock. 'Shall we show the young man what we can do, Mildred?'

She led the bird to an empty corner of the yard, and in a voice so serious as to be almost stern commanded it to dance. The goose blinked, then ducked its head and flat-footed in two precise circles. She fed it a few sunflower seeds before backing away to sit on the step. 'Now: tell me a secret.'

With a resigned air the goose waddled towards its mistress, who had turned her head sideways and tucked her hair back with her fingers, presenting her ear. At this sign the bird began to nibble at her ear with its beak.

'Is her name really Mildred?'

'Why would I call her Mildred if that wasn't her name?' Miss Duchâtel heaved herself to her feet, waving away Barney's offer of a hand. 'If you visit her every day, perhaps in a little while she'll do it for you too.'

They moved to return indoors, and as he passed one of the geese Barney brushed its head with his hand. Immediately the bird snapped down on his finger, making him cry out.

'Euphemia!' Miss Duchâtel smacked the bird. 'That's it: you shall be Christmas dinner this year.'

'It's all right,' said Barney, embarrassed. He squeezed his finger and was surprised to feel a warm wetness in his palm.

'There will be blood on the rug, and that is most definitely not all right,' said Miss Duchâtel, sitting him on the stoop. 'Wait there — I will find a plaster.'

After several minutes, she returned with a plaster strip and ball of cotton wool. Barney watched the top of her head as she dabbed at the bite mark, transfixed by the whiteness of her scalp against the chemical red of her hair. She pressed the plaster to his finger heavily, not like a mother. 'I'm sorry,' she said. 'That one has

140

always been unpredictable.'

They returned indoors to the waiting boxes. 'Was it your school?' Barney asked, keen to divert attention from himself. He picked up the photograph from the top of the stack.

'Those children were all orphans,' the woman replied. 'Either their fathers had been killed in the Great War and their mothers couldn't afford to keep them, or they had been abandoned as babies at the convent's weeping gate. We were taught together until the age of twelve. After that, the girls were sent into service and the boys had to learn a trade. That one, Francine, was a real bully,' she said, pressing her thumb in the face of a sad-looking child in the second row. 'She and I used to fight like street dogs. And he' — pointing at a boy with gossamer hair parted flatly down the middle of his head — 'he kept a cockroach as a pet. In a matchbox, you know. The cockroach was called Arnaud. I don't remember the lad's name.'

As Barney prepared a fresh journal with the date — Miss Duchâtel had said that dates were imperative — she began to tell him about the year the picture was taken. All through the winter, the children looked forward to their visit to the summer house, a convent in Normandy where they spent two weeks learning to swim and to build fires and lean-tos. A month after the photograph was developed, they had set off as usual for the summer house with no reason to suspect that they would return to Paris at the end of July short of one child.

'It was an accident,' said Miss Duchâtel,

141

pulling papers from the box and sorting them into piles. 'One of our favourite things was the flying fox. It ran all the way from a ledge on the lawn down a hill right to the edge of the pond. It wasn't that high off the ground — the taller boys couldn't use it, it was no good for them — but the little boys loved it, and some of the braver girls too. My sister saw me ride it a few times and wanted to try, but the nuns said she wasn't strong enough: she'd only fall off, and the hill was steep, so it could have been dangerous. Well, the minute we had all gone inside for our supper, what did she do? Only she was wearing one of those silly coats, the type with the little hood, and as soon as she reached for the handlebars the drawstring must have become tangled in the mechanism.' Miss Duchâtel was talking quickly now, not looking at him. 'When we took our places for dinner, we noticed that Simone wasn't there, so we all went out to search for her. We looked in the stables and the sheds where the jumping ropes were kept, and in the lean-to we'd built the day before. We checked the well and the root cellar, and a servant was sent into the village to see if perhaps she hadn't gone there to buy sweets. Then someone noticed that the cable car wasn't at the top of the hill where we always left it — and the boys ran down to the pond, but it was too late.'

The woman gave a little convulsive gesture and fixed him with a sideways look. 'But you didn't ask to hear all of that,' she said.

They continued to work in silence.

'Were you here during the war?' asked Barney,

turning over a sun-bleached photograph of a woman on a beach. The sky behind her was white. The corner of a picnic blanket jutted in at the bottom of the image, and on it were two champagne flutes.

She picked up a book and flipped through the pages, only to toss it back on the floor. 'I couldn't go to England when the island was evacuated, because I'm not a British citizen. But I wasn't going back to France, either. So I stayed here.'

'Some of the boys believe in a German ghost. The commandant used the school as his headquarters.'

'The commandant was not a bad man. His second-in-command, now — Botho Driesch.' She shook her head. 'I have things to do in town. You can come, if you like . . . '

'It's all right,' he said. 'I'll get on with this.'

'*Bon*.' As she pulled on her coat, she added over one shoulder: 'If you want to smoke, be sure to use a saucer. The floor will catch fire otherwise.' She smiled at his surprise. 'I saw your fingers. You're too young to smoke that much. During the war, we used Bible paper wrapped around coltsfoot, because the Germans bought up all the proper cigarettes — it was better, cleared out the lungs. Do you take Gauloises?'

'Woodbines, usually.'

'I'll see what I can do.'

When his host returned an hour later, he had finished sorting through the first box. He let her talk in her disjointed way, resisting the temptation to ask more questions. She seemed to

143

prefer to speak about the distant past — about the cutting attack in the alley behind the orphanage that left a J-like scar on her cheek when she was six — about the *femme galante* who taught her to play the accordion when she was fourteen — about the dance halls and cabarets of Montmartre — but as she spoke he took care to listen to what she did not say: there was no mention of friends or, indeed, of any other islanders.

At three o'clock she suggested that they go for a walk, and when they got back Miss Duchâtel made an early supper of cheese and saucisson followed by hot chocolate served in bowls, then excused herself while Barney worked on the maths problem Doc Dower had set him. He had neglected it until now — not because he hadn't wanted the *piastre* that had been promised to him, and not because he thought Doc would forget their conversation at the bottom of the muddy lower pitch — but because the thought of being unable to work it out was too disheartening. To attempt a solution felt akin to exposing himself to disappointment.

'Do you know how to calculate per-cent slope?' he asked his host when she returned to the kitchen.

'Per-cent what?'

'Never mind.'

At nine o'clock, they went to bed — but not before she suggested that Barney might like to visit his friend in the San that weekend.

'You could bring him back here for tea,' she said. 'If he's feeling up to it.'

144

★ ★ ★

3 June
Batting

This was not one of the older journals: he knew instinctively that it did not belong in the box of archives. A folded shopping list had been left between the pages allocated to the first week in July; a receipt for a car service was the only marker in the month of August. As the pages slipped through his fingers, he spied another note, written in blue ink on fine paper and folded in four, tucked into the diary's corner pocket.

THE TRUTH WILL OUT JEZEBEL WHORE

He refolded the paper with fingers that might as easily have been stung by a flame, but still the backwards writing stared through, ugly and insistent. He shoved the note into the corner pocket in time to hear the door open.

'How are you getting on?' Miss Duchâtel steadied herself in the doorway as she dragged her boots against the mud scrape. Barney returned the diary to the pile and reached for another book. 'It must be easier with materials unfamiliar to you. I stop to read everything — that slows me down.' She stepped inside and reached for the coffee pot. 'Perhaps when you are done there you would like to come with me to collect dinner? Maurice has put aside some coalfish for us at the kiosk.'

145

It was the closest Barney had been to the sea. When she saw the way his eyes lit up at the sight of the water playing upon the sand, she threw off her boots and rolled her trousers up to the knee. 'You're not going to let an old woman go in alone, are you?'

'Isn't it freezing?'

'What a silly question!'

They left their shoes and stumbled across the sand towards the water. The white moon was already beginning to emerge, like a circle of tracing paper pressed against the arc of blue. The waves rolled and receded upon themselves, tugged between two moons: the great spyhole in the sky and its watery reflection. The sea was so cold that it took several seconds for Barney to register the pain of it: the hint of heat first, then numbness, and then a piercing ache that made him wonder how long it would take to turn the blood in his feet to ice. Miss Duchâtel laughed and made for the far end of the shore, lunging at the water like a child. Barney's feet felt like stumps in the water, but still he followed.

By the time he had caught up with her, his host was sitting on a knoll of long grass, pulling on her socks and boots. 'This part of the island isn't so different from the south shore on St Just,' she said. 'They could fit together like pieces of a puzzle. If the grass here could speak to the rocks there, it would say: 'I remember you.''

'Places can't remember,' said Barney.

'Can't they?' She sniffed. 'Maybe not.'

'Robin says that's where POWs were sent. And Yids.'

'There were only two Jewish families who lived here. The first fled to England in a fishing boat. Chances are they are now lying at the bottom of the sea. The second family was deported to Germany — who knows where after that. Nobody put up any protest. I don't think they went to St Just.'

'Robin says there were secret massacres. They could have tested the bomb there, and no one would have known.'

'He sounds like a silly boy, your friend.'

They continued along the shore to where the cockle huts began, Barney thinking all the while that in just a few months, perhaps, he might be with Mum, walking along a beach like this, only one that was properly sandy and hot.

Miss Duchâtel had stopped to nudge at something with her toe. There, among the nacreous stones peeking out of the sand, it looked like a piece of membrane, a yellow and withered skin that was somehow at once dead and part of something alive and out of sight. 'A mermaid's purse,' she said to him, picking it up. 'Some of the old islanders call it a widow's purse, but I think mermaids are nicer.'

'What is it?'

She handed it to him. 'A catshark shell. It's the egg case that's shed when the shark is born. Would you like to take it home with you?'

Barney stared at the thing in his hands, feeling that it was repulsive and yet too fragile to be thrown back on the sand. It was almost weightless: a shining packet three inches long, shaped like a fish — pointed at one end, fanning into a tail at the other — with tendrils curling in imitation of purse strings. He nodded, and she gave him her handkerchief to bundle it in.

Finally they stopped at the last hut, where an old man was waiting for them, a tartan blanket laid out across his knees. Greeting Miss Duchâtel with a nod, he lifted something wrapped in paper that had turned pink and soggy and dropped it on the wooden countertop. The juices from the paper package seeped into the cracks in the counter. Barney watched as a fly landed on a puddle that had begun to collect in a knot in the wood and began rubbing its legs together, anticipating the feast.

'You are too good, Maurice,' she said.

The old man studied Barney. 'From the school?'

'That's right. He's being a great help to me.'

'Bad business,' said the old man. He leant upon his elbows so that his shoulders peaked about his ears. 'I heard it said this morning.' He drew a hand about his face, stretching the leathered skin that bristled with white whiskers right up to his cheekbones.

'We have so much to do,' said Miss Duchâtel. 'Barney is having a friend around tomorrow for tea.'

The old man remained silent, watching.

'Goodbye, Maurice,' said Miss Duchâtel, as she placed the fish into her net bag and started back up the slope towards the coast path. Trailing her, Barney stopped to squint at the grey strip hovering over the horizon and thought

148

how easy it would be to pretend that it didn't exist at all.

★ ★ ★

Miss Duchâtel made *choux amandine* and arranged them on a china plate with a dusting of icing sugar. 'I so rarely have the chance to entertain guests,' she said. She did not seem to mind that Ivor had brought Belinda with him, and she did not ask if her parents knew.

She had laid the table with a yellow cloth and scattered lavender sprigs about the bone china settings. She personalized the bowls of soup with their initials swirled in cream. She opened a bottle of wine and poured it into crystal glasses, which she handed over with a warning to sip around the chips.

Ivor looked well for an invalid, Miss Duchâtel observed, when Barney introduced them. She hoped that his illness would not affect his appetite. This made Ivor blush — a sight new to Barney, and gratifying — and he tried to change the subject by saying that he'd heard she kept geese.

'You must take some eggs back with you.' Miss Duchâtel indicated that they should sit. 'When I was a girl, at the orphanage on Rue des Hospitalières, there were several blind children who came to stay with us while their school was being renovated. Their teacher kept eggs in a little incubator so that when they were about to hatch the children could gather round and feel the little chicks coming through the shell. How

149

do you describe that to a little child of six or seven who has never even seen a chicken? The children spent a little time every day feeling the eggs in their hands, raising them to their ears, smelling them and even trying to taste them, waiting for this magic event that they had been told would happen any day.' She set the pot on the table and nudged the water jug toward Barney. 'I will never forget the morning the eggs started to hatch. We were allowed to come and watch, but not to touch them: that privilege was for the blind children only. The sight of that first tiny chick struggling against the shell — and the face of the little boy when he felt his finger pricked by the beak — well, I'd never seen anything like it. How often do we get to see the world so new like that? Once or twice in our lives, if we are lucky.'

'And you came here after you left the orphanage?' said Ivor.

'No, no. I worked in Paris. In the '30s I spent some time in Switzerland, publicizing a cabaret show. *Die Pfeffermühle*, it was called: *The Pepper Mill*. Perhaps you have heard of it?' Both boys shook their heads. 'It was produced by Erika Mann. Her father, Thomas, you might know from his books.'

Ivor was listening carefully. Barney was counting the number of bread slices they'd each had and wondering if it would seem greedy to take the last one.

'So how did you end up here?'

Miss Duchâtel blew a thin stream of smoke over one shoulder, tapped her cigarette on her saucer. 'One morning, I spotted a newspaper advertisement for a goose farm that was up for sale on Lindsey — I had never even heard of the place until that point — and I decided that I would take it. It was the beginning of the happiest five years of my life.'

'Until the war?'

'Oh, even with the war.' She squashed her cigarette on the edge of her plate and swept a few imaginary crumbs off the table into her palm.

Belinda did not speak for the first part of the meal, observing with cautious eyes and sampling successive courses only once she'd watched Barney and Ivor taste a bit of everything on their plates. Every now and then Miss Duchâtel would issue a pre-emptive correction or command — 'I will pour the drinks. Ivor, as the senior gentleman, will carve the roast' — in the manner of someone raised in an institution where you learnt to fight for what you wanted. It made them feel that they were part of a meal being staged from some other time in her life — that they were playing the roles of other guests. When she wasn't busy giving orders, she filled the silences with talk of the work she did for the Island Bat Ordnance Survey, counting colonies by night in barns up and down Lindsey.

'Batting,' said Barney.

'That's right,' she said, looking only slightly surprised.

Finally, Belinda started to eat what was left of the mint jelly on her plate. For several moments, the *tink* of her fork against china was the only sound in the room.

'Holland said you knew about the school ghost,' said Ivor.

'I don't know about ghosts,' said Miss Duchâtel. 'People like ghost stories because they are easier to believe than the crimes committed by the living.'

That was when Barney mentioned the baby that had been found behind the old kitchens. 'The police came, so it must have been a murder,' he said. Scarcely were the words out of his mouth than he knew that it had been a mistake.

'Why must you talk of such things?' she said, with a hard look. 'Boys — so fascinated by suffering. No — ' She waved away Ivor's attempt to help her clear the table. 'Thank you, I will do it.' She set her glass down too hard, and the last of the wine went splashing across the counter. 'Oh, hell.' Both boys offered their napkins; she used a dishcloth to mop up the mess. 'I'm sorry, I'm not feeling very well. You won't think me rude if I lie down for half an hour? Barney, perhaps you would like to show the others the mermaid's purse we found?'

'Widow's purse,' corrected Barney, worried that Ivor and Belinda would laugh.

Upstairs, Ivor was the first to comment that his room smelt odd.

'It's not my fault,' said Barney, crossing to the chest of drawers. The shell had shrunk since he'd brought it inside, but still retained its shape. 'Here. This one was a shark, apparently.'

'What are you going to do with it?' asked Belinda.

'I don't know. She thought I'd want to keep it.'

'Selkies shed their skins, don't they?' Ivor tested the membrane between his fingers. 'When they go from being seals to being human.'

'My gran says they're lost spirits of drowned people,' said Belinda.

They decided to go outside, to sit on the stile at the far end of the yard where the geese had gathered in search of feed. Beyond the farm grounds the land sloped down to the salt marsh, and from there to the beach dotted with cockle sheds. A cleft ran down the middle of a cliff rising from the water, and Ivor said that this was known as 'The Chimney', where men used to risk their lives lowering themselves on pulleys down the shaft to collect seabirds' eggs from the nests in the rock.

The wind was heavy with damp, so that the sea seemed everywhere: not just lapping at the shore, but in the small rain hanging in the air itself, seeping up through the ground, glistening in perfect droplets on the birds' beaks. Miss Duchâtel had told Barney that after January's floods they had been inundated with rats fleeing the salt marsh. They'd killed six of her chickens in a single week, leaving the yard strewn with feathers and entrails.

They made a game of keepy-uppy with a ball of wool that had become snagged on the wire tied to the gatepost. As they kicked it back and forth, Barney whispered a rhyme that Jake's friends used in counting games:

Red, white and blue,
My mother is a Jew —
My father is a Scotsman
And I'm a kangaroo.

Only it was hard to control this ball that wasn't a ball, and they only ever got as far as the third line. After several attempts, Barney kicked the knot into a puddle, scattering the geese, and the game ended. They were getting cold, so they decided to go back indoors.

Miss Duchâtel had appeared in the doorway and leant against the outside wall where the paint had started to blister. 'Before you come in, perhaps you would like to see Mildred dance?' she said with a sweet smile, winking at Barney 'You have told your friends about the tricks she can perform, I expect?'

They smiled and clapped exactly as she wanted them to, so that by the time she looked at her watch and said she had promised that Ivor should return to school before nightfall they were all in good spirits. They waved goodbye soon after, Belinda clutching a bouquet of goose feathers and Ivor concealing some dandelion wine under his duffel coat.

'I hope that you had a nice time,' said Miss Duchâtel to Barney, as they watched the two figures heading up the ridge.

'Oh, yes. Thank you.'

It was cold, standing there on the stoop, and after a minute he excused himself to return indoors. The woman made to follow him, but then she stopped, enchanted by something about

154

the sight of two dark heads bobbing along the horizon. Alone in front of the farmhouse, she watched them leave as one might a pair of ghosts.

★   ★   ★

Miss Duchâtel went to bed early that evening, saying that the headache still hadn't quite left her. 'You must do as you please now. Have you brought any books with you?'

'One or two,' said Barney. Robin had loaned him last year's *Boy's Own Annual*, but he didn't suppose this was the sort of thing she'd had in mind.

He followed her upstairs and retreated behind his own bedroom door. He hadn't had any intention of reading the annual — he had been put off by the large pages covered in dense lines of text; some of the stories only had one or two illustrations, and the puzzles were all too clever — but the clock on the bedside table showed that it was only just past eight, and he did not yet feel like going to sleep.

The first piece was called ' "Twixt School and College' and was followed by a column on caring for golden hamsters. Barney turned the pages, hoping for something on football or dogs. At last he landed on an adventure story called 'Heroes of El Alamein'. The title was obscured by a piece of card that had been inserted as a placeholder. Barney turned it over, recognizing the feel of its soft corners. On the one side was an illustration of a dark-haired youth, naked but for a fluttering loincloth, surrounded by shrieking, bare-breasted women. The youth's hands were pressed to his ears, and his eyes were bugged and frantic.

The reverse revealed it to be a postcard — blank, ORESTES PURSUED BY THE FURIES was written in small, square print at the bottom corner, followed by the single word: BOU-GUEREAU.

He fell asleep soon after, the annual still open on the bed and the postcard tilting between his fingers. That night, for the first time since arriving on the island, Barney slept solidly until dawn.

★ ★ ★

'I once read a story in a history book about a young English girl who was to be sent to Australia on a convict transport. She was a prostitute, yes?' Barney stirred more sugar into his porridge and nodded vaguely; he didn't want to hear an old woman talk about things like that. Miss Duchâtel was in an energetic mood and did not seem to notice his discomfort. 'Well, the ship sank and she washed up on shore somewhere in Namibia. Or perhaps it was Mozambique; I don't know. She was found by a local hunter who took her back to his house, and from then on she lived as a local queen. A white woman on the edge of the world.'

She poured the last of the coffee into his cup and watched him reach for the milk jug with a disapproving eye. 'You English, always ruining your tea and your coffee like that. You make a beautiful drink into nursery food.'

'Did she never go back, then?'

'I don't think so. England was her childhood. You can't go back to a place that no longer exists.'

'Of course it still *existed*.'

'Perhaps she did not think so, after many years as an African queen.' Miss Duchâtel rose and took the plates to the sink.

'Is that why you never went back to France?'

'Perhaps. It wouldn't be the same now. Sometimes it's better not to try to force the things you dream about onto real places, real people.' She ran the water. 'At the orphanage, a few days before Christmas one year, I discovered a box at the top of the dormitory wardrobe, hidden beneath some blankets. As it was wrapped in gold tissue I boasted to a friend that it must be for me, because gold was my favourite colour and the box was just the right size for the bisque doll that I coveted. But on Christmas morning the Mother Superior gave the box to another girl — no more than a baby, whose father was wealthy but lived very far away — while the rest of us had to make do with bags of glacé cherries.' She placed the dishes on the draining board, wiped her hands on a cloth.

'That's a sad story.'

'It's only a story now.' She looked at her watch. 'I have some shopping to collect in town. Would you like to come along for the drive?'

The car was parked on the verge at the top of the driveway, close to the main road. Miss Duchâtel told him that the door on the passenger side didn't open, so he would have to climb in across the driver's seat. The leatherwork was worn and gave off a neglected smell; the dashboard was furry with dust. But the engine made a good rumble, and as Miss Duchâtel slammed her door shut Barney felt the exhilaration of freedom through movement.

They were halfway to St Arras before the car shuddered and Barney felt his side begin to sink. 'Something's not right,' he said.

Miss Duchâtel had already decided this for herself. She braked, turned off the engine, and stepped out onto the road. 'Stay there,' she said.

He watched her inspect the front right tyre, and then the left. As she disappeared around the back of the car Barney watched the condensation from his breath form clouds in the window. Outside, the land and sky divided into two fat stripes: the frosty, dead-green of the empty field and the motionless grey of the sky. Inside, the air had turned still and cold, and Barney twisted in his seat to see what had become of Miss Duchâtel.

She had rounded the vehicle and now stood in the middle of the road, staring, horrified, at something he could not see. When she noticed him watching her she waved both hands at him. 'Stay there,' she said. 'It's only a puncture.'

But he was not to be fooled. Before she could prevent him from opening the driver's side door, he was out; and then, ignoring her admonishments, he went onto the road.

He did not register the slashed tyres, nor even the awkward tilt of the car. He only saw the

158

word, daubed in red paint along the passenger side in letters twelve inches high — and the ugly line scraped from fender to hub underlining them.

Instinctively, he looked around, though he might have known there would be no one there: this was not a place where people walked or stopped to take in the view, for there was no view to be taken. They were alone: grimly, awfully alone. The wind blew, a seabird shrieked — and then there was a gulping noise from Miss Duchâtel.

'Get back inside,' she said. 'I can get us home.'

'Who did this?'

'If I drive carefully we will make it.'

'What about the shopping?'

'The shopping doesn't matter.'

They did make it back to the farm, just. Miss Duchâtel asked if Barney had finished his maths prep, which he interpreted the way it was meant; he went upstairs to his room and closed the door. A little while later, he heard the front door open and footsteps on the path. At the top of the drive, Miss Duchâtel brandished a paintbrush at the offending letters, replacing them with broad strokes the colour of wet sand.

★ ★ ★

On the morning that Barney was due to return to school, Miss Duchâtel surveyed the stack of boxes in the corner of her living room and ran a finger down the margin of a workbook he had filled with dates and names. Her reading glasses rested on the table. 'Your eyes aren't so poor,' he observed.

'It's just as well you printed,' she said. 'I couldn't read cursive.'

'You could always get someone to type it for you.'

'Do you type?'

Barney shook his head. 'Morrell probably could.'

'Well, ask him if he wants the work one afternoon. It would be nice to see him again. And, of course, you must visit me too.'

As far as Barney was concerned, that was to be the end of it. The week had gone by quickly, and with two pound notes folded in his pocket he was the richest he'd ever been. Now he could look forward to seeing the others again and going back to a school where he was no longer the new boy.

Wandering up the drive that afternoon, he even thought he'd spotted the latest recruit: a child younger and scrawnier than him, wearing a thin jumper rolled up to show white elbows. *He'll be mincemeat by lights out*, thought Barney. 'You there!' he called after the newcomer.

Belinda turned round and flashed him a smile. After she'd lopped off her hair with some kitchen scissors, her horrified mother had taken her to reduce the damage at a salon in town — but she still looked like a prison-camp inmate. Now, for the first time, Barney saw how a plain girl could be transformed into a rather beautiful boy.

'It's meant to be like Erika Mann,' she

explained, as they continued up the drive together. 'I finished what Cowper started. Do you like it?' He'd nodded yes, although really he didn't know what to think.

They met in the fallout shelter that evening after supper, and Ivor told him about the idea they'd had for a secret society — a 'dining club', he called it, because every week they would pool their resources for a proper feast, replete with contraband food-stuffs, cigarettes and finest spirits. Then he and Belinda started spitting apple pips at each other, which seemed to Barney like an excuse to blow kisses. When Belinda rushed at Ivor for sending a pip down her front, he caught her in a gentle rugby tackle, pushing her onto the bench and making Barney edge away.

It wasn't clear when the girl had fallen in love with Ivor's taunts — the way he mocked them when he spoke, daring them not to understand.

'Adult moths can't take food, which is why they live for just a few days,' he was saying now. 'It only goes to show that we should enjoy ourselves while we can. I propose a bacchanal tonight. The masters aren't fussy about bed checks out of term, and most of the school won't be back until the morning.'

This was only partly true: Barney arrived at Medlar House that evening to find the dormitory already half full. Robin and Hughes were talking about the new lorry that had replaced the battered one Krawiec normally used to transport stones for wall repairs.

'Too smart for a groundskeeper, if you ask

me,' Hughes was saying.

'Perhaps old Cray bequeathed his estate to the school,' Robin said.

'Nonsense. He'd have to have a will to do that.'

'So?'

'And Cray didn't have an estate. He had a stack of postcards under his mattress and the same evil-smelling fruitcake in his tuck every half-term.'

Barney reached for the *Boy's Own* in his suitcase and left it on Robin's bed without bothering to interrupt them. If he wasn't to turn up to the feast empty-handed, he would have to get to the kitchens before they were locked at eight.

He was halfway to the shelter when he noticed the car parked outside the old kitchens. At the sound of his footsteps a door opened, and Belinda beckoned him. She sat with Ivor in the large back seat. Behind the wheel was Miss Duchâtel.

'Look who I found,' she said.

'What are you doing here?'

'That's no way to talk, Holland,' said Ivor.

Somehow, she must have found the money to replace the tyres. It was too dark to see the haphazard paint strokes concealing the offending word. 'Why are you here?'

'Inside that old building is the biggest horseshoe-bat colony on the island,' she said, pointing up at the roof. There was a box of recording equipment on the passenger seat, and Barney asked her to let him look at it, which she

162

did. They each had a go at talking into the microphone, until Miss Duchâtel spotted the first bats spilling out from the eaves and told them that they'd have to be quiet while she recorded them.

When they still hadn't left, she asked if it wasn't time they were in bed. But Ivor had spotted the thermos in the back seat and said he rather fancied some coffee instead.

'Well,' said Miss Duchâtel, 'you can have a drink, if you like, but I don't have any cups.'

That was how they ended up back in the fallout shelter with a flask of coffee that they divided into four jam jars. Finally, perhaps because Ivor added a little brandy to her flask, Miss Duchâtel began to relax enough to admit that she'd dined there during the war, when the Germans had used the old kitchens as entertaining quarters. Because the British government was too proud to admit that the islanders had been abandoned, they didn't drop food packages here as in other parts of Europe. The only food that came onto Lindsey arrived with the invading army — and even that stopped after D-Day, when islanders were reduced to killing stray dogs and cats to eat.

She said she'd been invited there to make up for the fact that a group of soldiers had stolen some of her geese. The commandant had heard about a Frenchwoman living on the farm, and because he had spent many childhood summers in the Auvergne he thought it would be nice to pass an evening reliving those times and practising his French. There was no point

163

refusing, so the commandant got his candlelit evening confusing his tenses and reminiscing about his Breton nanny, through mouthfuls of pâté and dauphinoise potatoes.

He was a handsome man, and impeccably well-mannered. But he spoke too much, seemed to want too much to be liked, and she was embarrassed by this. His lieutenant Driesch, on the other hand, was surly and breathed heavily through his nose as he ate. He had a drinker's face, Miss Duchâtel said. At the end of the evening, as she was escorted through the shadows to a car that would take her back to her farm, she heard him call after her — 'Madame', as if after three hours he still couldn't remember her name — but she had pretended not to hear. It was only when she arrived home that she realized she had left her purse behind. 'But by then the child was awake and it was long past curfew — '

'What child?' interjected Belinda.

For a moment the only sound was the hush of summer stalks brushing against the bunker door. *Cowper was right*, thought Barney. *It was a Jerrybag baby — and she killed it.*

'I looked after a neighbour's daughter,' she said. 'A very sickly baby. Infantile tetanus.' She downed the last of her coffee, and then she reached for the brandy bottle at Ivor's feet.

'You didn't tell us this before,' said Ivor.

'It was a long time ago. You know what happened to Lot's wife for dwelling too much on the past . . . '

That's why she used us to pretend, thought

164

Barney. *The tea party. Dinner. The commandant and Driesch and her together . . .*

'It's so late,' she said. 'What am I doing here,
still? In this hole in the ground . . . '

'We can take you back to the car, if you like.'

'Yes, that would be best.'

They waited until the headlights had disappeared over the ridge before returning to the
bunker. On the way, they spotted a colony of
land crabs digging up through the ground on the
first stage of their migration towards the sea. The
crabs would lay their eggs in the water, and once
these had hatched, the forest floor would tremble
with the bodies of tiny brown newborns
scrabbling their way back inland.

★   ★   ★

The question came unexpectedly, during prep.

'So what do you lot *do* in there?'

Robin hadn't bothered to look up from his
French conjugations, and so Barney continued
to draw lines in his geometry book, feigning
nonchalance. Still, a solution to the problem
Doc Dower had set that afternoon on the muddy
pitch evaded him. It occurred to Barney that
perhaps drawing lines was not the answer;
perhaps he ought to write down the figures as he
remembered Doc noting them . . .

'Where?'

'In the shelter. When you meet up in the
middle of the night.'

Barney set down his compass, then picked it
up again. 'Nothing,' he said.

165

'Rubbish.' Robin sniffed. 'Well, don't worry. I haven't told anyone.'

One hundred feet. One foot. Two-per-cent slope. Two over a hundred . . .

'You do know you'll get the sack if they catch you. Two chaps alone is one thing. Two chaps with a girl is another. Especially if one of them's a Mede. You can imagine how it looks.'

'It's not like that.'

Robin snatched the compass from Barney's desk and pressed the point against his bare thigh. 'What's he told you?' Robin held the compass in a fist, pressing harder against his leg. If it hurt, he didn't show it.

'Stop that. You'll cut yourself.'

'What do you care?'

'Idiot.'

Robin pressed the compass down so that the point buried into his skin. He let go, and it hung at a strange angle against his leg.

'Stop that. Take it out.'

'You do it.'

Robin twisted the point and levered the compass left and right. A moment later, a bubble of blood rose from the wound.

'Cowper says some of the girls at the fireworks display had stories to tell about her.'

'Stop doing that.' Barney reached for the compass, but Robin grabbed hold of it first. 'Cowper talks nonsense. You know that he doesn't like her.'

Robin eased the point from under his skin, drawing a line in the blood. 'So, does she talk about the baby?'

'No. She's heard the thing in the basement corridor, though.'

'There is no *thing*, you fool.' Robin rolled his eyes. 'Not there, anyway.'

'Give me that.'

Robin handed over the compass with a bored look and pressed one finger against the cut in his leg. Barney watched as he drew the finger across his lips.

'If there's a thing anywhere, it's out there,' said Robin. 'Cray saw it last year from the pumping station: a man in a grey coat. Cray watched him cross the field, but he vanished before he reached the fence.'

'Do you have a handkerchief?'

'No.'

Barney wiped the compass on his knee and tried to rub out the stain between his fingers. Robin watched wearily before turning back to his conjugations.

'So much fuss over a little blood,' he said.

★ ★ ★

When the post was distributed in the common room the following afternoon, Barney was aware of Cowper noting with interest the envelope handed to him by Mr Runcie — of the sort that sold for a penny at the post office. The paper inside had been torn from a notebook.

'First one this term?' said Cowper. Barney ignored him. 'Remind you of anyone?' Cowper said to Shields in a stage whisper, angling an open book so that Barney, too, could see the

167

picture. The novel featured illustrations in the Victorian style: broad-shouldered women with thick necks and small heads, and men with handlebar moustaches in tartan knickerbockers or canvas puttees. The picture Cowper meant Barney to see showed a giant hag being consumed by a pillar of flames, black hair fanning about her head, eyes rolling in torment, fingers splayed. The quotation at the bottom read '*I will come again*'.

Shields stole a glance over one shoulder at the girl sitting in the corner. 'Do you think *she'll* stick us in a hotpot?' he said.

'She'd have to transfix us with her beauty first,' came the reply. 'An unlikely prospect, with a nose like that. Rather too Semitic, don't you think?'

'Bog off,' hissed Barney.

'You'd better be careful, Holland, or she'll turn you into a pig with her voodoo magic.' Cowper closed the book. 'So, aren't you going to read it? Who's it from?'

'Mind your own business,' said Barney, tucking the envelope into his blazer pocket.

It wouldn't be safe to read in the house that night: Cowper would be waiting to grab the letter as he had grabbed the pamphlet in the toilets. So Barney asked Mr Runcie if he might be excused to go to the library. To his surprise, the housemaster nodded without asking any questions.

The library was locked. At the sound of the headmaster's door opening down the corridor, Barney ducked into the stairwell leading to the

168

laundries, then descended the narrow staircase to the dark bowels of the building, following the curve of the wall with one hand. All of the lights but one had been shut off, and that one flickered outside the main laundry. Barney unfolded the letter and tilted the paper away from him so that the shadows seemed to slide off the page.

Barn, old man

I'm sorry, I really am. Clive Brightly offered us the gig at the eleventh hour and I couldn't say no — you know how it is. You must have been gutted. Jake took it special hard, poor chap. He's all right now, but he asks about you every day. He'd love it if you sent him a letter some time — one just for him, you know. I'd read it to him, natch.

We enjoyed your last letter. Nice to hear you've made a few friends. Some of them will be your mates for life. I met George Mellow when we were nippers in Miss Knightly's class, you know. That makes me feel like an old man. He cut us a good deal at the Black Cap last week. You should have heard the skiffle and the Irish fiddles, it was a class act.

Mrs Metz had her record player going the other day, which made me think of you. Remember when she had it set up in the window for the victory celebrations and you went out in the courtyard with the other kids to dance to 'Bless 'Em All'? And the miserable old what's-it had the nerve to shut the window because the music was for her people, not the likes of us. She's not much improved with age

— but then I say there's something nice about certain things staying the same year in year out.

I hope you're giving the masters a good account of yourself and not messing about too much in lessons. We are proud of you, Barn — your mum too. Has she written to you yet?

Love from Spike, Jake and the lads

Spike should have known that Mum hadn't written. Perhaps he'd asked because he was worried that he was starting to forget them — in case London was starting to feel a lifetime away. Well, it did. Trust Spike to ruin it.

The wall had turned cold against Barney's back, so much so that it felt almost wet. Moving to one side, he felt his shirt catch on an object like a nail. He pulled away and was aware of his shirt clinging to his skin. There was no nail: the wall was smooth and dry.

The sound of flushing water rumbled overhead, followed by a trickle like laughter. Barney glanced up at the main pipe, which was flanked by two narrow ones that dripped at the join, where they veered to travel around the laundry door. Etched into the unpainted wood of the jamb, just above his head, were two sets of initials: *IM HC*. And on the opposite side, in the same hand, the words *hic fuimus*.

Noticing for the first time the depth of the darkness in the corridor — the kind of darkness that seemed to move, the kind of darkness that might have been alive — Barney shoved the paper into his pocket, not hearing the envelope drift to the floor.

* * *

They set off to Miss Duchâtel's straight after chapel, Belinda a few steps ahead and the other two trailing behind her. The girl pretended not to notice when Ivor kicked at a stone so that it skipped up against the back of her leg. Instead, she concentrated on the sea: the green flashes darkening to grey, flattening to a colder shade of blue. Whenever the sea changed colour before the sky, it was a sign that a storm would arrive quickly, with violence.

A movement to the side of the road made her stop. It was a moment before Barney perceived what she had seen, as the creature scuttling towards them weaved in and out of sight between the fencing. It had an arched, rust-coloured body, and between its jaws hung something pale and feathered, and limp.

'Is it one of hers?' whispered Belinda.

'It could be from anywhere,' said Ivor. 'But it's his now.'

He knelt, watching the fox, which had paused on the other side of the fence. Its spine bristled, and through its stuffed mouth came a low growl. For several seconds they remained like that — staring at each other — until Ivor lunged forward with a loud hiss that sent the fox loping into the undergrowth. He turned around, grinning.

'Eat or be eaten,' he said.

171

They could hear the Frenchwoman in the poultry yard as they approached from the road. She was chatting to the geese and occasionally snapping at the chickens.

Barney's hand was on the gate when Ivor touched his shoulder and placed a finger to his lips. 'Let's surprise her,' he said. So they crept around the back of the house instead.

Soon they heard her footsteps, and through the slats in the fence they saw her emerge holding a chicken under one arm. With a deft move she took it by the legs and swung it upside down, so quickly that by the time they had realized what was about to happen the bird was hanging in mid-air with glazed-over eyes, and the long knife was already in her hand.

There was not time to look away as Miss Duchâtel sliced the head off — backhanded, as if performing a tennis stroke — and the sight of it dropping to the ground with a thud, and all that blood pouring from the neck, made Belinda scream.

That was the surprise ruined. Miss Duchâtel told Ivor off for letting the girl watch, and tried to reassure her that the chicken had felt no pain — but Belinda shrank from the woman's arms and ran, sobbing, from the yard.

'What a display,' Ivor said. 'A child of her age.'

'Shut up,' said Barney, and followed her.

He found her at the front of the poultry yard, leaning against the fence and digging a groove into the earth with her toe. Something about her posture made him hesitate — if she ran away a second time it would be his fault — but when she heard him shoo away a couple of the hens she turned and said in a flat voice, 'Leave them alone.'

'I wasn't doing anything.'

She leant her head upon her arms and sighed deeply.

'You all right?' he said.

'It doesn't matter.'

They stood there for a while, watching the shadows brush the landscape, until Barney said. 'Why don't we go inside?'

'You can. I hate her.'

Perhaps she sensed it too, thought Barney. 'She lied about Switzerland,' he said.

'How do you know?'

'I don't. But I think she came over with the Krauts. Someone's threatened her. She's hiding something. Maybe the baby. Maybe she killed it, even.'

Belinda stared at the ground, surprisingly unmoved.

'Do you want to go into town?' he said. 'We're halfway there already, and I have sixpence.'

That seemed a good idea — until they were standing in a queue at the café. Noticing a pair of goose-pimpled calves like two small hams before them, Belinda tugged at Barney's sleeve.

'Never mind this,' she said. 'Let's go somewhere else.'

But Gloria had already turned around. Belinda would have recognized the pushed-up bosom in its mossy brown gym slip at a hundred yards.

'I say, Miss Haugherty,' Gloria said, with a

173

look of malicious delight. 'Look.'

The woman in the queue next to Gloria turned and regarded Belinda with a little lopsided smile.

'Belinda, dear. How lovely to see you again.'

Gloria's prune-coloured eyes slid back and forth in their deep sockets, from Barney to Belinda and back again.

'This is Barney Holland,' Belinda said.

'A pleasure to meet you, Barney,' said Miss Haugherty. 'Gloria, was it the plain scones or the fruit that Miss Home asked for?'

'The plain ones, Miss.' Gloria again fixed her stare on the pair. 'Fitting in nicely, are you?'

'I am, thanks.'

'Come along, Gloria. Do send my regards to your parents, Belinda.'

When they were gone, Barney bought two iced buns and suggested that they eat them by the sea wall.

'Friend of yours?' he said. For the first time, it occurred to him that perhaps being the only girl among boys wasn't what made her different: perhaps she had always been that way.

'I skivvied for her last year.' Kneeling over a square of newspaper to dig clumps of grass from Gloria's hockey boots while the sixth-former sat cross-legged on her bed and an American voice crooned 'Kiss of Fire' from the gramophone — making toast or restringing a lacrosse stick while Gloria pulled a brush through her dull hair, willing it to shine like Millicent Grady's, the head girl, rumoured to be at least a quarter Spanish. Everyone had to tiptoe around Gloria

174

because she was fat. This hadn't bothered Belinda so much as the way Gloria would snap her ruler against the backs of her legs as she knelt to lay the fire or grill her as to the whereabouts of a missing hairpin that Belinda knew full well wasn't Gloria's at all, but was pinched from her roommate.

'Big lass, isn't she?'

'That's one way of putting it.'

On the tiered walkway below, a young man was walking arm in arm with a young woman. The wind was blowing the woman's hair into her face: she had clearly given up tucking it behind her ears. She laughed suddenly, nudging into the young man's side, and he pulled her one way and then pushed her gently back.

'Do you suppose they're doing it?' she said.

Barney grunted through a mouthful of pastry.

'The girls in my dormitory used to talk about it after lights out,' she said. 'You know what.'

'Girls talk too much,' said Barney.

They wiped their fingers on the grass and walked along the sea wall.

'Robin knows about the dining society,' said Barney. 'He's seen us go to the shelter at night.'

'He said so?'

'I don't think he'll tell anyone else.' He registered her dimpling brow. 'Don't let Morrell know. He'd murder me.'

'Of course.'

The North Sea waters had turned a grungy colour. 'We should go to St Just,' said Belinda. 'We could rent a boat one day and come back when we felt like it. No one would have to know.'

'If you say so.'

'The top sets used to go there for an excursion just before exams started,' she said.

There would be walks and a visit to the paintings on the rock face where the centuries stacked upon one another; afterwards there would be a picnic by the midden strewn with oyster shells from Stone Age feasts. A local family would loan the senior form a two-masted schooner and the younger girls would wave them off enviously from the pier before trudging back to continue their revision.

'All right,' Barney said. 'We'll do that.'

They arrived back at the school gates to find Ivor already waiting.

'Where the hell have you been?' he said.

'We went into town,' said Barney.

'Without saying anything to us? Very nice.'

'Sorry,' said Barney.

'Don't apologize,' said Belinda. 'We didn't do anything wrong.'

'What would your father say?'

'Nothing, because you won't tell him.'

Ivor took her by the arm. 'I won't tell him because it won't happen again.'

'Let her go,' said Barney.

For a moment it looked as though Ivor was going to belt him, but then he just laughed and released his grip. 'Come back to the shelter. I've something to show you.'

They passed Robin teasing the Head's ginger cat with a piece of string. He was using the twitching, bodiless tail to lure it onto the fountain's edge, where the water had stained the grey stone green.

'Watch this, Holland,' said Robin. 'Watch the way he wiggles his arse when he thinks he's about to catch it. Bugger — he's stopped doing it now — '

'Later,' said Barney.

'You've been gone all day,' said Robin. But they were already halfway across the green.

In the shelter, Ivor showed them how he'd stuffed a fountain pen cartridge with match heads, sealing the ends with cigarette foil. 'This is just a prototype,' he said. 'A little sugar and vinegar would mean more power, and lighter fluid would give us a flame. Still, it's a start.'

They followed him outside to the bit of ground behind the shelter covered in a carpet of fir pines. Ivor cleared an area with his foot and placed the cartridge in the dirt.

'Stand back,' he said, pulling a lighter from his pocket and holding the flame near the butt of the cartridge. There was a whistling noise, and then a stream of smoke darted into the air, trailing out seconds later in a flourish of curlicues as it sputtered back to earth.

'You could try it up a pipe,' said Barney. 'There's one here — ' And they followed him around the side of the shelter, where there was a water tap covered with cobwebs. Barney tested the handle, which had rusted stiff. A spurt of brown water trickled to the ground. The stream dried almost instantly, and so they each gave the tap a whack and a kick.

Out spilt a thicket of legs: a nest of black

177

spiders, tumbling one after the other. There were dozens of them, it seemed, in that quivering mess of scrambling bodies. A voice from across the green made them turn in panic.

'What's going on down there?

Krawiec. He had a coil of rope looped over one shoulder and had stopped to lean on a spade. Through the trees they could make out the red handkerchief knotted at the groundsman's neck, the burr of white whiskers.

'I was just sending these two into Hall,' said Ivor. Then, in a low voice, 'If it turns out anyone spotted you in town, I didn't know.'

They emerged onto the green to find that Krawiec had already disappeared with his rope and spade. Only Robin remained where he'd been earlier.

'What were you doing?' he asked Barney as soon as the other two had gone inside. 'I heard something go off.'

'It was nothing. Where's the cat?'

'He heard it too. He ran away.'

'Did you tell Krawiec we were in the forest?'

'Honestly, Holland — you needn't be so precious about the company you keep.'

'What's that supposed to mean?'

'The way you and that girl follow him around everywhere. You're like a dog that thumps its tail to show its master he's still waiting. So very sad.'

'At least I don't go around with a mopey look on my mug all the time,' said Barney. *I know where you got that postcard*, he was about to add — but something stopped him. Robin was smiling.

178

'Fool yourself, if you must, but it's all in his file. Last year was his final warning. They're just waiting for him to try something like it again, and then he'll be out.'

'Like what?'

'Now you're interested.' Robin slid from the edge of the fountain and headed back towards the house. As he went, Barney watched him wrap the string around one finger and slide it into his pocket.

★　★　★

The following day during Scripture, Robin leant in to Barney and whispered, 'Four o'clock outside the Sixth Form common room. I told Maccleson we'd rake out the fire. Normally it's the ones in the First who do it, but it doesn't make any difference to them.'

Gumming at a fruit drop, Reverend Marrett turned to Barney. 'Holland: '*And he dreamed, and behold a ladder set up on the earth, and the top of it reached to heaven: and behold the angels of —* ''

'Elohim, sir. Ascending and descending on it.'

Reverend Marrett turned the fruit drop over in his mouth and resumed his pacing between the desks. When his back was turned, Barney looked again to Robin, but his friend had become suddenly engrossed in his psalter.

At four o'clock Barney stood outside the Sixth Form common room on the gallery overlooking the atrium. He watched the tops of boys' heads bobbing from one end to the other: hurrying to change for games, ducking down to hall for some bread and honey, a few conspiring in groups of twos and threes. Now and then a master would sweep through trailing a short gown with shoulder flaps like wings. Never before had he known that all this could be observed, invisibly, from above, and he wondered how many times someone might have watched him wandering by unawares.

'There you are,' said Robin, who had appeared at the top of the staircase with a newspaper tucked under one arm. 'Soon you'll see what Morrell's really after. His file will prove it.'

'I thought they were all kept in Pleming's study.' Hughes had told him so. There was one strongbox for current students, while another held the files of boys recently graduated: letters from estranged parents who used the school as a marital intermediary; requests for patience while fathers scrambled to scrape together payments that their wives did not know were overdue by three terms; confidences about delicate dispositions, family tragedies, embarrassing health problems; prep-school histories that had made applications to other institutions complicated; police records.

'They are.' Robin knocked on the door, which was opened by a bored-looking giant of a boy named Sackler. 'We're here to do the fire,' said Robin. 'Your usual chap is in the San.'

Sackler grunted and opened the door wide enough for them to enter.

Barney counted four sofas, on which lounged an assortment of senior boys. A rowing blade was

180

propped on the mantelpiece and would have given the room a distinguished air were it not for the various bits of clothing and gym shoes littering the floor. The smell of cigar smoke lingered by an open window.

'What's he doing here?' someone demanded as the junior boys approached the fireplace.

'Hove's ill,' said Sackler.

'Ill my arse.'

'Littlejohn shall do perfectly well,' said a sandy-haired boy in spectacles, who Barney deduced was Maccleson. 'Besides, I promised him a ride in the dumb waiter.'

'Not me,' said Robin. 'Holland here wants a go.' He shot Barney a look that warned him to be silent.

Maccleson considered the new boy. 'You're a big chap,' he said. 'Usually we only send kids from the First down. Most of them are half your size.'

'You forget Quilty,' said Sackler from behind a copy of *The Times*. 'He must have been ten stone.'

Maccleson rolled his lip. 'It's up to you. Ratty'll be out until five o'clock — he always takes tea at home with his wife.'

'Go on,' whispered Robin, who had unfolded the newspaper and was reaching for the fire brush. His back was to the room, and he spoke so low that only Barney could hear. 'The cabinet on your left. M for Morrell.'

Maccleson's finger was already on the call button next to a small door in the wall. There was a distant bang, and the door opened.

181

Maccleson slid up the grille to reveal a metal box about two feet wide and three feet deep.

'Slide in backwards,' he told Barney, who did as he was instructed. By now some of the other boys had looked up from their work to watch the cumbersome second-former squeeze into the lift. 'What you mustn't do is get out while you're down there,' he was saying. 'For one thing, we won't know when to call you back up, and for another, if Ratty finds out you've been poking about his study every single one of us will get sacked.'

'Will you give me a minute, at least?' Barney said. 'To catch my breath.'

'Fine.'

Once Barney was squashed inside the lift, Maccleson pulled down the grille and shut the outside door, leaving him in total darkness. There was a clang and a jolt, and then Barney felt himself being lowered through the shaft. The metallic scrape of the rails was piercing; the sway of the lift on the pulley enough to make him wonder how far he should fall if one of the ropes were to break. Just as he felt he might not survive it, there was another loud bang, another jolt — and the shrieking rails fell silent.

Barney pushed up the grille as Maccleson had shown him and nudged the outside door with his toe. It fell open easily — Mr Pleming had not locked it — and before him was the enormous desk, the table covered in green baize, the bay windows and the bookshelves.

The key was already already in the cabinet lock. Open. The files, tightly packed, in two

182

drawers: A — L, M — Z.

Barney pulled out the second drawer and began to finger through the paper tabs: there was Maccleson, near the front. Mason, Meyer, Middleton, Moat. Mowbridge — too far. He worked backwards: Moss, Mortlake, Morrison.

Morrell.

There were four items in the folder. The first was a letter, dated 1950, written by a Mrs E. Carr on behalf of Morrell's mother. On his last visit home, Ivor had reacted to news that his family had been forced to let go of a much loved footman with violent fury and tears 'befitting a snubbed schoolgirl'. She thought the Headmaster might like to know in case the boy showed signs of 'continued disturbance' when he returned. Mrs Carr went on to say that Mrs Morrell respected the Headmaster's decision not to grant her son's request for a change of personal tutor. She had every faith in Mr Swift and was sure that the boy would come to appreciate his guidance.

The next item was a typed complaint, dated 1952, by the parents of a boy who claimed to have come under attack by a senior pupil. Another boy reported to have been witness to the scene was believed to have lost a watch in a scuffle that followed, although there was no mention of his name. 'H. Cray lost a portion of one ear,' someone had written under a section headed 'Details'. There had been hope that the doctors might be able to reattach the missing piece, but it had never been found.

Last were two photographs of a damaged ear:

one taken side-on, so that a ridge of teeth marks stood out clearly against dark hair, the skin still blistered and swollen around the stitches; the other from the front, so that the chewed-down ear was barely visible.

There was a thud from the elevator shaft, followed by the echo of voices. Barney returned the folder and turned the key in the cabinet lock. He climbed into the dumb waiter head first, so that by the time Maccleson released the grille all they could see was the hunch of his spine. His reappearance was greeted by disappointed grunts. He wondered how many of the senior boys had hoped that he might have been caught, after all.

'So,' said Maccleson, 'Did you enjoy that?'

'Not half dark in there.'

'Once you could go all the way down to the basement.'

Barney waited for Robin to finish sweeping out the grate before they both thanked Maccleson and excused themselves.

'Well?' said Robin when they were in the corridor.

'You were there when he bit Cray's ear off?'

By the way he paled, Robin clearly had not expected this. 'It said that?'

'It said someone lost a watch.'

'And?'

'And he asked for a change of tutor. That's not news: I know Morrell hates Swift.'

'Well, excuse me for trying. I thought you ought to know you're friends with a maniac.' Robin clattered down the stairs. 'If you think he's got nothing else to hide, why don't you ask him yourself?'

★ ★ ★

Barney found Krawiec closing up the potting sheds as dusk was starting to fall.

'You should be inside,' said the groundsman, not looking up as he rattled at the lock.

'I wanted to ask you something . . . ' Barney hesitated, wondering if he should say 'sir': it felt wrong not to, but the groundsman was not to know that Barney himself was poor and uneducated. ' . . . Mr Krawiec.'

The groundsman looked at him, waiting.

'It's about Miss Duchâtel.'

The groundsman grunted and returned to fiddling with the lock.

'Why can't you ask her yourself?'

'Because I don't think she would tell the truth.'

'That is her right.'

'Please, sir.'

A hint of a smile. 'What do you want to know?' he said.

'When she came here. Why. Why she lives alone.'

'That is not 'something'. That is several things.'

'What she's hiding, then.'

'You are being impertinent.'

'I'm sorry.'

'You are a boy. That is the way it is. When you are grown up you will return to school and realize that the students never age: only the masters grow old.'

'You must know something. You were here. You worked for her.'

'They attacked her like animals. She didn't hurt anyone. She wants to be left in peace.'

'Who attacked her?'

The groundsman let the lock fall, shrugged at his reflection in the cloudy glass. 'Who didn't? Little children spat in the street. They cut her hair. That's why it is so ugly — she chooses to keep it that way.'

'Was it because of the commandant?'

Krawiec regarded the boy in the window's reflection, reading the curious inclination of his head.

'I don't know if you are very clever or very rude. Perhaps Mr Pleming will tell me.'

'Please don't tell Mr Pleming I asked you.'

'Then go back to your house.'

'Did he give her the painting? It belonged to the school before.'

'To accept a gift is not a crime. They destroyed so much.' Krawiec stepped past Barney to push a wheelbarrow round the side of the sheds. 'I have work to finish. Go back to your house, and don't ask me these things again.'

When he had left, Barney made his way to the shelter to think things over. The sound of voices inside made him stop by the outside door.

'You hate yourself because you don't feel guilt. But sin begets heroism.' There was the sound of a bag rustling — sweets being passed from one to the other — and a murmur that Barney could not make out.

'I can't help being horrid. I watch myself as if I were someone else.'

'Society's to blame. Margaret Mead saw it plain as day. You'd be all right if you'd grown up a Tau girl rather than an English one.'

A pause.

'So you'll do it?' the girl said.

'Of course. Cowper's a little shit.'

There was another pause, and laughter.

'Will you tell Barney?'

'What's the point? He'd stand there like a lump, as usual.'

'That's not very nice.'

'He can't imagine things on that scale. He can't even aspire to. The most he can aspire to in his whole life is a house in some vile garden city, or whatever it is they're calling them now — places with no centre, no history, for people with no imagination. Displacement camps for the working classes.'

'Why must you be so horrid always?'

'Always?'

'You talk about him all the time.'

He laughed. 'I've not the faintest interest in him, because I'm not like him. He's numb: that's how they breed them, because it's the only way they can go on living.'

'Tosh.'

'Do you know what his old man did, before the war? He worked in swampland. Day in, day out, pumping mud out of the Thames so more docks could be built. And to think he probably copped it doing the same thing for the Japs.'

'Just because his people are different from yours — '

'He *has* no people. His dad's rotting in a pit in some godforsaken jungle, and his mum's jaunted off to the other side of the world because she couldn't stand to look at her snotty-nosed halfwit kids one minute longer . . . '

'Why must you be so cruel?'

'It's not my fault that he's a parasite, clinging on to us as if we're his family. It's more than pathetic: it makes my skin crawl. He's like a hermit crab, squatting in someone else's shell.'

'You used him when it suited you. In fact, I think you rather envy him.'

'Whenever you try to be clever you end up sounding like a child.'

'I don't care. Better to sound like a child than a horrible old snob.'

Perhaps Robin was right; perhaps he should come straight out and demand that Ivor tell him what he'd been playing at. Slipping from the clearing, Barney told himself that he wasn't running away.

★   ★   ★

He went to Doc Dower's classroom, but the door was locked. Previously, Barney would have felt the dead handle with relief; he had never been one to seek the attention of adults, least of all teachers. He did not know why today was different. The *piastre* itself was worthless — Doc had said so himself.

Workbook in hand, he made his way to the masters' common room. He did not allow himself to hesitate before knocking. Several moments passed before a senior master whipped the door open. He peered down at Barney with disdain.

'What is it?'

'Please, sir — I'm looking for Doc Dower.'

'Has no one told you never to knock on this door? Boys must wait for a master to enter or exit before pestering us with queries.'

'I'm sorry, sir — '

The master did not reply; the door closed. Barney paused, wondering if he had gone to find Doc Dower or if he had left the second-former to wait to intercept the next passing master. So it was with some relief that he turned to see Mr Swift advancing down the hallway towards him.

'Please, sir — I'm looking for Doc Dower.'

'One minute, Holland.'

Once again, the door opened and shut.

'Holland, what?'

A trail of crumbs dotted Doc Dower's tie; in one hand he held a dainty china cup.

'I'm sorry, sir. It's the problem you set. About draining the pitch. With slope — ' Barney hated himself for babbling; he shuddered inwardly at the dampness of the book he handed over, pages crumpled by his clammy palms.

'Hold this, Holland.' Doc Dower passed him the china cup in exchange for the workbook.

'Two feet, sir. You have to double the slope. Dig down another foot at one end — '

'Quite right. Quite right.' He flipped the book

shut, returned it to Barney.

'Thank you, sir.'

'Wait here, Holland.'

Again, the door shut. Floating with relief, Barney grinned at a passing pair of Sagartians, provoking a smart clip round one ear.

'Look at us like that again and we'll report you for impertinence, new scum.'

Undaunted, Barney continued to wait at the door, rubbing his stinging ear.

'As promised, what?' Doc Dower reappeared, proffering a small silver coin between fat forefinger and thumb. He dropped it into Barney's extended palm, then clasped both hands behind his back.

'Thank you, sir.'

It was heavier than it looked. There was a garland on one side, and a woman in long robes with rays emanating from behind her head on the reverse.

'Not bad for a bit of mud work, what, Holland?'

'No, sir.'

'Keep it safe, will you?'

Barney did not need telling. He took it to the dormitory and wrapped it in a balled sock which he pushed to the farthest corner of his dressing-table drawer. Then he went to dinner, feeling every inch the engineer of Ispahan.

★ ★ ★

Moments after the dormitory lights were switched off, a commotion erupted from

190

Cowper's bed: a gulping, terrified noise and then the thump of Cowper tumbling to the floor, his legs tangled in a knot of sheets. There was the sound of something wet hitting the footboard, and moments later a putrid smell that made the boys gasp.

'Someone get the lights, for Christ's sake!' bellowed Cowper. Someone did — and the six boys blinked in amazement to see him in a heap on the floor, red-faced and sweating. Then Hiram Opie pointed at the cause of all this — the bloody mess of yellow skin pimpled with bumps where all but the smallest feathers had been plucked — giving rise to a chorus of disgust.

'What is it?'

'It's a bird, you idiot. Or it was.'

'Someone put it in my bed,' said Cowper, who sounded as if he might be on the point of tears. 'Some sick *arse* put it in my bed.'

The boys regarded each other.

'Not I,' said Shields.

'Not I,' echoed Percy, who still could not bring himself to look at that horrible mess.

'It was Holland,' said Cowper in a vicious tone. 'He did it for Belinda Flood. She worked her voodoo magic on it.'

'Don't be stupid — '

'The little slut did it to get back at me.'

There was a tense silence. 'For what?' said Barney.

'For nothing,' snapped Cowper. 'But you still did it.'

'I didn't,' protested Barney. 'I swear I didn't.'

'Liar. You got it from that woman's farm!' Cowper was standing, trying to decide whether to venture across the floor to confront Barney. In the end, he opted against it. 'You'll have to clear it up. I'm not touching it. It's probably got all kinds of plague.'

'I'm not touching it either.'

'You will, or else I'll report it to Runcie — and everyone here will back me up, too.' Cowper climbed into bed and pulled the covers around him. The others followed suit, watching Barney with nervous delight.

'If I do, it will only be because the rest of you are being such wimps about it.' Barney made for the dustpan and brush kept by the door. 'And because then I'll be the only one to know where I put it.'

He put it outside with the other rubbish, of course, taking care to rearrange the contents so that the carcass wouldn't be seen when it came time for the bins to be emptied.

He returned to the dormitory to find Cowper and Shields blocking the door, arms folded across their chests.

'Not so fast,' said Cowper. He looked past Barney to Hughes, who had emerged from the adjoining dormitory.

'Fairborough's got it going nicely,' said Hughes.

'Well done,' said Cowper.

'Leave off,' said Barney. 'Let me in.'

'When you helped her with that bit of witchcraft? Not a chance, Camden Town. You'll be tried by ordeal, just like all witches.' He

192

grabbed Barney by the collar and shoved him backwards. Shields and Hughes grabbed his arms, and between them they bundled Barney into the other dormitory.

A fire blazed in the grate, casting shadows on the faces of five boys sitting up in bed: a grim and silent jury. Barney did not know these boys well. He certainly could not count any friends among them.

'Sit him down just there,' ordered Cowper, indicating a spot in front of the fire. 'Fairborough, lend a hand.'

Barney had begun to struggle, but between the four of them they managed to pin him down. Cowper tore off his slippers and rolled Barney's pyjama cuffs to the knees.

'You're lucky we hadn't any hot coals,' he said. 'Though this shall do just as well, I'll wager.'

Hughes sat on Barney's chest while Cowper and Shields lifted his feet to the fire: close enough that he could feel the wall of heat against his soles.

'We shan't let you blister, never fear,' said Cowper. 'That would give Runcie something to ask about.'

'Let go — ' The blood rushed from his raised ankles down his legs, deadening his feet even as ripples of white heat stung his soles.

'Admit that you did it, and say you're sorry.'

'I *didn't* do it — '

'We'll see if that's what you're still saying a minute from now.' Cowper threw a glance at the clock on the wall.

'Let go!'

'Hush, or Swift will come. Then we shall have to tell him about your little prank, and you'll really be in for it.'

Cowper waited for more than the full minute before heaving Barney's feet over his head and saying, 'Now will you apologize?'

'Just say it, Camden Town,' hissed Shields, who was getting the worst of the heat.

'I'm sorry — '

They allowed him to struggle to his feet and stumble back to bed, all the while looking to each other with grim satisfaction that justice had been done.

In the morning, inspecting his feet before the others were awake, Barney was distressed to find no marks, even though it stung to touch the soft skin under his toes. Even the knowledge of the *piastre* at the back of his dressing-table drawer was not enough to distract him from the lingering pain. He found some calamine lotion in the toilets and doubled his socks so that he would not limp; when Robin asked about the ordeal he shrugged and said Cowper gave himself more credit than he deserved. When he told Ivor about it after lessons, the Mede threw back his head and laughed in a way that made Barney suspect he was as much a butt of the joke as Cowper had been

★ ★ ★

It was around this time that Mrs Morrell paid her first visit to the school.

She was greeted by a cluster of junior boys

194

who paused to gawp at the woman in the fox fur: an interloper, foreign by virtue of her sex and ostentatious Englishness, and the fact that she had arrived in a private car. Make-up clumped at the corners of her eyes and mouth; most likely it had been applied in the pre-dawn dark before catching the first ferry of the day. At first she did not appear to know what to do. Several minutes passed before the Head emerged from the school, pulling at his tie, and with a flustered air extended his hand in welcome long before he was close enough for her to take it.

Later that evening, Barney spotted Ivor waiting grimly in the atrium, wearing a duffel coat and Jonty's fedora.

'Mater's in town,' said Ivor, in response to a curious look. 'Jonty's anniversary. She's taking me out.'

'All right for some,' said Barney.

'It's only her hotel,' said Ivor. 'Dismal place.'

Barney didn't see him again for two days.

On the Sunday morning, Mrs Morrell appeared in time for Chapel, flanked by the Head and the Head's wife.

The junior boys had been discussing executions as they waited to file in. Robin wanted to know if Barney had joined the crowds outside Wandsworth Prison when that poor idiot was hanged for murder. ' 'Let him have it' — that was all the bugger said, and he got the drop.' Robin shook his head. 'What do you think of that, Holland?'

Barney was about to say that he didn't know — but then he felt Robin's fingers lacing around

195

his neck and instinctively grasped the boy's hands by the wrists.

'Snap! Just like that — eh, Holland? If you're lucky.'

Barney twisted, feigning a struggle against the collar formed by Robin's fingers. His hands were hot, but not clammy, and there was something thrilling about wrestling him across the lawn. He stopped when he heard the Head's wife address Mrs Morrell by name and shook Robin off to get a better look.

Next to Mrs Pleming — as usual, in sensible shoes and inexpertly applied lipstick — Mrs Morrell exuded a wildness barely repressed by tasteful jewellery, a dove-grey suit and a badger-pelt coat. Her rolled and lacquered hair had golden lights, and her nails were painted red. She appeared restless, opening and closing her purse to check for something that was never there, and more than once Mrs Pleming cast a quick, nervous glance in her direction as one might throw at a child on the brink of some disgraceful behaviour.

When the Fifth filed in, Ivor was too engaged in conversation with Potts to acknowledge his mother, although she soon spotted him and gave a little lurch as he passed her.

Barney looked for Belinda, who sat at the far end of the pew and did not appear to have noticed Mrs Morrell. He thought the girl looked small and sad, lost among the rows of fidgeting boys. She did not move her lips to murmur the prayers, but stared straight to the front as if imagining herself somewhere else. Now and then she shivered. A wind was coming in from the sea, licked fierce by tall waves, and the stone walls of the chapel seemed to feed the cold air, spreading a smell that made the grown-ups whisper in worried voices about another storm tide. Detritus was still being cleared from the floods that had claimed twelve lives that year. Barney breathed into his palms and rubbed them on marbled knees, wincing as he stamped his feet upon the flagstones.

Mrs Morrell sang discordantly through the hymn, attracting looks from the adults and obvious smirks from the boys. It was only after a few bars that they realized she was following a different tune altogether and investing it with her own words. In counterpoint to the mighty 'Kingsfold', her voice rose louder and louder.

'How desolate my life would be,
How dark and drear my nights and days,
If Jesus' face I did not see
To brighten all earth's weary ways!'

Barney searched for Ivor in the rows behind and found him staring, grey-faced, straight ahead. As his mother's voice strained higher, he closed his hymnal with a snap.

'With burdened heart I wandered long,
By grief and unbelief distressed;
But now I sing faith's happy song,
In Christ my Saviour I am blest!'

By now only the masters and their wives

197

continued with the hymn, while the boys stared. As the organ thundered the final refrain, they watched Ivor shove past the other Medes in his row and make for the exit. The final chord sounded as the panelled door slammed closed behind him.

Afterwards, Barney noticed Mrs Morrell standing before Jonty's plaque. She betrayed no emotion: only a rigidness as though she had been caught off-guard by something unanticipated and unpleasant. He watched Mrs Pleming join her, take her gently by the elbow and whisper a few words in her ear.

Soon after, the driver returned with the car and Mrs Morrell made her departure, waved off by the Head and his wife. Ivor remained nowhere to be seen.

★　★　★

Swift followed the boys as far as the patch of scuffed grass circling the Medlar steps and watched them file in through the common door. Try as he might to dismiss it, the scene caused by Mrs Morrell preyed on his mind. To the boys, it had been a laugh; to the masters, a mild embarrassment. A broken woman always was. The Head's wife had handled her admirably, considering how frightened the other masters' wives looked. Mollie Flood had watched Mrs Morrell standing before Jonty's plaque, and though Swift had tried to look away before she noticed him, she had seen him and paled. One mother observing another's grief.

Passing in front of the housemaster's study, Swift was stopped by the sudden, shrill sound of a telephone. He counted six rings, each in its way louder and more desperate than the one before it. He waited for several moments, believing that every plaintive peal must surely be the last. Fourteen, fifteen. He placed his hand on the doorknob; but as soon as he did the ringing stopped.

As though by some strange premonition that whoever it had been at the other end of the telephone line had not given up the pursuit, Swift remained where he was. Sure enough, less than a minute later the telephone shuddered into life again. He tested the door, which was open, and entered the study.

On the fourth ring, the deputy housemaster lifted the phone from its cradle. 'Medlar House — '

'Is that you?' It was a woman's voice. 'I hoped you might be there — '

The phone slipped in his hand; he fumbled, pressed it to his ear. She was already mid-sentence.

' — in town said it must have been hers. It must be. She came here often in those days, didn't she?'

'I don't know who you're talking about.'

'It must be hers. Please say it is. I may go mad otherwise — '

'Why are you calling?'

'I'm sorry — I don't know what I was thinking — '

There was a sound in his ear like an accordion

199

being squeezed of its air, then the click of a line going dead.

The study door remained open, and a leaf skittered across the gravel and over the threshold. Outside, the chaplain walked across the drive, his cassock stiff and rustling. It occurred to Swift that it would not do for Mr Runcie to find him here like this: answering his telephone with the door open, letting the leaves in.

Someone was emerging from Ormer House: the girl, Belinda, dropping her satchel to pull on her coat. She slung the bag over one shoulder, turned on the step and saw him there, telephone in hand, staring through the open door at her across the empty drive.

There was no reason to feel caught out. He acknowledged her with a nod, returned the receiver to the cradle and pretended to busy himself with some papers in a tray on Mr Runcie's desk. When he looked up again she was already halfway across the green, heading towards the forest path.

He waited for her to disappear into the gloom before tugging sharply at the phone line until at last it pulled clean away from the wall.

★　★　★

The inner door was scarcely ajar, but the sound hummed through the gaps in the panelling. It was a grotesque murmur, urgent and unceasing like a heartbeat. As the second door opened, it raised to a drone: and then a hundred black

200

bodies were swarming and darting towards the light, hitting their faces, skimming their open mouths. The flies were fat and hairless, intoxicated on sugar.

The toffee tin lay open on the floor, the last few squares lumped together where the paper wrappers had begun to sweat. Four days had passed.

'You were supposed to bring it back,' said Ivor to Barney. 'The other night when we had our hands full, I told you to bring the rest.'

'I thought I had.'

Shielding his face with his arm, Ivor grabbed the tin and chucked it onto the ground outside the shelter. 'It'll have to air out now. No point coming tonight.'

'The sandwiches won't keep,' said Belinda in a small voice.

'We could have them somewhere else,' said Barney.

'Perhaps in Ratty's study? Honestly, Holland.'

Barney looked up at the sky. The clouds hung so low it seemed that from the top of the highest tree it would be possible to touch them. 'We could go to the rock pools,' he said. 'It won't be too cold tonight.'

To his surprise, Ivor agreed. Later that night, he even took the precaution of bringing along a sinister-looking bottle, 'to keep out the chill'. Settling into a ledge in the rock face — out of sight from the school's attic windows and shielded from the wind — the others regarded it with suspicion.

'That's not brandy,' said Belinda.

'It hasn't even got a label,' said Barney. 'He's probably filled it with bog water.'

'Don't have it, then,' said Ivor.

High above loomed trees bent inland by the wind. The tide was out, and the muddy sand gleamed slick. By night, even the sea seemed to know to keep silent.

Belinda shivered, and Ivor passed her a jar filled from the bottle he had brought. 'It will warm you up,' he said when she hesitated.

First she tasted a certain sourness, then the hint of something sweet, like bruised plums. After that her tongue was hit by a burning ginger tang, and finally a bitter aftertaste that made her want to drink more, if only to replace the sensation.

'It's fortified,' said Ivor. 'I got it off Krawiec.'

'Why would he give it to you?' said Barney.

'I didn't say he gave it to me. I said I got it off him.'

'You stole it?'

'We have an understanding.'

Belinda tore open a bag of sandwiches and shoved it under the boys' noses. 'Take one,' she said. She drank again from the jar.

Food had become their obsession: sweet things for Belinda, and for Barney the fattier the better. No wonder some of the masters had begun to comment that Holland had put on some weight, or that Mollie Flood often found another popped button on her daughter's gym blouse. For the first time in her life the girl had pimples, and dark rings circled her eyes. For his part, Ivor did not seem to need sleep: he neither gained nor lost weight. Only the younger two were steadily fattening up.

'I've never been here by night,' said Ivor, shooting Barney a look. 'In the summer it would be a fine place for a swim, don't you think, Bel?'

'It's too shallow to swim properly,' she said. 'But people throw anything down here thinking that the water is deep. I found a bracelet once.'

'Odd thing to throw away.'

Belinda shrugged. 'The wine is making me thirsty,' she said. 'If only I could drink just a little of that water down there.'

'That's what one of the POWs on St Just thought,' said Ivor. 'He was already starved, so the seawater knocked him right out. While he was unconscious, a couple of the other workers killed him.'

'Why would they do that?'

'Because they were famished. They ate him then and there.'

All that on an island visible on a clear day from Miss Duchâtel's bedroom window, thought Barney.

'You're making it up.'

'I'm not. Krawiec told me. They ate rats too — and birds, when they could catch them. But this lad was young, and there was still meat on him.'

Belinda looked at Barney. 'I don't believe it,' she said.

'Why not? The Japs ate their own troops when things got really bad in the East.'

At this Barney chucked the stale heel of bread

203

into the water. There was no sound of a splash. 'Don't listen to him,' he said.

'It's slippery here,' said Ivor, scuffing his soles to illustrate the point. 'If you fell and hit your head, you'd drown without anyone knowing. Even if you called out for help, most likely no one would hear.'

The sea released a sudden, hungry rumble.

'What did you mean about having an understanding with him?' Barney asked. 'Krawiec.'

'We see through people. And we're both good at keeping our mouths shut.'

Belinda snorted.

'If only you knew,' said Ivor.

'So tell us. Who have you seen through?'

'Henry Cray,' said Barney.

Ivor looked at him. 'Cray was a kid. He had nothing to hide.'

'Who then? Doc Dower?'

'My father?' said Belinda.

'Ratty?'

Ivor looked away.

'Swift,' said Barney at last. 'That's why you wanted to change tutors.'

'Who told you that?'

Now it was Barney's turn to stare out to sea. 'Littlejohn.'

'Liar.'

'So what's Swift got to hide?'

'Weakness. A guilty conscience.'

'For what?' asked Belinda.

'I don't know. All I know is that he tried to top himself. Here, in fact.' Ivor kicked a stone down to the water. 'Four years ago now: I was in the First.'

'That's when I started at St Mary's,' said Belinda.

Ivor frowned. 'You can't have been old enough.'

'I was almost ten. Mother was ill.'

'Get back to Swift,' said Barney.

'Krawiec's the only other person who knew. "Just as well for her, he failed": that's what he told me.'

'Just as well for who?' asked Barney.

'God knows. A lover.'

They stared at the water, lost in their own thoughts.

'I'm not hungry. I think I'll go back now,' said Belinda at last.

'Me too,' said Barney.

They began to pack their satchels as Ivor drained the remains of Krawiec's wine. Suddenly he leapt to his feet. 'Listen. For God's sake, *listen*.'

They stood stock still, straining after what Ivor had heard through the sound of the waves worrying the shoreline.

'Do you hear them coming through the forest?' Ivor shambled closer to the rock face. 'Can you hear what they are saying?'

Again, they listened.

'*We will eat you if we can*,' said Ivor. '*We will eat you if we can* . . . '

'Come on,' said Barney to Belinda. He slung both their satchels over his shoulder and offered her his hand. 'Watch your step.'

'We can't just leave him in that state,' said Belinda. 'He's drunk.'

'We can.'

'Try it,' said Ivor, hurling himself at Barney and pinning him against the rock face. 'Just try and leave me.' His breath was hot and sweet. 'Do you know what we do with spies, Holland?'

'Get off,' said Barney.

'Shan't. You'll stay there until you tell me.'

'What are you talking about?' said Belinda, who was regarding them with a frightened look.

'Nothing to worry about,' said Ivor. 'Follow the breadcrumb trail.'

'Barney?'

'I'm coming.' As he straightened, Barney felt a hand tighten around his arm.

'Try that sort of thing again and you'll be sorry, Holland.'

★   ★   ★

Six boys emerged from the boarding house with the slightly crazed look of prisoners let out on day release — fists balled, tightly coiled, ready to fight the world — and at Opie's cry of 'Bundle!' Cowper and Littlejohn made a beeline for the Audley family vault. They argued loudly over the rules as they went. No props, and once a man was down he was out. Using the wall was fair play, but no more than one rush and no ganging. It went without saying that Shields and Cowper would be partners. Robin claimed Barney before he had a chance to object, leaving Percy and Opie to pair off together.

'You're bigger than me, so I'll be the rider,' said Robin to Barney when they reached the vault, which was like a little yellow chapel built of stone with windows that were caged behind wire guards. Barney's face lit with the wary if delighted look of an explorer among savages: his ears pinked as Littlejohn pushed him towards the ground.

There was no clear start to the fight, only a sudden scuffle and a few shrill cries from the crowd of onlookers that had gathered behind the vault — around the far side, away from masters' prying eyes, where the yellow paint had begun to flake and the concrete underneath was turning green — before Opie and Percy were thrust towards the wall, sending a shudder through the stone down to the generations of Audley family members resting below. As they fought, the crowd started up a chant, snatches of which Barney recognized, even though he could not remember having heard it before:

'*Coatsworth, Comfrey, Curless,*
Dockett and de Bock,
Frankland, Hess, the fine boy Just
Kors-Kingsley, Lennert, Loft,
Morrell, Overbay, Previn,
Potts and Savin next,
Standring, Thorup, Thrane and Voigt,
Voysey — then the rest:
Widdows, Williams, Wilbermere,
No more after those;
Their glory in our memory set
And day by day it grows.'

It was Barney who stumbled first, and Robin who lost his grip. All Shields had to do was stick out his foot, and Barney was sent flying at the wall. Robin had farther to fall, and it was a spectacular dethroning: Barney saw the flush of fury and humiliation in his friend's cheeks as he dragged himself from underfoot to shelter by the stone steps that led to the vault's only door, which had been bricked up long ago.

'All right?' he asked, once the others had retreated.

'You let go too soon,' snapped Robin. He pulled up his shirt to examine his chest. Barney tried not to stare, wiping the blood from his nose with the back of one hand before offering to help him up, but the gesture was silently refused.

Pushing through the crowd on his way back to the boarding house — there was just enough time to clean himself up before the next lesson — Barney came face to face with Belinda, fighting to stand her ground against the dispersing crowd. She took something out of her tunic pocket and handed it to him. It was a silver Buren.

'Where'd you find this?' he asked.

'In the stream that comes off the towpath. Ivor was looking for a watch with a timer — perhaps you'd give it to him.'

'It's Robin's.'

She blinked, then took Barney's hand and closed his fingers around the watch. 'Never mind Ivor,' she said. 'You have it.'

★ ★ ★

She had drawn the inner door closed but left the other ajar in order to hear them approach. She waited for ten minutes, listening to the foxes' screams, and then poked her head outside, wondering why the other two were late. When she began to get cold, she returned to the bunker. She lit a candle and warmed her hands over the flame, thinking all the time of the delights promised for the feast: hard-boiled eggs and a box of sticky dates, which the French-woman had sent to Barney that week.

She didn't hear him approaching through the trees and stopping before the shelter. She didn't hear him testing the hatch, pressing his ear to the concrete wall. She sat very still, watching the shadows flicker on the ceiling, feeling suddenly and strangely nostalgic for this moment.

Leaving the house that evening, her mother had asked where she was going — defensively, and also with a hint of something Belinda might have recognized as envy, if only she had been attuned to it. The woods, she'd replied. And her mother had said she didn't want her playing there after dark, and not out of sight of the house. Why not, Belinda had said, even though a voice in her head told her to stop. Because I say so, her mother had replied. Belinda could tell that she was ready to be angry: primed to slap the girl for rudeness, impatient to shout and send her to her bedroom without tea. Belinda had toyed with her mother's anger, relishing the prospect of a scene in which, as always, her mother should be the first to snap. In the end, though, she had opted for peace: she did not wish to miss tonight's feast. She felt that her mother could not love her, and she basked in a feeling of martyrdom because of this.

Filled with a delicious melancholy, she pulled her coat more tightly around her and drew her knees to her chin. Soon the others would arrive, filling the cavernous space with their schoolboy smell of gravy and boiled greens and gruff whispers, and Ivor would toss sugared almonds for her to catch in her mouth while Holland busied himself with the brandy, pretending not to watch them.

There was a slam, and a sudden draught that extinguished the candle.

It was the silence more than the darkness that frightened her as she followed the wall to the inner door. It swung to easily, but there was no rush of sweet forest air. The outer door would not open.

'Ivor! I know it's you. Open the door.'

She pulled harder at the handle, expecting to hear laughter, a scuffle of feet.

'Barney, tell him to open the door.'

She waited until it became frighteningly clear that her eyes would never adjust to this darkness.

'Barney! It's not funny — '

She stumbled back to the inner chamber, feeling the bench for the box of matches. But what if the candle were to fall over — what if a fire were to start? Suddenly she was clinging to a cave wall as waves flooded in from the sea. The same waves that had swallowed up the strip of beach which only minutes earlier had charted a safe course to the coast road. The water was creeping up, up the rock face, and she saw too clearly how it would end . . .

She crumpled against the door and buried her head in her arms.

'Mind out!'

She was toppled by the opening door, stunned by two bright lights. Torches.

'What a stupid place to sit. What were you playing at?'

They pressed into the main chamber together. Candles were lit, satchels unloaded. She wiped the damp from her cheeks. They were not laughing at her: they had not detected her terror.

But Ivor must have noticed that something was amiss, as he chucked her under the chin with a reassuring grin. 'Buck up, little one! I've brought chocolate.'

And then, as Barney ducked outside to bring in the last of the blankets, he told her what he'd learnt that day, and how easy it would be after all to do that thing they'd discussed over the half-term. There was a tub of weed-killer in the gardener's lodge; sugar could be bought in town. All that remained to be found was a fuse.

★　★　★

It was Miss Duchâtel who told them about the sabotage attempts during the war: carefully engineered explosions and acts of vandalism — slashing car tyres, cutting cables, bricks through windows — that made the islanders feel less complicit in the occupation. 'It gave us something to do, to remind ourselves what it was to be free,' she said. 'We scattered leaflets under the banner 'Lindsey Island Freedom Front', and we circulated newsletters 'to all our loyal readers', even though there were only a few subscribers and they were the editors!'

That day she had begun by offering fried whitebait and mayonnaise, which Ivor tucked into with relish: biting off the heads with their staring eyes and giving great grunts of pleasure just to see the younger girl squirm. She followed this with boiled eggs dipped in salt, which she made a show of tipping over one shoulder to ward off witches.

Barney said nothing. Now all he could ever think of when he came back here was the message that he should not have seen, the word painted on the side of the car. 'They cut her hair,' Krawiec had said. Barney barely heard the Frenchwoman recall the long nights during the Occupation when there was no radio and the only films playing at the cinema were German ones. 'René Christiansen would make a show with his magic lantern — we had to stuff the gaps under the doors with newspaper so no light would show — and old Mrs Klausen devised some interesting delicacies out of lavender and kelp, no doubt just as the Stone Agers did, once upon a time. We had forgotten how to survive off the land for too long — we who are supposed to be so advanced, with our televisions and our atom bombs . . . '

By the disparaging things she said about the islanders being abandoned to their usual life after the war, Barney wondered if it wasn't actually his sort, and not the Germans at all, whom she really hated. Was he part of a new invasion, of holidaymakers and boarding students? She had lived here long enough to consider herself a native: had earned this right by enduring the Occupation. 'You only have to look at the islander diet to see how soft we have become,' she said. 'Forget the fish and the sea birds. Now everything is imported: boxes of tea, packet biscuits, meat in tins . . . '

Then she and Ivor began discussing the fate of families like his after the war: grand dynasties who had lost their properties and staff while unscrupulous young businessmen watched their profits soar. England was no longer a land of heroes, Ivor said, no matter how many empty memorials were erected to the shades of past triumphs; no matter how many attempts to freeze time in the silent noon of their finest hour. Out with the colonies, where once men had proved their worth, and in with the welfare state. Not that the poor didn't deserve every opportunity to help themselves — a glance in Barney's direction — but the new order was squeezing out any room for those with true ambition. ''The future's not what it used to be' . . . ' he concluded. 'All we have to look forward to now are free spectacles in our dotage.'

Barney suggested that perhaps he should go to America — or one day, when it was possible, outer space. 'Shields says there will be colonies on the moon,' he said. 'Like India.'

'Colonies on the moon,' mused Ivor, 'would be the final insult to poetry.'

213

'Or you could dispense with civilization altogether,' said Miss Duchâtel. 'And move into that little house of yours in the forest. Living the Utopian dream.'

'The only people who believe in Utopia any more are Reds,' said Ivor.

Curled on the sofa, their stomachs full of *pot-au-feu* and farmer's loaf, it wasn't long before the sound of the rain outside and the crackling of the fire lulled Barney and Belinda to sleep. As always, Miss Duchâtel had served watered-down wine with the meal, and neither had yet developed the ability to drink without dozing off straight after. Miss Duchâtel sent Ivor to bring the blankets from the bedroom, and these they arranged about the shoulders of the drowsy pair by the fire.

How much Barney dreamt that afternoon and how much he absorbed from the conversation at the kitchen table, where the other two continued to speak in low voices, was difficult to say. There appeared before him a narrow underground shaft and two great points of stone. Beyond these was a vertical drop and the sound of water crashing against rock hundreds of feet below. The tunnel became filled with voices, and he saw that between the two points of stone was a man. Around his body was a belay line. He had been trying to drop through the vertical section, perhaps to clear a route for others. But he was stuck — *It's the locking device*, he was saying, *it's jammed against the rock* — and even though he struggled, it was clear from his expression that he knew there was no use.

214

There had been too many voices in such a small space, too much urgency in the press of bodies, the cool walls becoming wet with condensation. In the end the handsome young man fell asleep, his head tipping to one side just as if he had nodded off — it did not look as though he had suffocated, even though that is exactly what happened — and immediately the others recognized that if they did not retreat back up to the open air they too would die in the tunnel. There was a scramble of feet, a murmur of voices.

A little while later came the distant, muted sludge of cement being poured down the shaft, creeping under the young man's fingernails and soaking through the fibres in his uniform — a British uniform, always meticulous: a master at his school had always commented on the pride he took in his appearance, even as a boy — and soon the cement grew cold, hardened in the spaces between the rock and the darkness below. It was the only way he could be buried, by filling him in like this. More importantly, it was the only way the tunnel would never be discovered by the enemy.

When Barney woke, he looked without turning his head to where Miss Duchâtel had dragged her chair around the kitchen table to draw an arm around Ivor's shoulders.

Barney squeezed his eyes shut, counted to sixty and rolled over.

'Sorry,' he said. 'Must have nodded off.'

Ivor did not turn around.

'Don't apologize,' said Miss Duchâtel. 'We

215

have been having a good talk. And Belinda has been reading.'

Ivor did not turn around. Barney saw that Belinda had sequestered herself in the horsehair chair with a brightly coloured tome she had found on one of the shelves, *Mediterranean Food*. Now she stood up to show Barney a picture of a skinned hare. As she passed the book across the sofa, her sleeve pulled back to reveal a fine, white wrist, circled by a bracelet of blue glass beads.

'Where did you find that?' said Miss Duchâtel, crossing the room.

Belinda paled, covering the bracelet with her other hand.

'In the rock pools,' she said.

'You stole it.' Miss Duchâtel's voice was loud and hard.

'No, I didn't.'

Miss Duchâtel slid her fingers between the girl's skin and the bracelet, gave a single, hard tug. 'Take it off, now.'

'It's mine.'

'It is not yours. It's hers, it was on her — take it off, take it off!'

Her voice was ugly, and in her fright Belinda slid the bracelet from her wrist and let it drop to the floor. The Frenchwoman grabbed it and shoved it in her pocket.

'Stealing from the dead,' she spat. 'From a helpless baby!'

'I didn't know,' said Belinda.

'It's all right,' said Barney.

'It's not all right,' said Belinda. 'I didn't steal

it. I didn't.' And before anyone could say anything else, she tore from the house.

'I'm sorry,' said Ivor to Miss Duchâtel. For the first time Barney noticed how red his eyes were. 'We'll talk to her.'

But Miss Duchâtel only nodded, and said that they should probably leave too. It would be dark soon, and the girl needed watching.

'Didn't your mother tell you the story of the three little men in the wood?' said Ivor once they had caught up with her, tugging her to a halt at the crest of the hill where the kittiwakes screamed overhead. 'About the ungrateful girl who spurned the elves' gifts, so that they punished her by making toads spill out of her mouth?'

'So she *is* a witch,' said Belinda.

'And you're a spoilt, rude little girl.'

But by the time they had reached the road, the boys could hear her footsteps rushing to catch up.

'I'm sorry,' Belinda said. 'You'll still let me help, won't you?'

★ ★ ★

It had been Ivor's idea, inspired by Miss Duchâtel's stories and a passage he'd come across in one of his books about something called Greek fire. The firecracker he had set off behind the shelter was just a trial.

Like a snail that builds its shell by turning round and round, he had begun to talk himself into a burning disgust for anyone who wasn't

217

prepared to 'act'. According to Ivor, such people represented all that was wrong with their parents' generation: their dreadful silences, and also their fundamental lack of heroism. Ivor wanted to create something that would defy silence. In one glorious act of destruction he'd show everyone how the young, too, could find freedom in a pile of ashes. Never again would the masters assume that the war was something that they could own exclusively. The young would reclaim it for their own, for the dads and brothers that they'd lost, for the awful fear that they left behind: the dread of silence and the bomb.

After they saw the girl off at the road, he and Barney decided to wander back up to the school past the old pumping station.

'That bracelet,' said Barney. 'She did find it in the rock pools. She told us so before.'

'So?'

'So nothing,' he said.

It had been almost two weeks since Barney had last come here with Robin, deliberately flouting the rule that boys weren't to wander the grounds in pairs. Robin had offered his hand as they crossed the narrow bridge together, holding on just long enough as they landed on the main platform to squeeze Barney's fingers. As they'd sat fashioning sailing boats out of twigs and leaves, Robin had confided about his terrible dreams: about firequakes that would break the island like a piece of chalk and terrible, walking sea monsters caked in black volcanic sand. The sea claimed its due by swallowing them all before belching them out again and smashing their heads on the rocks. Barney mentioned this to Ivor now, hoping that the older boy would say something confident and wise. But Ivor only laughed.

'*Don't be afeard*,' he said, heaving himself up from the crossbar onto the upper ledge. '*This isle is full of noises that give delight and hurt not . . .*'

Barney rubbed the smooth face of the silver Buren between finger and thumb. He swallowed his annoyance, wishing that for once Ivor might speak in a way that did not make him feel dull by comparison. Just then he hated the oppressive emptiness of this place: the thick silence, the stench of rotting kelp and a river that was still and glassy, dotted with kingcup straining after light through the gloom. From the forest floor, it seemed as though he could hear the click and rustle of a thousand tiny bodies battling against each other for survival. The ground under their feet seethed with insect life: every footstep provoked the crack of tiny membranes.

Ivor was in a buoyant spirit. 'They won't know what hit them,' he was saying. That was the plan: like the crab that throws a pebble into an oyster yawning at the full moon, he was setting a trap. Barney chewed at his nail, afraid to meet Ivor in the eye.

'You're sure nobody will get hurt?'

'Oh, I see.' Ivor was busy lighting a cigarette. 'It's that *bijou* of yours, isn't it? Littlejohn.'

'He's not my anything.'

'I'm only having a laugh, Holland.' He passed

219

the cigarette to the younger boy, standing close enough for Barney to smell the smoke on his breath. 'You do know that, don't you?'

Barney nodded, unsure. He felt small and pathetic, because he knew his fear was to do with failure — with failing to stand in the middle of the woods talking as an equal to a boy like Morrell. The Mede was standing too close now.

'It's getting late. We should go back.'

Ivor reached for the cigarette between his fingers before grabbing Barney's arm. His other hand locked on the back of his head, pressing him forward as he planted his mouth on Barney's. They remained like that for what seemed for ever, though it was only a few seconds: the warm, sweet taste of smoke laced with Miss Duchâtel's chocolate éclairs, the pressure of the older boy's cool lips, the scrape of teeth on his mouth, the scratch of regrowth against downy skin. A twisting branch was heard — a whisper, a rustle of leaves underfoot . . .

They pulled apart in time to see Cowper and Shields sprinting off towards the drive, and Hiram Opie's copper-coloured eyes staring back at them through the silent forest gloom.

★ ★ ★

If Ivor hadn't delayed things by going after Opie first, perhaps he could have caught up with the other two before they reached Runcie. As it happened, they reached the boarding house just as Runcie was emerging from his study to take a lesson, and by their flushed faces and dishevelled state it was obvious that they had something serious to relay.

Since it was a Saturday, supper was a little later than usual. There were no masters present, and the boys were free to return to the common rooms as soon as they wished. This was precisely what Barney did, pursued by whispers and meaningful glances. As he extricated himself from the dining table, Cowper started the chant —

Temptation, temptation, temptation,
Holland went down to the station . . .

— while Robin stared into his kedgeree with a mouth like a cat's arse. When Barney got back to Medlar he made a beeline for the toilets, where he threw up his supper and all of Miss Duchâtel's tea to boot. Afterwards, staring into the bowl as he tugged down on the chain, he found himself wishing that there might be some way for him to squeeze himself through the piping and flush himself out to sea.

If he hadn't been so stupid as to spend the money Miss Duchâtel had paid him on cakes and ginger beer and cigarettes, he could have afforded a cab to Port Grenen and a ferry ticket to Grimsby, and perhaps also the train fare back to London. It was Ivor's fault that he couldn't even run away from this place — that he was trapped here, a most despised prisoner among murderous inmates. He would have gone straight to bed just to escape the significant silences of the prep hall, but no one was allowed in the dormitory until the bell had rung. When at last it did, he climbed the stairs two at a time and buried himself under the covers without bothering to change out of his clothes. There was no point in that, he knew.

Sure enough, within half an hour Runcie's footsteps could be heard on the staircase. It wasn't as if Barney didn't know what to expect — like so many things, the cane held greater fear for the uninitiated — but right now that made little difference. The lamp at the end of the corridor was switched on: there was a knock at the door.

'Holland. My study, please.'

Nobody spoke as he laced his shoes and tiptoed past the row of beds, his hand slipping as he turned the handle.

The housemaster was at his desk when Barney entered, squinting in the glare of lights turned up to daylight brightness. For the first time he noticed the rattan cane sticking out of the umbrella stand. Runcie did not invite him to sit.

'I received a disturbing report this afternoon,' began the master, returning his pen to the inkwell. 'No doubt you will have some idea as to what it involved.' Barney hung his head, concentrating on the swirl of vines patterned in the carpet. 'I will, of course, have to ask you if it is true. That you were party to indiscretions with another pupil? A senior boy.' Barney nodded. 'And the name of this boy?'

'Morrell, sir.' At last Barney looked up, sensing his opportunity. 'He started it, sir. We were just having a fag, and the next thing — '

'I see. But then why did you not come to me?'

'I don't know, sir.'

'You understand, don't you Holland,the fabric of our instruction in chapel, about the sins of the cities of the plain?'

'Sir.'

'In that case, Holland, I struggle to understand how you could have exposed yourself to such a situation without at least some expectation of wrongdoing. After all that this school has offered to you. I shudder to think what your father would make of it.'

Barney swallowed.

'Mr Swift brought me this the other day.' Mr Runcie opened a drawer, withdrew the envelope addressed to him in Spike's awkward handwriting.

'Sir.'

'He found it in the basement corridor. How do you suppose it got there?'

'I was reading my letter, sir. I must have forgotten it.'

'You do know that junior boys are forbidden from frequenting the basement corridor after supper?'

'Yes, sir. The library was locked, sir, so I — '

'Was Morrell with you then?'

'No, sir.'

'So what happened this afternoon was an isolated incident, was it?'

He's looking for a way out, thought Barney with relief. *His heart's not in it.* 'Sir. I'm sorry, sir. It won't happen again.' He wondered if Runcie could hear the imperceptible ticking of

Robin's watch in his pocket.

The housemaster rose and walked around the desk, pausing in front of the boy, whose ears were now quite red. 'Unfortunately, I would be remiss in my duty if I did not take steps to ensure that we are quite clear on this point. That you have put me in this position is a cause of deep regret for me.' Runcie turned towards the umbrella stand. 'The matter can be laid to rest quite simply, right now. Six strokes for regular infractions: three each for straying in a group of fewer than three boys and for smoking. Four strokes for an act of perversion.' He sounded weary. 'I hope you'll agree that it's quite fair.'

'Sir,' said Barney, his throat now quite dry.

'Hands on the desk, Holland.'

There are worse fates, he told himself, as Runcie sliced the air behind him in two deft practice strokes. Death marches through the jungle. Bamboo shoots under the nails. Watching a Jap slice your gut open and eat your liver right in front you . . .

The first cut was sharp, but the second landed with razor precision. Barney gritted his teeth, sucking in his cheeks and refusing to make a noise. They would be listening upstairs, taking grim pleasure in the sounds of muffled yelps or sobbing, and it was for them, more even than for Runcie, that he refused to show weakness.

Mass graves filled with decapitated bodies. Samurai swords filleting a man as if he were a fish. Faces shot off, sending teeth into the back of blown-in skulls. Fly-blown heads rammed on pikes . . .

224

He heard himself whimper, and at the next stroke he cried out. It was too much now: he would be severed in half . . .

'Up you get.' Runcie returned the cane to the umbrella stand and opened the door. He stood by as Barney shuffled past him into the dark hallway, each motion shooting pangs of agony down his legs. Master and pupil heard the creak of springs overhead as five bodies scrambled beneath the covers, the excited whispers and impatient admonishments to be quiet, but neither gave any indication that they knew what awaited upstairs: the excruciating process of undressing against his classmates' taut silence, the awkward tumble into bed, and eyes that ached with the swell of tears that wouldn't come.

★ ★ ★

She did not ask him why he suddenly wished to go now: if anything, she seemed relieved, eager to join him. It was only when they were halfway down to the shore that she suggested Ivor might have wanted to come along as well.

'Ivor can go to hell with the rest of them,' said Barney.

'Why?'

They had stopped at the edge of the beach, and the sand under their feet crunched with broken shells. 'You don't have to do this if you don't want to,' he said.

'You can't go all that way on your own. You'd never make it.'

225

'I don't care. I don't want to see any of them ever again . . .'

'What about Robin?'

'Robin most of all.'

'But *why?*' She squinted at him, hands on hips. 'Have you two fallen out?'

'I've had enough of people not telling the truth. Miss Duchâtel and Ivor and even you.' He could see that she was hurt, and ignored this. 'I had to take the blame for that stupid prank on Cowper, even though it was nothing to do with me. It would have been all right if one of you had bothered to tell me.'

'He said he had. You should have told Cowper it was Ivor's fault.'

'Bit late for that — and anyway, Cowper will believe what he wants to believe.'

'I'm sorry, Barney.'

He considered the almost imperceptible quivering of her irises, the tufts of black hair that had begun to grow back feathery and untamed about the tops of her small, white ears. For some reason at that moment she reminded him of a baby bird.

'You don't have to come. It's probably better if you don't. But don't go back to him.'

He continued towards the kiosk, his satchel banging heavily with tins of condensed milk and a few apples they had stopped to collect from the wrong side of the garden wall. There was a bottle opener with which he'd make a harpoon to spear fish, and some matches to start a campfire. Doc Dower's *piastre*, wrapped in his balled sock, was there too — a reminder, should he need it, that he was more than capable of building anything else he might require on the island. A moment later, he felt a hand on his arm.

'There,' she said, pointing. 'We won't have to drag it far.'

It made a terrible noise, the splintered wood shrieking against the pebbles. Barney tossed the satchel in beneath one of the benches and knelt to soothe his palms in the cold water while Belinda peered out across the sulphur-coloured sea.

'There's a fog coming in,' she said.

Barney squinted at the horizon, willing the hump of land to reveal itself against the pale winter sky. 'It will change in a minute,' she added, sensing his impatience.

Last year, there had been talk of delaying the St Mary's boating trip to St Just because of high winds reported on the north side of the island. In the end, the morning had dawned warm and fair and there was no suggestion of any problem until much later, when the supper that had been laid out in the dining hall was discovered, still untouched, at a quarter past midnight by the last member of staff to secure the building.

'Let's have one of those apples,' said Belinda.

'They're meant for later,' said Barney, who nevertheless tossed her one of the smaller ones. She polished it against her tunic before biting in with a loud, satisfying crunch.

There had been talk of a storm, which another student, who had a ham radio, was able to infer from the shipping forecast. The late ferry had arrived as scheduled, which sparked off whispers that its wake might have forced the lightweight schooner to capsize. The owner, rumoured to have been found with the stink of alcohol on his breath, had been asleep below deck at the time, where the horrified cries of the girls on the shore failed to reach him.

'It's starting to move, do you see?' said Belinda, tipping her head at the yellow haze.

'Hadn't we better get started?' said Barney.

'Let me finish this.' She took another bite and tossed the core into the long grass. 'We'll have to aim for the north side,' she said. 'The harbour still hasn't been cleaned up from the floods, and there's nowhere to dock on the south shore.'

Barney shunted the boat forward another foot. St Just was almost visible now: an eerie grey line on the horizon, surrounded by a strange, thermal haze. Elsewhere in the world, there were islands used as graveyards for broken ships, as quarantines for people with polio or tuberculosis. Islands for displaced tribes: places that turned out not to be safe but poisonous. The water in those lagoons could burn your skin right off.

He had started to heave at the resisting vessel when a voice called out from the bluffs.

'Well. *Fancy that.*'

There was barely time to scramble into the boat before Ivor had caught on to the stern with both hands.

'Let go,' Barney said.

'And be the last one to watch you two paddle off to your deaths? Get out of there.'

'Leave us alone.'

'Preston said he saw you skulking off together

before the second bell. You stopped for apples at the garden wall, he said. Fine way to treat a friend.'

'We're not friends,' said Barney.

Ivor turned to the girl. 'Is that what you think?' he said. But before she could answer the bells of St Arras began to sound, making her hesitate. 'So, you're going to live in blissful nature, like Paul and Virginie?' continued Ivor. He stepped towards her. 'You little tart,' he said. 'You ought to be ashamed.'

'Don't talk to her like that,' said Barney.

Ivor laughed — an awkward, sneering laugh — and said, 'What a pair you are.'

He grabbed the satchel from Barney and pulled it open.

'At least you remembered the tin opener this time,' he said. He took out the matchbox and threw it into the water. 'Shame those got wet, though.'

Barney lunged for the bag but Ivor pulled out of reach. 'Catch,' he said, tossing one of the apples far over Belinda's head. 'No? Try again.' He lobbed another apple into the long grass, followed by a volley of three, four, five more.

'Stop it,' said Belinda, even now clambering out of the boat to chase after the apples that skittered across the pebble beach.

'Never mind them,' called Barney after her — but she wasn't listening.

Ivor smirked, waiting until she had disappeared from view before rounding the rowing boat.

'How many'd they give you?' said Barney.

229

'Twelve of the best, my boy.' Ivor sat himself on the edge of the boat and pulled a cigarette from his pocket. 'Listen, Holland . . . ' He stared straight ahead to light the cigarette, which he didn't offer to Barney. 'You do know it didn't mean anything, don't you?'

'You might have told Runcie that.'

'Runcie knows it just as well as I do. You make things worse by going about looking so damned shifty about it all.' He blew a mouthful of smoke towards the sea, so that the wind lifted it like a piece of grey gossamer. 'You're not to know, I suppose, never having been away to school before: so you'll have to take my word for it. Or ask Littlejohn. He knows more about it than he's willing to let on. It's *faute de mieux*.'

'Screw you.'

'Only you wouldn't be able to keep yourself from thinking about the old geezers sitting round the pub in Camden Town — about what they'd say if they found out. There's no such trouble for a toff like me.' Belinda had returned, apples gathered in the pouch of her tunic. 'At least she's not dead inside.' A nervous laugh. 'She's not dead, full stop . . . '

What an idiot he had been not to see it at the time. The girl, gamine and shorn-headed, as a substitute for the boys who had come before her: Henry Cray and Robin, and God knows how many others. He had redirected his love for his family's sacked footman onto Henry Cray — and then, onto the fallen child, Belinda Flood.

'And to think, if I'd arrived here a minute later

230

you'd never get to see this,' Ivor continued in a loud voice, pulling something from his satchel: a wind-up alarm clock with a couple of wires sticking out of one end. 'You set the time as the alarm, and when the minute hand strikes an electrical signal is sent to the speaker, jumps onto the other wire and — provided there's a spark — ignites it. Rather clever, don't you think?'

'Let me see,' said Barney, grabbing the clock from Ivor before the older boy had the wit to resist. Instead he inched closer, looming over Barney like a protective shadow, while Belinda craned her neck from across the boat like some small animal sniffing curiously at the air.

Barney felt the weight of it in his hand, rolled the wires between his fingers. He turned from Ivor, resisting his overbearing hulk, his hot breath and salty musk. The wet sand beneath their feet had darkened: the wind nipped at Barney's bare fingers, wrapped around the metal timepiece. There was a toxic, fishy smell, and he looked up to see that the yellow haze had not drifted but spread.

He did not know how many seconds passed before he hurled the timepiece at the water so hard that the mist swallowed it before it broke the surface. No sooner had he done that than something hit the pit of his stomach, and then he felt the sudden shock of cold. He was lying face up in the shallow water before he saw the older boy come after him again, and behind him Belinda with the paddle . . .

And then there were fingers around his throat

and salt water pouring into his mouth, and all the while it was freezing. *So this is how death starts*, he thought. *Will it feel like this until it's over, or is there worse to come?*

What happened next did not seem real — perhaps because they were both under water, perhaps because he was struggling for breath. But even if he had imagined Ivor's teeth sinking into his cheek with the clarity of a sewing needle drawing stitches through flesh, there was no denying the plume of blood that spread about him in the moments that followed, or the ripping noise that made his insides heave.

He did not know what made Ivor detach himself so suddenly, but by then there was such terrible pain that he didn't care. It was only seconds later that he perceived an outline against the setting sun, shouting and waving its arms.

Already the rowing boat had started to drift, teased along the shore by the uneven waves, and meanwhile Ivor had pulled Belinda away from it and was guiding her quickly up the slope towards the shouting man.

'She's safe,' the Mede was saying, in a clear, loud voice. 'It's all right. I've got her now.'

Barney rushed to his feet, only to be pulled back by the waves: he struggled, righted himself, stood again, clutching his cheek with one hand as blood ran through his fingers. The figure was still shouting, pointing at the boat which continued to drift farther down the beach. Ivor had flung his school blazer around Belinda's shoulders and held her by the elbow, shielding the back of her head with his other arm as if to protect her from the soaked and shivering thing on the beach: a flayed spectre in dripping shrouds, blood spilling into his mouth, naked legs whipped raw by the wind, feet sinking deeper into the rushing sand.

* * *

He was put in isolation in the San and instructed not to touch the stitches. That was what came of playing in the water, Matron told him: the beach might look sandy, but the rocks beneath the surface were sharp. If it hadn't been for Morrell, one shuddered to think what might have become of the poor girl.

There was only one other boy in the San at the time, in a bay on the other side of a curtained partition: Sanger, who was laid up with a throat infection. On his second morning Barney heard Matron tell him that he would be sent back to lessons that afternoon. Immediately he tore a page from the primer on his bedside table and scribbled a few lines in the margins. Once Matron had left the room, he tiptoed to the curtain and poked his head into Sanger's bay.

'Give this to Littlejohn, will you?' he said.

Sanger stared up at Barney with eyes still ringed pink from all the hacking and wheezing of the last six days. He wet his lips and straightened himself beneath the covers. 'What's it worth?' he said.

'Next week's tuck.'

'Two weeks.'

'Fine. But you have to give it to him straight away.'

The trick would be to laugh it off. If he played his cards right, Robin might ask to touch the scar, his war wound, and then Barney could take the watch out of his pocket and press it into his hand . . .

As a starting whistle shrilled from the games pitch that afternoon, he wondered if Robin had chosen to ignore him. Perhaps Sanger had never even delivered the message. Barney thought of Ivor in his set, revelling in the fact of being a hero, and Belinda recovering in her child's bedroom, doubly scarred and never likely to trust him again — neither sparing a thought for Robin Littlejohn, who had only that minute excused himself from the sidelines complaining of a stomach ache.

He must have cut back to Medlar behind the old kitchens, which is why Barney didn't see him as he watched the drive from the San window. Now as on every other day of the year, the horseman and his mount were emerging from the fountain's green water: the rider still pointing at the moon, which wasn't a moon now, but a brilliant white sun.

As Barney waited, he noticed how the water brightened as the noontime sun emerged from behind the clouds. The change filled him with hope. In a few weeks it would be Christmas and he would get to see Spike and Jake again. By the time the new term started, everyone would have forgotten the fuss with Ivor.

There is a fountain filled with blood
(filled with blood, filled with blood).
There is a fountain filled with blood
flows from Emmanuel's veins!

He felt the silver watch through his pocket, this thing that had lived against the other boy's skin and marked the seconds to the rhythm of his quick, adolescent pulse. In that moment he decided that he would return it to Littlejohn as soon as he arrived. Not as an apology, nor even as a gift. It was his, after all.

And sinners plunged beneath that flood
lose all their guilty stains
(lose all their guilty stains,
lose all their guilty stains).

A bird shot out from the treetops seconds before the explosion, as if it had detected the first ripples of a collapsing star, sensed the death tremors before the final, violent event — and in the same moment, Barney heard the window shatter, felt his mouth filling with the taste of ash. On the lower playing field, boys and masters raised their eyes to the clouds, believing the sound to have been the roar of approaching thunder. But the sun was shining more brightly than ever before, and for several moments they chose not to believe the rising wail of the air-raid siren, the black plume unfurling against an untainted sky . . .

★ ★ ★

235

Once Swift had reported to the headmaster that Robin Littlejohn wasn't accounted for, the entire school cleared to the lower pitch. Now only Pleming remained to consider the smouldering ruins: the unseated stone rider face down in the green water, its outstretched arm flung over the fountain's edge as if grasping after his mount, which had fled. A monstrous crater opened up to the corridor that had once linked the main building to the old kitchens. Picking up a piece of metal casing that was still warm to the touch, he considered the surviving ironwork grilles that braced shattered windows, the contorted drainpipes and flooded gutters. It did not match any of these, either in colour or weight. The tragedy seemed to point to the explosion of a UXB.

By the time the ambulance arrived, Barney had already regained consciousness beneath a dusting of broken glass. He had fallen from the bed and was staring in bewilderment at the sparkling floor, unaware of the blood that trickled from his nose and wondering how to stop the ringing in his ears.

He was quickly transferred to a bed against the opposite wall, away from the window, and an hour later he lay beneath a fresh sheet that Matron had tucked tightly beneath his hips, so that at first it appeared to his housemaster that there was only half a boy there, severed at the abdomen.

'Well, Holland.' Runcie seated himself in the chair next to the bed. 'You've had a lucky escape.'

Barney cast his eyes downwards. He was fiddling with something in one hand, and the housemaster gently prised his fingers open to see what it was.

'Is this yours?' he asked. Barney shook his head.

'It's Robin's,' he said.

'What were you doing with it?'

Barney opened his mouth and shut it again.

'I was going to give it back to him,' he said at last. 'It had fallen into the river.'

A shaft of sunlight widened through the window, cutting into his eyes. Runcie stood up and lowered the blind. When had they become such suspicious creatures, he wondered. From the kitchens below wafted a smell of tripe and boiled meat: a smell from his boyhood, an odour that took him back to swimming lessons in the black tank on frosty mornings, to knee baths in a communal tub and socks hardened to the shape of the wearer's foot — the scent of an institution larger than himself. These lads today had nothing in common with the bonny little men of his youth.

'The funny thing is that Morrell wasn't at the house match when it happened. I don't suppose you'd know where else he might have been?'

'No, sir.'

The Head's cat had been preening by the fountain, warmed by the hazy noontime sun. In the second before the blast, it was as if someone had flipped a switch and shut off all the sound. The last thing he remembered was the cat opening its mouth to release a furious wail

237

— though to Barney it appeared only as a soundless yawn. He had never expected Ivor to pull off an explosion of such immensity.

There was a knock, and Mr Pleming stuck his head around the door. 'I'm sorry to interrupt . . . ' He regarded the boy, who was staring out beyond the blinded window, and the housemaster. 'Holland.'

'Sir.'

'Nasty business. Brave lad.' Pleming hesitated. He sensed that his smile was over-zealous, but he was not a man confident at relinquishing a concentrated smile.

'Headmaster?'

'Mr Runcie. Mr Swift has caught up with the pupils who weren't accounted for.'

Runcie nodded and rose slowly to his feet.

'It came out of the ground, sir,' said Barney.

Runcie sensed the Head shift impatiently behind him. 'What do you mean by that?'

Mr Pleming eased the door open at a wider angle and stopped it with his toe.

'It exploded *up*, sir.'

'Well, it didn't fall from the sky, now, did it?' said Runcie, forcing a smile as he stepped across the threshold past the Head, who did not appear to see the funny side.

★　★　★

Scrums and penalties and picnic baskets, skinned knees gleaming pink through mud, striped socks and the captain's coin toss, reedy voices raised in cheers and middle-aged faces set

238

in grim satisfaction — all this was a world away, on another island in another sea. Here, there was only the little house, the open door . . . and the girl and the wolf inside, together.

Always, he had witnessed and done nothing. He had maintained his composure where others would have tried to rescue the innocents being locked in churches and burned alive. He had filed reports, infiltrated meetings, gained and betrayed trust. When it was all over, he had come home — to a position in the school where his name was engraved in gilded letters on the Captain of Games roll, where even today there were those who could remember the time he had kicked a rugby ball clear over the roof and where he had continued to witness and turn a blind eye to those petty cruelties that he knew made men of boys.

Swift had heard the voices, low and conspiratorial, and detected the shuffle of bodies through the concrete wall. The girl had been the first to notice him peering around the corner, and her hand had shot to her mouth in fright.

How much she had looked like her mother then, he thought.

The boy he sent directly to the headmaster. He took Belinda by the shoulder and steered her firmly towards her father's house.

'Don't,' she said, shrugging him off. 'Or I shall tell Mother.'

He felt a rush of panic. 'Tell her what?'

'About that day after the tea, when you followed me there.'

When the earth had shifted beneath their feet

— when the ground had cracked open to reveal a terrible secret.

'I did no such thing.'

'Didn't you?' She looked at him, and he noticed how her irises reflected the same glassy colour that bewilders the eye when the sun hits the sea.

'This is ridiculous.'

'I don't suppose the school could do with another scandal.'

'A boy *died* today.'

Belinda paled. 'Barney — ' she said.

'No, but it was a damned close thing for him,' said Swift.

'Who, then?'

At last, the balance of power had shifted. 'There will be plenty of time for questions later,' he said. 'Right now, if I were you, I'd take the position that the less said the better.'

He felt her scowling ahead of him, and he pitied her father: befuddled and perhaps frightened by his daughter's impending maturity. The girl harboured a quiet, bitter fury at her impotence as a child and a female: that much was clear. Perhaps that was what had attracted her to Morrell, who shared her anger and who could be charming as well as cruel. Swift had heard the news of the boating accident that spring — two girls and a schoolmistress very nearly drowned at sea — but had never considered the possibility that Mollie's daughter could have been involved. It was what she *hadn't* done that was the problem — and then Swift remembered

240

Mollie's words: 'We don't *have* to do anything.'

Five years ago.

★ ★ ★

They had both been younger, of course: Mollie particularly, with only the one daughter and island life still a relative novelty. Flood had married late, and there was a significant age gap between them. She was not lonely — at the drinks party where they first met she had dared the young French master to suggest as much — and she was not, strictly speaking, bored. She had the little girl to look after, and letters to write to her family in Norfolk. And books — so many books. Poetry, she had told him. Anyone in particular? Christina Rossetti, she had said.

'*This close-companioned inarticulate hour,*' he quoted.

That wasn't Christina, she told him. That was her brother.

He couldn't think of one of her poems, he admitted.

Not even 'Goblin Market'? she asked. About the little girl lured to eat fruit from the goblins — '*But when the noon waxed bright, Her hair grew thin and grey . . .*'

Children's poems, he said.

It's not really a poem for children, she told him. And then she had asked him what he intended to do in his spare time on the island.

'I should like to see you,' he replied. In

241

hindsight, it had been a ridiculous thing to say: but it had not sounded so bold at the time. It couldn't have, because she had laughed.

★ ★ ★

In the interview, Ivor insisted that he'd only intended to protect her — that when they had heard the explosion their first thought had been to take cover. He'd seen something as they headed for the shelter — a man in a long coat, not one of the masters, hurrying across the field towards the fence — and he'd sensed then that there was an emergency at the school, and that the main building was the last place they should go.

The dreadful irony had been that the alarm which was set off by the blast hadn't been the air-raid siren but the thin, plangent all-clear. As for the clothes she had been wearing, 'borrowed' from the lost-and-found chest — they were simply part of a theatrical game they'd devised. A pantomime, was all. 'It wasn't what you think,' he said, more than once, until at last Pleming placed his hands on the desk and said: 'What do you suppose we think?'

The Courvoisier bottles told their own story, of course. There was enough in Ivor Morrell's record to paint a picture of the category of boy he fell into. Boys who made heroes of their victims, who took equal delight in torturing and rescuing the objects of their desire.

'She was panicking,' Ivor said. 'She kept saying

that she'd felt something. There was a smell — a rotting smell — right after we heard the explosion. She said she'd smelt it before, in the basements.'

'She took fright at a smell?'

'Not just a smell. Something pungent. Sick. I felt it too.'

'Do you normally *feel* smells, Morrell?'

'Not usually. That's why it seemed so . . . unorthodox.'

'Perhaps you'd like to tell me about the unorthodox materials found in the shelter,' Pleming said. 'Weed-killer, tin canisters, petroleum. The police are going to want to ask you about this.'

'It was an experiment, that's all. Just a bit of fun.'

'And was Barney Holland involved in this bit of fun?' Pleming frowned. 'For boys like you, school may seem just a diversion. For the Flood girl, I imagine it's mostly an irrelevance. But for Barney Holland, it may just be his only chance at a better life. Thanks to his little escapade with her last week, he may have lost that opportunity. I don't suppose your brother would have made much of this sort of thing,' the Head continued. 'Playing dress-up and experimenting with explosives.'

'No, sir.'

Pleming settled himself behind the desk and opened the green folder that lay between them.

'Well, then. Shall we begin at the beginning?'

★ ★ ★

243

Perched on the armchair beneath a framed reproduction of *Madame Monet*, Mollie Flood worried at her wedding ring around a finger that was already red and swollen.

'Honestly, Belinda, if this is another lie — '

'I tell you, it's not a lie.'

It was just the same as before, thought the girl: the disbelieving adults and the terrible pictures in her head . . . Miss Gallo in the dark water with seaweed swirling about her arms, flooding her mouth, tickling the soles of her feet, sinking like a boulder to the bottom of the sea — *oh it was sad, so sad* — and the beautiful Millicent Grady floating calmly on the water's surface, like Ophelia, with her hair fanning out in a magnificent black halo. The North Sea waters were so cold you'd die of shock. Mary Compton had said so. Your heart would freeze before your brain knew it, and then you'd be asleep and never know the difference.

'Morrell also mentioned seeing a man on the far field shortly after the blast.' Swift remained in the doorway. 'No doubt the police will look into it.'

'Forgive me, Michael. Please, do sit.'

The three-piece suite was arranged around a coffee table still draped with a plastic cloth from the younger child's tea. Swift seated himself at the far end of the sofa near the radiogram, facing Mollie and leaving Belinda no option but to continue to stand awkwardly in the middle of the room.

'Who gave you these things to wear? Was it that Holland boy again?'

'It wasn't Barney's fault,' she said. And then, in a small voice, 'I wanted to be like the others.'

'Don't be ridiculous. Go up to your room and change into something appropriate.'

The adults sat in an uneasy silence as the girl's footsteps retreated up the staircase, along the corridor to the far end of the house. A door slammed.

'I'm sorry about this. Would you like a coffee?'

'Thank you.'

It was his first time sitting in this room since he had arrived as a teacher at the school. He found the Flood family's home particularly oppressive. He had visited many houses like this to report the deaths of sons on battlefields half a world away: houses kept too tidy, fusty with ambition and self-regard, OMO box on the windowsill. The curtains here had been replaced with fabric printed in diagrammatic patterns, and a new pink lampshade had been bought for the standing light. The mud-room, leading to the kitchen, had been recovered in a garishly red wallpaper. But the clock remained on the mantelpiece, flanked by a framed photograph of Belinda — and there on the side table was the cut-glass ashtray where once he had stubbed out her cigarette.

'Is it true, then? That one of the boys . . . '

'He almost certainly wouldn't have known what hit him.'

'My God, how ghastly.' A terrible realization. 'It could have been any one of us. At any moment — '

'It could have been much worse.'

'Is that what Mr Pleming will tell his parents?'

Swift picked up his cup and set it down again. 'Belinda is safe, Mollie. You have nothing to worry about now.'

'No, of course not. Apart from running away to sea in a clapped-out rowing boat. And hiding in a shelter in the woods with a boy old enough to be called up for service.' She sipped her coffee, and Swift wondered if she was also remembering a moment's indiscretion five years ago.

'She's been a different child since all of the horridness last year,' Mollie said at last. It was the English mistress at the root of that, she knew: Miss Gallo, who had chosen to die a heroine, to be loved and mourned by generations of loyal students. Belinda may have seen the damage to the side of the schooner as it set off from the shore — she knew she had been wrong not to mention it to anyone; knew it well enough as to have almost drowned herself running away from school — but for how long must she be eaten by this guilt? 'Enormous appetite, compulsive washing — two baths a day, sometimes three. And then to have found . . . that awful thing. From the war, wasn't it?'

He regarded her and made no sound. She waited for him to confirm what she had said, but he did not so much as tilt his head in either direction. She swallowed, folded and refolded her hands — still watching him, always watching him, not blinking. When the silence grew too long she filled it, breathing out the words so that her voice would not crack. 'I'd thought that

246

things had started to improve since half-term . . . '

It occurred to Swift then that although Mollie was the sort of woman others should have described as a model wife, he had never heard anyone refer to her in this way. When they first met, she had already realized the futility of basing her life around her daughter. But what had this left her? The restrictions of a boarding-school environment, sharpened by the memory of who she had been before, in the heady days of the war. Neither one of them had anticipated this disappointment at the future: this ennui with what had been won and what no longer remained to fight for. The first time he met her he had known that that was something they shared.

'This Morrell boy,' Mollie said. 'Tell me about him.'

'He has a rather curious moral framework. He's very keen on the ancients. I get the sense he'd rather like to be able to live his life according to their rules, rather than to ours.'

'I see.'

'He's a slave to his own rhetoric, that's all. I imagine some of it might have rubbed off on the younger ones.'

'And why do you suppose he should have had any interest in her?'

'He enjoys looking out for the friendless.' The dregs were bitter, puckering the inside of his mouth: he didn't know why he was still going through the charade of drinking. 'I imagine he thought he was a comfort to her. That's a normal schoolboy fantasy, isn't it? Saving the girl in distress.'

'Is it?'

Swift could bear it no longer: the porcelain slippery in his sweating palms, the ticking of the grandfather clock in the hallway. He stood up. 'I'm sorry to have kept you,' he said.

'Michael,' she began — but there was something half-hearted in her voice. 'Tell my husband not to worry about us, if you see him?'

'Of course. Please, there's no need to see me out.'

As he passed the fountain, the French master paused to consider the felled horse and the rider severed from its back, trying to imagine the fire and the hundred small gods to which it had given birth. The bombed-out wing might have passed for a Gothic ruin now: the surviving corner with its blown-out window like a blinded eye, the brickwork silhouetted against the blue glow of moonlight reflecting up from the sea.

'Do sit,' said Pleming, indicating the chair. He liked Swift, approved of his manicured hands and mobile nostrils, derived personal satisfaction from the fact that his name was written in gold letters on the games board. No wonder he'd never rubbed along particularly well with Morrell. 'So. You're here to inform me of what we both already know.' He tapped the open file. 'Mrs Morrell.'

'Psychologically, I gather she's rather fragile.'

Pleming flipped the file closed. 'I have found, Swift, through long years of experience, that nearly all behavioural disorders can be traced to psychological fragility on the mother's side.' He peered over the rims of his spectacles and lowered his voice. 'Between you and me, Flood's girl is a prime example. You've seen what she's done to her hair. There is something agitated about her mother — it's no secret, you needn't look so embarrassed — and this, I feel sure, has affected the child considerably.'

'I couldn't begin to comment.'

'Of course not. And that's not what we're here to discuss, is it?' Pleming considered the deputy housemaster gravely. 'Mrs Morrell requested a change of personal tutor for her son at the end of his first year. I declined the request. You were not informed of it.'

Swift waited with mounting impatience. *Have it out and let's be done with it*, he wanted to say. 'Was there a complaint?'

'Nothing specific, no. Can you recall anything that might have upset him at the time?'

'Upheaval at home — the family was forced to let go of staff that year. I imagine things must have been difficult with his father's return, and Jonty . . . '

'Potts and Coatsworth and de Bock also lost brothers in the war. Several lost fathers. None of them have conspired to detonate a bomb on school grounds. He said it was to destroy silence. What do you suppose he meant by that?'

'I haven't a clue.'

'Might he have been keeping any secrets?'

'Headmaster, Morrell is a deeply unpleasant boy. A quiet bully. No one would wish to sully his brother's memory, but — '

'I see.' Pleming closed the file. 'The irony, of course, is that if it hadn't been for that damned UXB, none of this would have come to light.'

'Either way, we'd be sitting on a time bomb.'

'Then we are decided.'

Later that same day Ivor, high-shouldered and looking surprisingly small in his brother's army coat and wide-brimmed fedora, climbed into Krawiec's van to be taken to Port Grenen. Watching the vehicle draw an arc around the cordoned-off rubble of the old kitchens, Barney wondered if memory was something that could be unlearnt. Before, he had yearned for some recollection of his mother's war. Now, he wished he might tear from his mind's eye the burnt-on image of that leaping flame, that bolt of light, the clouds of choking dust.

Not for the first time he knelt upon an empty bed, observing the vapour trail of one life drifting out of his own. The night before she left, his mother had crept in next to Barney on the mattress he shared with Jake and slept, curled around him like a cat, until the small hours. Only in the blue light of dawn had he been aware of her slipping away, and through sleep-crusted eyes he had traced her outline against the light in the hallway before watching the door shut.

★ ★ ★

Heading up the coast road with her arms weighed down by shopping on the one hand, and by Lucia's insistent toddler pull on the other, Mollie recalled the tipsy acrobat that had

250

balanced upon her bookshelf as a child: a slender figure on a bicycle that dipped at the slightest touch before righting himself, balancing by an invisible law of physics explained to her many times by her father yet to this day never fully understood. At Lucia's stop-start infant pace the walk had taken twice as long as usual, and Mollie's thoughts had diffused into bleary fog. There was the sound of her daughter's voice, and the vast silence of the sky — the silence was louder, reducing Lucia's babble to distant chirping — and her own feet slapping on the pavement. A melody looping at the back of her mind — a violin study her husband had been practising the previous evening — and words, unfocused and unrecalled, like text pressed through blotting paper.

So the sound of the horn came as a rude invasion — and as she blinked at the tank-grey lorry powering towards her, the sight of his outline through the windshield woke her from the reverie with a jolt. The pavement had run out a hundred yards back, so she tugged the child onto the verge and pretended to fumble with the shopping as the lorry slowed to pass. There was someone in the passenger seat next to the Pole — a figure in a grey coat whose face was obscured by the long rim of a hat — and a trunk rattling in the open trailer behind them.

There was room for just one vehicle at this point in the road, and no turning space. It was only civil of the Pole to slow down as he passed the woman with her child. It was not necessary for him to stop. To switch off the engine. Staring at her.

'Come, Lucia.'

They edged sideways past the vehicle, and as they passed behind it Mollie looked back, waiting to hear the engine start up again. Neither head moved, and she sensed that he was still waiting. She did not know for what. Not bread: those days were past. An acknowledgement? She commanded the muscles of her mouth to form a smile. Almost instantly, a hand was raised in the rear-view mirror — *Good day, prosze pani* — and the lorry shuddered on, sinking down the coast road until it disappeared between the horizon and the sea.

★ ★ ★

Swift had overheard himself being described with grudging respect as one who had 'done his bit'. He had headed straight for France when others had retreated to England to train the next generation of heroes. His schoolmates remembered him as a romancer, though this reputation had faded as one by one they left for mediocre jobs and degrees at provincial universities, or died on battlefields thousands of miles away. Thankfully, it did not have the staying power to be passed on to the next generation, which was ready to choose its own myths. Among the masters there were better targets for schoolboy gossip that was idle and salacious, cruel through the laughter.

An afternoon five years ago: an afternoon of

watery, early summer sun. Cow parsley like wedding confetti in her hair. He had kissed the strawberry stains from her fingers. Even then, in that most perfect of moments, his thoughts had thrust forward to the future, when their time would be over. One way or another, everything ended up in the past: the things he wanted to, and those he didn't.

When the worst thing happened — not the pregnancy, but the news five months in that she had lost it — he had asked her what they should do. That was when she'd replied that they didn't have to do anything. It had looked after itself. She had barely begun to show — she was slight of build, and her husband was not attuned to these things — and she had buried it in a quiet spot where it would not be disturbed. Mollie had been strong for just long enough before the fever took hold — before she found it too hard to feel Belinda's gaze peeping around the bedroom door and she had told her husband that she thought it was time the girl went to school, learnt some independence.

She had been strong, but he had not. He had only heard her voice repeating to him the words she had recited at the gravesite — *Plant thou no roses at my head, Nor shady cypress tree* — and felt despair.

He had got as far as the rock pools. Standing barefoot in the shallows, he had stared out to St Just and thought how easy it would be to join his child. The island was a fine line separating the impending sea and boundless sky. In poor light it would disappear altogether, like a mirage. He could dream himself walking out to it.

And if thou wilt, remember,
And if thou wilt, forget.

He chose the stones carefully, weighing each one in his hand, feeling its smoothness, judging its colour. Some he threw back into the water immediately, but a few he put in his pockets, testing their pull. He supposed it would be better to be pulled down by the shoulders, head first, to make quick and sure work of it, and so he filled his jacket — inside and out — before beginning the search for flattish rocks to fit his trouser pockets. But most of the flat ones he chose were light: better suited to skipping, not death. Instead, he collected handfuls of small stones and stuffed his pockets until they bulged.

It was at that point that he had heard the sound of a foot slipping on the chalky ground of the cliff edge, and a scuffle as a body righted itself. He had turned and peered up in time to see a boy, petrified, looking down at him with a look of peculiar recognition. A junior lad, new that year: Jonty Morrell's brother. The sun had been high in the sky, and Swift shielded his eyes against the glare, gesturing with his free hand as a clutch of stones scattered to the ground. With that motion, the boy had turned and fled.

He had felt ridiculous, then, standing barefoot in the rock pools, and his sagging pockets had struck him suddenly as something rather shameful: he might as easily have been caught parading in women's clothing. Stirred by a rush of self-loathing, he had tipped the stones back into the water and watched them settle to the shallow sea floor, jostling their reunion with a muted clatter.

★ ★ ★

Barney had been working the crown on the silver Buren with his fingernail for what seemed hours, and still it wouldn't budge. The ticking grated in the silent San, where any sound besides the trickle of water in a basin or the occasional turning of a page in a book felt somehow profane. An hour earlier, as Mr Runcie had retreated behind Matron's starched bulk, through the door and down the stairs to the house — to the others, Cowper and Shields and Percy, Opie and Hughes but not Robin — the ticking had become more than irritating. It hadn't even had the decency to freeze: wasn't that what was supposed to happen when the owner died? *You rotter, Robin*, Barney thought, fumbling with the seal behind the watch face, desperate only to make it stop.

Now there would never be a burst of flame that was theirs and only theirs, their one chance at beautiful destruction. The explosion, contrary to first appearances, had had nothing to do with Ivor: the bomb had lain beneath the drive for years, waiting for its moment — and it had taken Robin with it, to spite them.

Why this sickening guilt — why now? Memory is nothing but ashes and dust, he told himself, banishing the memory of the blaze. Trolley lights through the smoke, the silhouette of a fire engine ladder, an ARP warden's helmet like a cymbal hitting the ground. Since earliest childhood he had had a waking dream: running through a house pursued by flames and chasing after a woman's voice, driven by the urgent need to get to her before the fire.

Ashes and dust. And nothing after that.

The watch slipped, warm and slick in his clumsy fingers, and for an instant Barney was tempted to hurl it through the window. He thought that he should like to smash it through the glass of the Audley family vault. No one had been able to tell him whether or not anyone was actually buried there, and if there wasn't what the point of it was, besides it being a place to play Bundle. Dad had no gravestone, nor had Robin — blown to smithereens so that there were bits of him floating in the very air Barney breathed.

★　★　★

'There is a seed cake and that horrible ginger beer you like so much,' said Miss Duchâtel, setting a basket on the stand next to his bed. 'For you to share with the other boys if you wish' — she cast a glance around the empty San — 'or with Belinda, perhaps.'

Matron's expression betrayed judgement: she recognized the Frenchwoman, though she had never spoken to her. What had the housemaster been thinking, sending the boy to stay with a pariah? Had it been his idea of a joke? Or had he not known? To have said that Miss Duchâtel had no friends on the island would have been untrue: there was old Maurice at the fisherman's kiosk, as well as a lady from the Nonconformist church who sometimes made an exchange of home-brewed rum for fresh eggs and her famously boozy fruitcakes. She was also known to have offered work to Krawiec, the school grounds-man, whom most of the islanders avoided as much as possible because he reminded them of the past. But that did not require the Frenchwoman to leave her farm. Her visits to St Arras were always restricted to a prompt tour of the shops, where she placed her orders in advance for collection.

The laundress pouring sheets in a rolling bin hovered at the far end of the San, watching. But Matron was determinedly civil. Most people treated the Frenchwoman with polite coolness. There were exceptions: the butcher, who refused to serve her himself and would call for his wife to take her money, or the postal warden, who always made her complete a customs form for letters to France, even though these had not been required since the war. 'She made her bed,' said Matron's glance at the hesitating laundress. 'The war wasn't easy on anyone, but at least we kept our noses clean,' the girl's silence seemed to imply.

'We'll put the ginger beer in the tuck locker,' said Matron, taking the basket without waiting for either one of them to object. When she had gone, Miss Duchâtel sat down.

'Did they tell you about Morrell?' said Barney.

'No.' She followed Matron with her eyes, down the corridor between the beds to where a roster hung on the wall by a little roll-top desk. 'Why? How is Ivor?'

'They sent him away. For good.'

'For what reason?'

'It doesn't matter. We weren't friends any more.'

'Why ever not?' Barney looked away until it became clear that she would not press the point. 'Well, that is a shame.'

'The police told Pleming it was a German bomb that didn't go off when it was supposed to.' A red arrow that began at the top of his neck, behind the ears, flushed down towards his clavicle. 'Which means that it was no one's fault. Ivor's not going to rat you out now.'

Miss Duchâtel stood up abruptly, gaze trained on Matron's back as if to avoid looking at Barney would somehow quieten him. 'You are tired, and still upset,' she said in a low voice. 'I understand. You want to be left alone, yes?

'Not especially.'

'I must go now. I didn't realize it was so late — '

'Do the police know as well?'

'Know what?'

'About you and the commandant. The painting was a gift from him. There were two glasses in the photograph of the picnic — the other one was his. And the baby didn't belong to a neighbour, it was yours. You killed it — '

'She died — '

'You never fought in any Resistance. You were an orphan — a model in Paris. Poor. You came over with the Germans. That's why the islanders cut your hair off after they'd left.'

'Stop this, Barney.'

'The one thing I don't understand is why the bracelet you said belonged to her was down in the rock pools. That's where Belinda found it.'

A strange look passed over Miss Duchâtel's face: almost a smile.

'It's where she was buried,' she said.

'Then how did she turn up behind the old kitchens?'

'Lower your voice, Holland,' barked Matron, having reappeared from her trip to the linen hanger, as Barney and Miss Duchâtel turned on her with pale faces. 'I'm sorry, Miss Duchâtel. Perhaps the morning would be a better time to visit. The boys get too excited when they're tired.'

'Yes, of course.' She collected her purse from under the chair and slung her coat over one arm. 'That was another woman's shame, Barney, not mine.'

He expected that she would return — if not the next day, then surely the day after that. But by the time Matron agreed that he could move into Wool House with the others there had been no more baskets of cakes and ginger beer, no invitation to tea at the farmhouse. It was not until the following week that his housemaster approached Barney with a card in a red envelope.

'It's from Miss Duchâtel,' Mr Runcie said. He

259

waited until the housemaster had turned away before tearing it open and devouring the words in a few quick glances.

My dear Barney,
  Still I have no word from Ivor, who I suppose has forgotten all about us now that he is back in England. That ferry ride is so convenient for some people: the way the sea eats up the past. While the earth remembers everything, the land and the trees and the things we leave on it, the sea remembers nothing.
  I have decided that I owe you the truth about those things of which you accused me. You were right about many things, but not about her death: there was nothing I could have done to prevent that. Funerals were prohibited on the island — the enemy considered large gatherings too risky — and so we had a choice: either to hand her over for 'disposal', or to lay her to rest ourselves. The ground on my farm was too hard, and toxic because of that photographer's chemicals. So we turned to the sea.

When I get to the end, I will tear this up, thought Barney.

  The person to ask about the body that was discovered by the old kitchens is called Swallow, or something like that — I'm sorry I can't remember. I don't know whether he is a master or a student at the school, perhaps

260

neither. Mr Krawiec once mentioned the name to me in confidence. I was one of the few people who offered him work in exchange for food after the war; he came to trust me, I suppose, despite my reputation.

Believe me when I say that I am sorry for all that has happened. My heart aches for that poor boy and his family — and for you, Barney, because I know that he was your friend.

At the bottom of the page was a signature that resembled a hair fallen across the paper, formless as breath.

★   ★   ★

In all likelihood she had not known, when she wrote to Barney, that that week's ferry had been delayed by high winds and thick fog. By the time the alarm was raised, the vessel carrying Ivor Morrell was already out of radio call.

Gales would often hold things up by an hour or more: if there was fog, then the captain would be relying on signals from the mainland. Perhaps he was being overly cautious, explained the porter to waiting passengers, but better safe than sorry.

The search boats' lanterns were no use in such fog. A call was put in to the Skagerrak coastguard to be on the lookout. Almost immediately, the reply came through: a fifteen-mile ice sheet had made the coast there quite inaccessible for several weeks.

Repeated radio requests to the vessel itself resulted only in static silence. The next day an ice-breaker was summoned from Esbjerg, but after six hours on the water no sign of the Lindsey Island ferry, its captain or sole passenger, had been detected.

It took several days for the news to filter back to school. Even then it did not become common knowledge among the masters until a day or two before the end of term, when the last ferry before Christmas looked likely to be delayed by similar conditions. Ominous mutterings about wayward gales and heavy pack ice trapping the vessel — freezing the motor and luring panicked passengers onto the floes in the mistaken belief that it was safer on the sheet — did not seem to hint at tragedy until, halfway across the strait, Barney asked Mr Runcie if Morrell's ferry had also been delayed for very long. At that point, Mr Runcie became suddenly very concerned about Percy, who had started a nosebleed, so that Barney's question was left to hang in the air, crushed by the creaking of frost-bitten chains and the motor's tormented groan.

★ ★ ★

The island of St Just is little more than two miles long and a mile wide. Its deep pits and valleys are frequently flooded by rain and tidewater that seeps through the loam and trickles through burrowing streams that worm through the rock. If the climate were ten degrees warmer, the air itchy with tiny buzzing creatures, there might be

262

something of the bayou to its weird, floating aspect.

It is a primordial landscape in which human visitors are made immediately aware that they are the aliens. Three doomed settlement attempts have been verified on the record. Pottery artefacts suspected to date to the Viking era have been found in two caves on the island's northern face. The Domesday Book records that a Templar Order gave the island a name and established itself here for a number of years. In the early 1600s, Danish settlers attempted to appropriate the island, along with Lindsey, though the mission was poorly planned and haphazardly executed. Their expulsion a decade later was said to have been swift and merciless.

Vast colonies of rare seabirds are known to nest here, along with a particular breed of Scandinavian seal, small and heavily whiskered, that can be spotted sunbathing on the flats in summer. A small freshwater fish known as the Tollis Pink is said to thrive in the pools and gullies in the centre of the island, although parties of visiting schoolchildren rarely manage to return with any in their nets, even after long days of searching.

Scant reminders of human visitation only add to the island's mystique: stone circles left in several of the caves conform to remains from Continental witchcraft ceremonials. A triangle carved into the bark of the tallest tree on the rocky South Slope is assumed to represent some form of distress signal — though its precise cause remains unclear.

A clapboard house no larger than a beach hut, buttressed with rocks in the island fashion, once stood high atop the South Slope. A photograph, reproduced here, exists in the Lindsey archives of an unidentified woman in front of this house. Undated and unsigned, it is said to have been contributed to the collection by a German official.

The clapboard house, alas, no longer stands. Found to obstruct the German line of fire across the sea from St Arras, it was demolished some time in 1942. Now its foundations provide a haven for hermit crabs and a popular picnic spot for day tourists.

★　★　★

Having pasted a borrowing card over the flyleaf, Swift found the *Angler's Guide to St Just* its place on the shelf. He wondered if anyone would seek out this book when the list of acquired titles was posted on the Library door the next day. Spy novels were all the rage, now: stories about Englishmen philandering their way through the most perilous corners of the world, notching up romantic conquests in the same way that small boys collected bottle tops.

A shuffle of feet made him turn to find Barney Holland standing awkwardly to attention by the desk. Now that the pale days of the summer term were upon them, he saw that something about the boy had changed — a growth spurt, perhaps. He could not have been standing there long, and had probably been trying to think of a way to alert the master to his presence without having to raise his voice.

'What is it, Holland? You know the library's not open now.'

The boy made as if to advance, then stopped. All along the window ledge books were piled in balusters, and his gaze had lighted on a stack left for sorting at the end.

Swift noted his embarrassment and followed his gaze to the book at the top of the pile. 'Ancients,' he said brusquely. 'Romans.'

'Byzantines, sir.'

'What is it you wanted, Holland?' Swift said. His tone made the boy straighten instantly, his expression tinted with a look of surprise and — could it be? — hurt.

'It's about the cross-country team, sir. I wanted to know if I could join, sir — properly, I mean.'

' 'Properly'?'

'Not just in games, sir. I'd like to train properly. Enter in for races and things, you know.'

'I see.' This was unexpected. 'And why the sudden interest in running, Holland? You've always brought up the rear, from what I recall of your efforts last term.'

'Yes, sir. I want to get fit. All the others have something they're good at, sir — Shields with maths, and Cowper at rugby . . . ' He swallowed. 'I know I'm not the brightest, but I've got two legs and I'm not half as fat as Hughes, sir.'

'Very well. I'll see you at six o'clock tomorrow morning, warmed up and ready to go. We'll take

265

the route along the chalk ridge. Do you think you'll be up to that?'

Of course he didn't. 'Thank you, sir. Six o'clock, sir.'

Swift watched him leave the room. The silence now seemed changed. For several weeks last term the sea had gone strangely quiet, as though the frosty air had frozen out all possibility of sound. Since the thaw — since the breaking-up of the ice sheets, the lifting of the grey-green mist — it was as if the water had found its voice again.

They paused at the summit of the chalk ridge the next morning so that Barney could refasten his shoelaces. From here, it felt as though they should have been able to survey the whole island, like an equation solved and laid bare on a blackboard at the front of the classroom. It frustrated Barney that he couldn't. The main road wended out of sight where the land curved — real, but invisible.

High up on the far plateau, a figure stalked towards the Chimney, a dog circling about his legs. Now and then the dog would break away and tear ahead along the ridge, stopping at the edge to bark at the waves as if to fend off the encroaching tide. A whistle from its owner brought it looping round. Barney thought how nice it would be to have a dog and wondered if Mum would allow it.

He was surprised to have made it this far without his chest tightening under the exertion: his breath had settled into a rhythm that reflected the pitch and roll of the sea. On the ferry at the beginning of term, Barney had watched the thin hump of land rise out of the water with a shiver and a sense that something remained there still. For an instant his thoughts drifted to the vessel that had spent the winter stranded many miles to the north — the carcass had been retrieved in the spring, regurgitated ashore in some dreary Swedish village; the captain and his sole passenger long since disappeared — but it was hard to detect its spectre here today. The laughing waves did not frighten him: day by day, summer was muffling the undrownable voices that had haunted the winter ice.

'This must be the hardest bit, sir. The slope, I mean.'

'It gets steeper.'

'That's gradient, sir. You could calculate it if you timed the run. You'd have to have someone measure it, though, sir.'

'Paying attention in maths, now, are we, Holland?'

'It's more common sense than anything, sir. Like evening out the lower pitch.'

'Doc Dower's project, you mean.' Swift smiled with something resembling condescension.

'What's funny, sir?'

'Nothing, Holland. It's just I can think of more productive uses of precious time than adjusting the gradient of the landscape. Particularly when it's only going to be trodden over by boys scrumming over a rugby ball.'

'You say that, sir . . .'

The air buzzed with the metallic hum of

crickets, like so many rattling electric wires, and it carried a sweet scent: a lusty smell of the earth bursting to crack. Through the whispering grasses, over and around the ancient screes, they carried on along the island's north face.

'We'll cut inland at the next turning,' said Swift. Rivulets of perspiration illuminated his pink skin, and his eyes seemed bright as the spangled waves far below. Out here among the kittiwakes and the cowering gorse, they were like masters of a wild planet: blood thinned by North Sea winds, their hearts drumming to the sound of their own steady footfall. 'Past the barn with the red roof. The road comes out by that farmhouse.'

Even from here Barney could make out the grey dots of the Frenchwoman's geese muddling through the waterlogged run, the languid curve of their necks flexing to and fro as they pecked after seeds sunk into the mud. There was the stile near which they had played keepy-uppy.

They gathered pace when the land became flat, and Barney sensed Swift pulling ahead at a heady speed. The island was flush with light now, only a short half-hour from when they had set off in the gloom of a forest dawn, and as the main road came within view he sensed the beginning of a slow transformation back into their ordained roles: master and pupil, ruler and oppressed.

'Have you seen the plaque, sir?'

Clusters of boys had been drawn to it all week: a shining brass plate screwed to the chapel wall

268

next to the list of glorious war dead. *In memory of Robin Littlejohn*, it read. And beneath this, a quotation from Job: *'For inquire, please, of bygone ages, and consider what the fathers have searched out. For we are but of yesterday and know nothing, for our days on earth are a shadow.'*

'I have. It's very dignified.'

'Cray didn't get one, sir.'

'Cray didn't die at school, Holland. Or at war.'

They continued in silence for several minutes, reflecting on this.

'Morrell could have been a hero, sir,' Barney said, as they rounded the bend past Miss Duchâtel's farmhouse. The blackout curtains were drawn, and the feed bucket rolled empty on the step, clattering on its handle. 'If only things were different.'

'What things are those, Holland?'

'If there'd been a war he'd have been a brilliant spy.'

'The secret service doesn't recruit loose cannons, Holland.'

'Well, you would know, sir.' Barney scrambled to match Swift's long stride as the master began to pull ahead. 'That's what you did, wasn't it, sir? Hughes said so, sir.'

'Did he.'

'It's only clever chaps who get to do things like that, sir. The not-so-clever ones get put in the army.'

'That doesn't make them any less brave,' said Swift.

He had not fought, he had not saved a single

269

life. While others had fought bravely and died, others like him had enjoyed an uneventful war. That was a thing surely worse than death. Despite the dormitory rumours which he pretended not to hear, the only weapon Swift had ever carried had been an Enfield — and even that he had fired just once, taking pity on a fox which had been hit by a vehicle and which he later found lying in the middle of the road with its long, flat jaw hinging open and closed in the desperate trance that precedes a slow and painful death.

He had caught up with young Morrell that day at the rock pools: shaken him so hard as he made him promise not to breathe a word of what he'd seen that he feared the boy's neck might snap. For five years Swift had forced silence upon him. Wasn't that what schools everywhere taught? That membership to the group depends on an agreement of selective silence? The Headmaster had instructed his staff not to be drawn into discussions about the ferry that had become stranded in the ice that winter: the school had wiped its hands of Morrell now.

Shadows raced across the darkening screes, and Swift found himself thinking how much the island resembled the modern-day young: sulking and dwelling and guarding its secrets jealously. He consulted his watch. 'You'll have five minutes to get changed before breakfast, Holland,' he said. 'We've made slow time today. We'll aim to do better on Thursday, shall we? Less talking might do the trick.'

* * *

Barney arrived at breakfast to discover a letter propped against his plate.

'Well, would you look at that: Camden Town's got post,' said Cowper. 'From your girlfriend, is it, boyo?'

'Kissy-kissy,' said Shields.

' "To my dearest, darlingest Barnaby, I dream of you day and night. How do I love thine icicle Barnaby toes and icicle Barnaby nose? Let me count the ways . . . " '

It didn't take much to tell that the letter was indeed from a girl: the envelope was printed with a decorative border and the seal illustrated with a pig and a turkey in a vicar's collar squatting atop a hill. Four lines of curlicued text were printed at the bottom corner.

The Owl and the Pussycat went to sea
In a beautiful pea-green boat,
They took some honey and plenty of
    money,
Wrapped up in a five-pound note.

The seal had been deftly split by Runcie's letter opener, the pages returned to the envelope as good as undisturbed. At the top of the first page were four more lines of script.

They dined on mince and slices of quince,
Which they ate with a runcible spoon;
And hand in hand, on the edge of the sand,
They danced by the light of the moon.

271

'What does she say?' said Opie.

''My best-beloved Barnaby-boo . . . ''

Pretending not to watch them from the other end of the table, Swift monitored the taunts and Barney's failure to rise to them. Those boys fussed over concocted gossip like carrion birds pecking vainly at pieces of driftwood. All the time on this island, people talked about the wrong things.

'Be that way,' huffed Cowper finally, and the others followed him, rising from the table.

The letter was brief, the first page limited to bland greetings. *I hope you are well and that you will send my best wishes to the others. My new school is very nice and the girls are friendly.* On the second page she had drawn a picture of the pony that she was learning to ride and a floor plan of her dormitory. It was signed *from B.* The postscript added simply that she thought she might have forgotten to stamp a borrowing card for the book about the bear tamer's daughter, and would he mind doing this for her so that Mr Nunn's library records were up to date?

The card he found between the pages of the chapter on the early campaigns of the general Belisarius — and with it, two pieces of paper, folded in thirds. The handwriting here was the same, only slightly larger and more carefully executed.

Do you know the story of the schoolteacher who offered his students as ransom? Their city was under siege and he was desperate. The enemy general was so disgusted by the schoolteacher's offer he had him stripped and provided the children with sticks to beat him with, all the way home.

That's why they have sent me away, Barney. Mummy knows that I know. That's why she didn't mind me being sent to school in England this time.

Will you keep this for me, just in case?

And on a separate sheet of paper:

Herewith follows the last will and testament of Belinda Margaret Flood:

To Lucia, I entrust my Saucy Walker doll and Julip horses and any books she might like (apart from my School Friend, which I already promised to Joyce), as well as my patent, shoes.

To Mummy, the paste brooch that I stole last year (it is in the papier-mâché box in the second drawer from the bottom in Lucia's room).

To Daddy, my paintings.

To Barney, the four shillings and sixpence in the change purse that I left under the bench You Know Where.

He shut the book and returned it to its place, pocketing the note with the resignation of a spy who has just been given his arsenic pill. Was this what she had been practising for all along, those nights in the rock pools? Was keeping her mother's secret so corrosive? Of course she was not about to die. The will was nothing but a piece of wishful thinking. At the end of term a bottle of Pentazine tablets would be found in her bedside drawer and confiscated. She had attempted only one tablet before penning the letter, and it was so large it had made her gag.

It must have seemed a terrible insult to her. Never mind that the lesson she ought to have learnt from all this should have been the wonder and unlikely miracle of existence: life, against terrible odds. The thing that those two small souls buried on this island had never known. Before the UXB carried off Robin, Belinda probably would have said that they'd been spared a double disappointment: the guilt of living through war, and being the shame that would scar the peace. Best to die young. He wondered if she still believed this. Once, she had told Barney that in the Narnia books Susan didn't die as her siblings did, because she finally lost faith in that other world: instead of death, she progressed to adulthood. She had said then that she should be ashamed of such a fate, so mundane as to be almost offensive.

★ ★ ★

On the first day to feel like summer, the bells of St Arras and Port Grenen pealed back and forth across the high plateau. While the boys of the Carding House School were busy helping to set up the tables and chairs for the Sports Day tea, Barney found himself between assignments and idle in the shade of a blossoming apple tree. His pocket was stretched to contain a stiff, square

274

shape that pointed at the corners, and now he pressed his thumb into the uppermost point with a warm sensation. It was his release form, his ticket out of here — this school, this island sinking under its own memories. In one week he would return to London to collect Jake and to say goodbye to Spike (the tired linoleum, the chattering gas meter, the Jamaican family with those offensive parcels shoved through the letterbox), and a few days after that they would take the train to Portsmouth, and from there board a ship to Cape Town. There would be a swimming pool for dunking the uninitiated, and parties after supper and a cabin with twin berths that he and Jake would fight over — there would be deck games and no masters. And then, at the end of it, there would be Africa, and Mum.

'Buck up, Holland!' A passing Mede whose arm was slung with four metal hurdles bumped him. 'Get the flag from the masters' common room, will you? Dolly'll know someone's coming for it.'

'Buck up, buck up!' chanted Hiram Opie from behind the flapping canvas hoarding, where he steadied a stake that two older boys were struggling to force into the ground.

'Shut up, Opie,' grunted Barney, heaving himself reluctantly into action. In recent weeks he had begun bullying Hiram as the others did: what had begun as a means of confirming his membership in a group now came by second nature.

He had already become a curiosity for escaping death and being judged to have grieved

Littlejohn discreetly, without pretence or affectation. The drama with Ivor, the white scar that cupped his cheekbone, had further gilded his reputation by his association with rebellion. It seemed a shame, on the eve of a happier year, to have to give up all that he'd endured for: the respect of his peers won when, over the heads of a group of boys huddled around the notice board, his name had been called out as the only Lydian to make the cut for Swift's elite runners. Tomorrow he would race against three Sagartians and two Medes in the long-distance meet: five miles up the spine of the island and five miles back, to be greeted at the finish line by the entire school — everyone, at least, who wouldn't be playing in or watching the cricket match on the upper pitch — and, if he won, to be awarded a plaque with his name on it for the cross-country register that hung in the atrium. Many times already, he had attempted to render the words in Copperplate Gothic letters on the back of his English jotter — Barnaby Holland, 1954 — but it was still difficult to imagine just how the thing might look, immortalized behind glass. Whistling to himself as he passed through the headmaster's corridor, he paused by the registers to count the names on the cross-country list. Twenty-four in total, and none at all between 1940 and 1946. Opposite was the Games Captains' roll of honour, and he spotted Swift's name in the middle: Michael Swift, 1937. The letters had been etched in the pewter and painted over in dark ink that showed the dust.

'Waiting for someone, Holland?' said a voice

from across the hallway Mr Flood stood in the doorway of the masters' common room with an armful of mark books clutched to his chest, crumpling the canary-yellow tie that looked as if it might be a gift from his wife. 'Otherwise I'd have to ask what business brings you indoors when there's setting-up still to be done . . . '

'It's just that Rowe said we needed the flag, sir.'

'Ah, yes.' Flood had kept the door propped ajar: now he pushed against it, executing a ballroom manoeuvre into the common room and indicating that Holland should follow him. 'It's on top of the bookcase,' he said, peering over the rims of his spectacles. 'Do you see there? You might need to use a chair.'

This was a rare incursion into a sacred domain, and Barney suddenly felt that he must make a special effort to take in as much as possible in the short time he would be allowed access to its secrets. The masters' common room was laid out in an L-shape, with the approach through the shorter section, furnished sparsely with pigeonholes and shelves and two occasional tables. It was hazy with pipe smoke; newspapers were left draped over armchairs on which broad backsides had left their imprint and piles of marking teetered beneath chipped teacups.

'Don't dawdle, lad. Here's a stool you can use.' Barney mounted the chair and steadied himself against the bookshelf. 'Do you know what day it is?'

'Wednesday, sir, the twenty-sixth of May.'

277

'It's the same day that Hunt's chaps got to within 300 feet of the summit of Everest before having to turn back. Not enough oxygen, you know.'

'No, sir.'

The boy eased himself down to the floor with the flag draped in one arm. There had been a disturbance of dust atop the bookcase, and the boy stifled a sneeze. When, years later, he would read of the master's sudden death on holiday in France (a history of high blood pressure, a day of record temperatures in the Cévennes), it was that moment of dust motes dancing in the pipe smoke and a canvas flag pressed heavily into the crook of his arm that would come rushing back to him.

'Running tomorrow, I see, Holland?' He glanced at Barney over the top of his spectacles, and not for the first time Barney wondered why he bothered to wear them at all, if not to look through them.

'Yes, sir.'

'Good for you, lad. Endurance sport and all that. How the war was won.'

'Sir.'

Now Barney saw the meekness in the master's eyes, behind the wire spectacles. *He will never know*, thought Barney. *He was never a collaborator, or an adulterer. He has probably never broken a rule in his life, and so he can be happy.*

'Off you go, then, Holland. And good luck tomorrow, if I don't see you.'

'Thank you, sir.'

Flood waited for the boy to disappear ahead of him down the corridor and into the daylight before making his own way through the archway, towards home. Pleming had hosted a drinks party the previous night to celebrate the housemaster's birthday, and his head still throbbed with a faint ache behind the eyes. Against his wishes Mollie had brought along her husband's violin, and under pressure from his colleagues and their wives Flood had finally been convinced to play two short pieces: some Corelli and a silly little study by Kreutzer. His palms had slipped along the neck of the instrument and his fingers had squeaked and slid over the strings in a way that had made him annoyed and embarrassed, though if anyone else had noticed they hadn't let on. The wine had been flowing for just long enough to dull the edges of formality with which the masters normally interacted before the boys, and their wives had been understandably eager to make the most of this opportunity to relax. All night, Mollie had laughed with the other women in a way that expressed a strange kind of relief — and at the evening's end she had slipped one arm through Swift's and with her free hand pinched his chin in a fond, maternal manner. He had noticed the way Runcie watched for his reaction, like a dog seeking permission from a herdsman to nip at the heels of an errant sheep. 'Time for our Mikey to find himself a companion his own age,' he had sniffed to Flood, who thought it a strange thing to say.

But all that was not the cause of what he felt

now: this gnawing hollowness insulted by the bells and smugly glaring sun, the gloating beauty of a day designed for the enjoyment of the young. As he made his way across the green, pursuing a line amid the bustle of boys and masters ferrying chairs and tables and bunting and assorted sporting equipment, it was the shaded window that held his attention, gazing out beyond the tree line and across the sea to another school many miles away.

He pushed through the kitchen door, which had been left on the latch, and called upstairs to Lucia so that he might swing her in his arms and never let her go.

★   ★   ★

The story was that Shields had put Cowper up to it. A month's supply of Crunch bars from his tuck and bragging rights in perpetuity: that was the agreement, if things worked out exactly as planned.

The caper was not an original one, but it had been so rarely pulled off that there was still a promising sense of challenge about it. As the school assembled in a semicircle in front of Ormer House, Cowper took pains to arrange himself at the far end of the standing Lydian row. The first form sat on the ground in front of the second, which perched on benches flanking the masters; the overspill had to stand behind them with the third. Behind them, Medes and Sagartians stood atop benches which creaked and tipped under their weight, hovering over the smaller boys below with relish.

In the middle of the semicircle, the photographer had set up his camera. He pointed it to face the far end of the group, then stepped back as it began its slow rotation. Once the shutter had fallen, Cowper waited for the photographer to consult his watch before ducking behind the teetering back row and running as fast as he could to the other end of the group. Only the boys who were privy to the plan detected the *thump-thump-thump* of his footsteps, but they continued staring straight at the camera's wandering eye as if by keeping still themselves they might hasten his progress. Time seemed suspended in the moments it took for him to emerge at the far end of the Lydian row, next to Holland. By now, the camera had almost finished its slow sweep of the group, and the boys at the end where the picture had started began to shift and fidget. Another second passed, and another, in which each one imagined his moment in history between one flash of light and another yet to come.

When the rolled-up prints arrived for collection, they were greeted with yelps of glee: for there was Cowper glowering in concentration at the far left of the image, and there he was again — grinning, only slightly blurred — at the far right. Like a mischievous spirit nagging at the fringes of the group, at once here and elsewhere: a memory that would not be shaken off.

★ ★ ★

The starting pistol had misfired, and the Medes on either side of Barney had both set off at the click and muffled *pfft!* of the cap scuttling back into the barrel. The others, bewildered by the delay, followed a second later. There had been no attempt to arrange a restart, as it was the slower two who launched off seconds ahead of the rest — and sure enough, by the time Barney reached the forest outskirts he had already overtaken them both.

He'd had every intention of running to win that morning. Winning would mean proving Swift wrong — it would mean a medal to show to Jake and to give to Mum — it would be his farewell to the island, which at last he was about to leave for good. He had nothing against the other runners — the Sagartians were solitary boys, aloof but not haughty, and one of the Medes had even stooped to offering him running tips (lengthen your stride downhill; do press-ups to improve lung capacity; never watch the feet of the runner in front) — but it wasn't them that he'd be defeating.

Most of the crowd had drifted away within seconds of the race: there was nothing to watch unless they intended to sprint alongside the runners. Prefects had been recruited to keep posts at four points spread over the course, the first of which would be waiting at the main road on the other side of the forest. By then the Medes were far enough behind him not to notice Holland duck off the path.

Initially he had stayed away out of a sense of guilt, then it had simply become habit. There

282

had been no point in bunking off runs since Barney had announced his desire to compete, and most of his free time was now spent with Cowper and Shields, smoking at the pumping station. It was only the thought of Belinda's four shillings and sixpence that lured him there. There was plenty of time to duck in and collect his fee: there was no rule against it.

Sure enough, there was the money in a coin purse under the bench. Tucking it into his shorts, Barney glanced around the shelter and considered how much smaller it seemed now, even though it should have felt more spacious without the other two there. Deprived of emperor and muse, it was now neither a palace nor a shrine. The matches left on the upturned crate were too damp to strike, so the only light there was filtered at strange angles through the Judas window. Although the materials for Ivor's sea-fire experiment had been removed, it looked as though no one had been here since to tidy up after them: the jam jars and detritus from their last feast still cluttered the space between the packing crates, and a bottle stuffed with cigarette stubs glinted in the dim light like an apothecary's vial. Barney sat on the bench and rested his head against the cool wall beneath the rash of plague spots, listening to the clatter of leaves and clicking of beetles through the mulch. There was a funny odour that must have been trapped in here for months, which reminded him of old Brillo pads and putty, only stronger. Belinda had thought it might have been a ghost, because it was murky and rotten. But Barney didn't believe in ghosts — particularly not ones in grey coats who vanished hurrying across misty fields.

Nevertheless the silence felt heavy, resonating with something at once there and not there, and he was overcome with the visceral awareness of a presence. It was the same feeling he'd had once or twice in the basement corridor, where bodies stirred and voices whispered long after the laundresses had gone home. It was a tangible stillness — a visible silence.

'Robin?'

But Barney knew that it wasn't a ghost. The thing that haunted the corridor and the field opposite the pumping station, that lurked in the darkest corner of the fallout shelter, had nothing to do with what had happened ten years earlier, but everything to do with what had been happening all along, in front of their own eyes.

For so long he had unconsciously thought of this place as Ivor's. The Mede's rule here had been absolute — not least at those times when he became cruel, said cruel things and they thought him ugly and hated themselves for being his pets. Was that why they had kept returning to him, because there was no other escape?

He began to run again. He hardly noticed the prefects cheering them on from the checkpoints, or the razor grass that sliced at his bare legs — he did not hear the toot of a horn as a car overtook him on the main road or register a flock of bull-necked fulmars fouling a vehicle abandoned in the lay-by. At one point he pulled ahead of the two Medes, and for some time he ran abreast one of the Sagartians, though he too must have fallen behind at some stage above the chalk ridge. Beyond that, Barney did not notice his fellow racers. There was the taste of salt on his lips and rawness in his throat as he charged up the incline of the school drive towards the fluttering bunting and the crowds — and then, at last, there was the whisper of ribbon streaming across his chest and the clap of palms against his back, the cheers of the Second Form.

Two hours later, hair slicked flat against his head from the shower, smart in the new civvies his mother had sent him, which he would wear when they disembarked from the ship at Cape Town, Holland heard his name announced over rising applause. The bailiff's wife made her slow voyage across the stage towards the trophy table draped with a billowing Union Jack, swinging fat, sunburnt hands like paddles. This was one of the moments Spike had warned him about: Doc Dower's enormous head nodding at him in approval; the upturned faces of his classmates as he approached the stage — smiling for him, at last.

How many years before they would brush shoulders over a tray of canapés at the school reunion, greet each other by their surnames? Some of those Old Boys would come to seek out what had been lost or changed, some wouldn't have stopped thinking of their schooldays since the prize-giving on the lower pitch: the elation and anxiety of freedom amid the glorious hopefulness of high summer, and a terrible sense of time passing and lost, of an ending that wasn't, a sense that perhaps this was as good as things were ever going to be, on this tiny island that both was and wasn't England, on a summer's day in 1954. Even now, Barney knew that a part of him would be forever nostalgic for that moment.

Time held still just long enough for him to grieve its passing, dispelled by scattering clouds and cheers from the front benches. The bailiff's wife's hand was clammy, and he had to take care not to let the trophy slip through his fingers as he stepped gingerly from the stage. Still the school was clapping: they would continue to do so until he reached his row, and then even in the hush that followed there were whispered congratulations from Shields and Cowper, Percy and Hughes and Sanger, friendly smacks on the back, fingers ruffling through his hair.

Forty years on, what would they talk about? One of them might bring up the death of a French tutor — an overdose of sleeping pills, it would be rumoured. *No doubt something to do with the war: must have seen a few things.* Or the time a UXB took out half the drive and part of the east wing. Then someone might also remember the boy who vanished from the ice-stranded ferry, never to be heard from again. They would not mention the noises in the basement corridor, which for so long were passed off as the flutterings of a ghost.

Barney sat through the remainder of the prize-giving with the trophy pressing heavily into his knees. By the time he stood up his legs prickled with pins and needles, and he had to

286

hobble out of the tent like a decorated veteran: broken though glorious. Barney didn't mind. By the following term, his name would have appeared on the Games board as if etched by some divine hand: and from that moment on, a shade of him would live there for ever.

★ ★ ★

The Medlar House boys made him King that night, to rule over the bacchanalian disorder that was the Topsy Turvy: an evening of inverted roles, of pranks on the masters and shameless pelting of the prefects, of gorging on limitless tuck and forgoing every one of Matron's twelve sacred Dormitory Rules. As if in a blissful dream, Barney sanctioned the turning-forward of every clock in the school by one hour so that lessons the next day would be missed — then, egged on by Shields and Cowper, he ordained that the school be condemned to a blackout, with only Lydians permitted candles by which to wreak their rightful havoc. Shadows were thrown down every corridor, warped and flickering so that from one end of the school to the other it was impossible to tell what had created them. Like orphan shades dancing out of their parents' reach, they made riddles of the rooms.

The kitchens were raided for pans to serve as tambourines, and in place of a gun salute, birch canes were removed from every classroom to be broken across desks with resounding cracks. They used charcoal to make ghoulish masks of their faces and threw open the windows so that the glass hummed with echoes. There were no little girls dressed as foil-helmeted Britannia, but Cowper showed the others how to make paper hats like the ones they'd had for the Coronation celebrations in his village, and these they wore on their rampage through the school. Again and again the chant went up:

> Coatsworth, Comfrey, Curless,
> Dockett and de Bock,
> Frankland, Hess, the fine boy Just
> Kors-Kingsley, Lennert, Loft,
> Morrell, Overbay, Previn,
> Potts and Savin next,
> Standring, Thorup, Thrane and Voigt,
> Voysey — then the rest:
> Widdows, Williams, Wilbermere,
> No more after those;
> Their glory in our memory set
> And day by day it grows.

Just as their energies seemed about to be spent, someone suggested that it was time for the bonfire, which the Sagartians — their slaves for the night — had already been put to work constructing on the lower pitch.

'All hail, the King of Camden Town!' bellowed Cowper at the assembled seniors. 'Kneel before him, knaves and wretches, and beg his mercy!' And Barney watched benevolently as Ivor's friend Potts, and Jordan-Smythe who had come second in that day's race, and Mattheson who couldn't pronounce his Rs, knelt before him on the cold grass.

Then the head boy handed Barney the torch for lighting the straw dummy that had been tied to the stake atop the bonfire: a stuffed pillowcase with a whorishly painted head and witch's hat. The junior boys let up screams of exhilarated bloodlust as the dummy was set alight, and as they danced about the flames they cast long shadows over the vast island plateau, transforming it into a playground of dark spectres, a landscape of wandering lunatics.

Other titles published by
The House of Ulverscroft:

SMOKE PORTRAIT

Trilby Kent

It's 1936. Glen Phayre, in her twenties, has come to live with her aunt, who runs a tea plantation in Ceylon. Among other charitable tasks, Glen writes letters to a Belgian prisoner. But the letters go astray and are received instead by teenager Marten Kuypers, whose brother, Krelis, has vanished and is presumed dead. Marten replies to Glen in the guise of the grown-up prisoner she expects to hear from. Their correspondence evolves, both using false identities whilst remaining true to their own selves in other ways. Gradually they come to depend on each other, and their pen friendship proves to be crucial when events in their real lives take on a darker, more threatening turn in the shadow of the impending world war.

THE GUEST LIST

Melissa Hill

** No bookjacket record is available. (91)

THE COMPROMISE

Zoe Miller

Childhood friends Juliet, Rebecca, Rose and Matthew grew up in a small village outside Dublin. Now privileged, wealthy and powerful, they appear to have it all. But when Juliet is involved in a suspicious accident and lies trapped between life and death at the bottom of a cliff, a secret that has been hidden for years threatens the seemingly perfect lives of the close-knit group. For the beautiful, fragile Rose, Juliet's accident draws unwanted attention to the sins of the past. For her husband, the ruthlessly ambitious Matthew, it removes a critical obstacle from the path of his political career. And as Rebecca discovers more about what happened to her friend, she begins to wonder if she ever knew the real Juliet . . .

SENSE AND SENSIBILITY

Joanna Trollope

★★ No bookjacket record is available. (91)

THE FOSTER HUSBAND

Pippa Wright

Kate left her seaside home town of Lyme Regis for the bright lights of London when she was eighteen, and never looked back. She had it all: glamorous career, the lovely townhouse, the gorgeous husband. But now she's back: unemployed, separated, and holed up in her dead granny's bungalow. Worse still, she's forced to share the bungalow with Ben, the clueless and domestically challenged fiance of her bossy sister Prue. Ben is a man in need of simple instruction. And Kate is a woman in need of a project. So, she decides to train Ben, her foster husband, as a selfless pre-wedding gift to her sister. But Kate may still have a few lessons of her own to learn . . .

HOW TO FALL IN LOVE

Cecelia Ahern

Adam Basil and Christine Rose are thrown together late one night, when Christine is crossing Ha'penny Bridge in Dublin. Adam is there, poised, threatening to jump. He is desperate — but Christine makes a crazy deal with him. His 35th birthday is looming and she bets him that before then, she can show him life is worth living. Despite her determination, Christine knows what a dangerous promise she's made. Against the ticking clock, the two of them embark on wild escapades, grand romantic gestures and some unlikely late-night outings. Slowly, Christine thinks Adam is starting to fall back in love with his life. But has she done enough to change his mind for good? And is that all that's starting to happen?